PRAISE FOR

Summer of Lost and Found

"A sweet, sparkling setting, a historical riddle, and a quirky cast make this little gem of a mystery a pure pleasure to read."

—Jodi Lynn Anderson, author of
My Diary from the Edge of the World

"The mystery of the Lost Colony of Roanoke becomes an engaging backdrop for a preteen experiencing her own losses. . . . This blend of history with mystery and fantasy with realism is a good find indeed."

—*Kirkus Reviews*

"Behrens's deft writing gives the book substance. . . . This intriguing mix of historical and realistic fiction with a dash of the paranormal makes this well-written novel appealing to a wide range of middle grade readers."

—*School Library Journal*

"For middle-graders finding their own summer vacations less than exciting, Nell's investigation will be a pleasant diversion."

—*BCCB*, recommended

ALSO BY REBECCA BEHRENS

When Audrey Met Alice

COMING SOON

The Last Grand Adventure

SUMMER OF
LOST and FOUND

REBECCA BEHRENS

ALADDIN
NEW YORK   LONDON   TORONTO   SYDNEY   NEW DELHI

ALADDIN

An imprint of Simon & Schuster Children's Publishing Division

1230 Avenue of the Americas, New York, New York 10020

First Aladdin paperback edition May 2017

Text copyright © 2016 by Rebecca Behrens

Cover illustration copyright © 2016 by Robyn Ng

Also available in an Aladdin hardcover edition.

All rights reserved, including the right of reproduction in whole or in part in any form.

ALADDIN and related logo are registered trademarks of Simon & Schuster, Inc.

For information about special discounts for bulk purchases, please contact Simon & Schuster Special Sales at 1-866-506-1949 or business@simonandschuster.com.

The Simon & Schuster Speakers Bureau can bring authors to your live event. For more information or to book an event contact the Simon & Schuster Speakers Bureau at 1-866-248-3049 or visit our website at www.simonspeakers.com.

Cover designed by Laura Lyn DiSiena

Interior designed by Steve Scott

The text of this book was set in Bodoni 72.

Manufactured in the United States of America 0417 OFF

2 4 6 8 10 9 7 5 3 1

The Library of Congress has cataloged the hardcover edition as follows:

Names: Behrens, Rebecca, author.

Title: Summer of lost and found / by Rebecca Behrens.

Description: First Aladdin hardcover edition. | New York : Aladdin, 2016. |

Summary: Nell is a city girl forced to spend her summer in Roanoke, North Carolina, but when she meets historical reenactor Ambrose, they explore for clues as to what really happened to the lost colonists, turning her once boring vacation into an adventure.

Identifiers: LCCN 2015036440 | ISBN 9781481458962 (hardback) |

ISBN 9781481458993 (paperback) | ISBN 9781481459020 (eBook)

Subjects: | CYAC: Vacations—Fiction. | Mystery and detective stories. |

Roanoke Colony—Fiction. | BISAC: JUVENILE FICTION / Social Issues / Friendship. |

JUVENILE FICTION / Historical / United States / Colonial & Revolutionary Periods. |

JUVENILE FICTION / People & Places / United States / General.

Classification: LCC PZ7.B38823405 Su 2016 | DDC [Fic]—dc23

LC record available at http://lccn.loc.gov/2015036440

For Blake

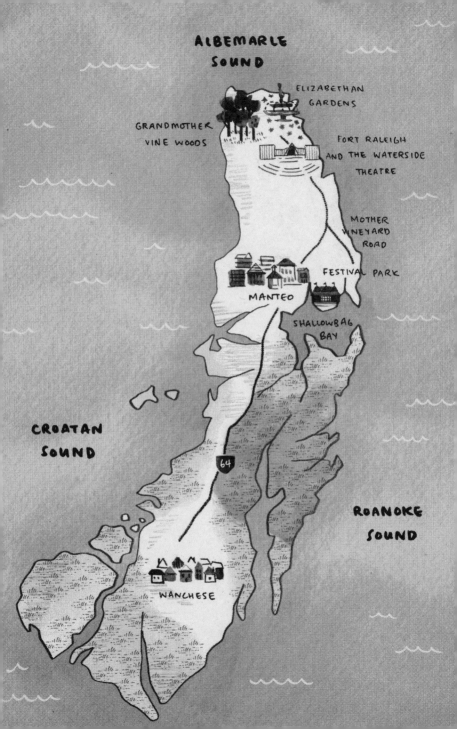

SUMMER OF
LOST and FOUND

CHAPTER ONE

You don't expect your life to change because of a toothbrush. But that's really how my summer of lost and found started, with one missing object.

My mom had let me stay up late watching TV. My dad was out at a book signing—or so I thought. After a rerun of a detective show started, I shuffled into the bathroom to brush my teeth. But when I pulled open the medicine cabinet, my hand reached toward only two toothbrushes in the tree-shaped holder. The third, my dad's, was missing. I checked to see if it had fallen behind the sink, but it wasn't anywhere. It was gone on purpose.

Wasn't it late for my dad to not be home?

And who brings a toothbrush to a bookstore?

I marched down the hall and knocked on my parents' bedroom door. Pushing it open, I found Mom lying on her back on the floor, one hand over her eyes. Scanning the room, I noticed that the big suitcase, which usually has their laundry piled on top of it, was also missing.

"Where's Dad? And why did he take the suitcase?" He'd been home at breakfast, reading the paper and asking me about school. Now he was gone overnight? I chewed at a hangnail.

"Everything's fine, Nell. But something came up . . . and he had to go out of town for a little while."

"For work?"

She pursed her lips, like she was about to tell me something important. But then she yawned and said, "It's getting late. I promise we'll talk more about this tomorrow, okay?"

"Okay." I noticed how much her shoulders slumped after hugging me good night. I went to bed, but my mom stayed up late tapping the keys of her laptop and puttering around the kitchen making buttered toast. She only nibbled at the slices, which I know because I found them, minus a few dainty bites, on the top of the trash can in the morning.

Her sleeplessness was contagious. It's hard to conk out when you can sense someone else being restless in the space you share. The street noises, like a wheezing garbage truck and the trill of a siren, startled me. I swore our apartment was echoier, and there were all these sounds that never bothered me before: air-conditioner hisses and floorboard sighs. Apartment 5A is the perfect size for three people. With only two, there is a strange emptiness. I kept listening for the scrape of a key in the lock.

I woke up to a message from my dad. He said he was sorry about leaving so suddenly, that everything was fine, but an opportunity came up and blah, blah, blah. Whenever my dad e-mails or texts me, he tries to include a quote from Shakespeare, his favorite writer. It's our thing. The cryptic one in that message was: "There is nothing either good or bad, but thinking makes it so." I think he was trying to help me stop worrying, but I know that the play it was from, *Hamlet*, is not exactly a feel-good story. We saw it performed in the park last summer.

That's when I started to second-guess what this was all about. Sometimes Dad travels for work, but it wouldn't happen so suddenly, in between breakfast and dinner. Also, if he had sold another book, I would know about it because that is a Big Deal in our household. Whenever my dad gets a contract, he always comes home with cupcakes or cake pops or whoopie pies or whatever the latest dessert craze is. Then for days we find him sprawled around the apartment, pecking at his laptop. Always smiling. He loves getting work, even if it's only to write a little article in some magazine so obscure they don't sell it at News & Lotto. The time he finally sold his novel about a spy mystery on the *Titanic*, we went out for a dinner cruise. Ironically, I guess.

The disappearance of the toothbrush happened right before my mom was supposed to go to Roanoke Island for a month, to study some kind of special vine. The plan was for me to stay in the city with Dad. But while she was making dinner the next night, all that changed. Wandering into the kitchen, a half hour past our normal dinnertime, I found my mom hunched over the stovetop, haphazardly heating up a bag of frozen tortellini. She straightened and forced a big smile.

"Dinner's almost ready."

I sauntered over to the cupboard and pulled out the place mats, then started to set the table. "Three place mats? Or . . . two?"

Mom clattered the pan, turning some of the tortellini into hot little missiles. "Two, tonight."

I put one back before plopping into my worn wooden seat. "So where'd Dad go?"

Mom squeezed her eyes shut for just a moment, which is her tell. "Well, he's— Ow!" She cursed the size of our tiny New York City kitchen and ran her hand under cold water, having accidentally brushed the burner. I grabbed her some frozen peas from the freezer and forgot that she was in the middle of an explanation. Once we were seated at the table, she delivered the news: I was going with her to Roanoke, and we would leave a week from Thursday.

"But, Mom, I have plans for the summer! I'm going to the Junior Keeper Camp at the zoo. And Jade and I were supposed to take tennis lessons." Summer is my favorite time in the city, full of frozen treats and street fairs and fireworks sparkling over the river. I didn't want to miss a minute of it.

My mom made a valiant attempt at faking enthusiasm, but her eyes suggested she also felt this situation was not ideal. "You'll have plenty to do there—Roanoke's a vacation place— and you can help me. Think of it as a summer job. I'll even pay you a stipend."

I begged her to reconsider and let me stay in Manhattan. "What about all our plants?" I feared for their lives. Dad was horrible at remembering to water them. We call him the Plant Killer. And because my mom is a botanist, we have a lot of really cool ones—a sensitive plant whose leaves curl up if you touch them; a big, hardy Venus flytrap; four different types of orchids; ficus and mini palm trees. We live on the top floor of a brownstone, and our apartment has roof rights. Mom babies her flower beds, succulent plantings, and little vegetable garden so much that they are practically my siblings. In fact, her term of endearment for me has always been "sprout" because I'm her little plant. Anyway, we couldn't just give the super the keys and ask him to water the plant members of our family while we were away.

Mom shook her head. "Sorry, sprout, but you have to come with me." I would be spending my summer in North Carolina; my plant sibs would have to fend for themselves. Mom assured me that her colleagues were excellent, responsible plant-sitters.

I went into my bedroom and called Dad's cell, but it went straight to voice mail. So I did some snooping in our living room, which doubles as his office. Rummaging in the desk drawers, I found that in addition to taking everything essential with him, like his notebooks, he'd also taken his passport. Something very strange was going on. I was ready to call the cops and turn this into a true-life detective-show episode. But when I stormed back into the kitchen, I found my mom's laptop open. In the blur of type, I saw the word "separation." Suddenly I didn't want to read any more.

Thursday afternoon, I broke the news to my best friend, Jade Brathwaite. It was hot outside, the kind of sticky-sweaty, humid-like-the-locker-room hot that means New York summer has finally started. Jade and I were dragging ourselves to the frozen-custard place on Columbus. I texted my mom on our way, to see if there was a line—sometimes it snakes out of the store and stretches down the block. Mom's office window in the Natural History Museum faces the shop, so we have a system: She looks up from her plant samples to see whether people are crowded on the sidewalk across the street; if she reports that there isn't a custard-waiting clump, I get her a to-go dish and pop it into the freezer for an after-work treat. Despite the heat that day, Jade and I were in the clear.

"That's probably because nobody wants to get custard when it's this hot out. It's too thick and milky. This is Popsicle weather," Jade said.

We shuffled inside the store and got in line to order. I went with heirloom-tomato custard because I love their weird flavors. My mom does too, so that's what I got for her. Jade got chocolate with cookie crumbles. "Did you get the e-mail about tennis racquets?" she asked.

"Um, about that," I started.

"About what?" Jade grabbed a couple of napkins. "You're still signing up for the lessons, right? You know"—she leaned toward me—"Sofia told me there are always lots of cute boys at the tennis place. This might be the summer we finally meet some." Sofia was Jade's friend who lived in the same building. I didn't know her well because she went to private school.

We grabbed our custard and headed back into the heat, slowly making our way down the block toward my apartment. I couldn't wait any longer. "I have to tell you something, actually." I paused to slip the handles of the bag with my mom's cup around my wrist, so I could take a bite of mine. The custard would give me strength to break the news to Jade. "I'm going away for the summer."

"What?" Jade flailed her arms up in the air and lost a spoonful of chocolate in the process. "Are you kidding me?"

"Nope." I shook my head and spun my spoon around the fast-melting scoop. Custard soup already. "I have to help my mom on her research trip to North Carolina. Roanoke Island. She told me last night."

"Did you remind her about our plans? We're going to be Central Park zookeepers for a week! We might even get to feed the red pandas!"

I nodded. "I reminded her, but she's not budging. We leave in a week."

"Can't you just stay at home? Your dad's not going, right?"

Hearing Jade mention my dad made me feel something sharp in my stomach. My mom was still being cagey with information about where he went. Or when he was coming back. Or *why* he left. The specifics were a mystery, not unlike the ones he wrote. But I didn't want to tell Jade what was going on—her parents are perfect, the type who always hold hands at school events and refer to each other as "darling" around the house. My parents like to squabble, and even when one of my friends is over, they'll roll their eyes at each other and argue about whose turn it is to take out the recycling. It's not like they have big dramatic fights all the time—just lots of little bickering ones. *Maybe even more than usual lately,* I thought.

"My dad's away for a bit, for work."

She narrowed her eyes slightly. "You haven't mentioned anything about that before." Jade knows me too well. But I didn't want her nosing into this . . . whatever it was. Situation. *Separation?*

"It came up really fast. Tight deadline."

"I'm bummed," she said, leaning over to wrap her arm

around my shoulder. "We were going to have so much fun this summer."

"We totally were." I ran upstairs to put Mom's custard in the freezer, then came back down. Jade and I sat on the steps to my building, slurping up the dregs of our dessert. Her phone buzzed, and she smiled. "Well, now Sofia might get to do zoo camp too. She was on the waiting list. We'll text you lots of pictures."

I stuck my spoon in my dish like it was a white flag of surrender. My stomach was getting that awful stabby feeling again. Now my best friend and Sofia would bond all summer while feeding zoo animals, and they'd probably get tennis-player boyfriends, and meanwhile I'd be collecting leaves in the boonies of North Carolina.

Great.

The night before we left, in a last-ditch effort to salvage my plans, I e-mailed my dad. Maybe a list of the reasons why summer is the best time in New York City could convince him to hightail it back from wherever he was. I wrote about the joys of the ice-cream truck and outdoor film fests, listing all our favorite warm-weather activities and city traditions. I left out the negatives, like free-range cockroaches and the constant drizzle of air-conditioner water onto the sidewalks.

All I got back was this: Great list. You're making me

homesick, Nelly. We'll take full advantage of the fun summer stuff when we're both back in town. Because as you know: "Summer's lease hath all too short a date." (That's from a sonnet.) Love you, Dad. When I showed it to Mom while she was folding pretrip laundry, her mouth screwed up into a grimace. "I'm sorry that he's homesick, but . . ." she started, leaving the sentence unfinished.

She cleared her throat. "Have you finished packing?"

In truth, I hadn't started. Normally I love filling my suitcase for a trip, but there was too much weirdness surrounding this one. "What do I need to bring to North Carolina?"

"Clothes! Good shoes for walking! Swimsuit! Sunglasses! Bug spray!" Mom kept rattling off a list from the other room as I wandered back to mine. "Toothbrush! Toothpaste! Dental floss!"

"Okay!" I cringed, remembering when I first noticed what had gone missing in our medicine cabinet.

She called, "Plenty of books!" I thought about how the first time I went to sleepaway camp for two weeks, I'd packed six books. Dad had told me I'd be out having too much fun in the great outdoors or by the campfire to read, but I'd still insisted on bringing them all, just in case. "If you send us lots of letters about how many books you've read, we'll take it as a sign that you need rescuing," he'd added.

I really hadn't liked that camp, so I'd sent four letters on stationery from my new personalized set. By the fourth letter, I had written to say that I'd finished all my books and was in desperate need of rescuing. Unfortunately for me, the letter hadn't arrived until two days after I'd gotten back to the city.

So while packing for Roanoke, I swept the whole pile of books on my nightstand into my suitcase. The thing was, if I ended up reading them all in a miserable first week, who would come and rescue me?

CHAPTER TWO

*W*e stood in the world's longest rental-car line at the Norfolk airport. I wandered over to the free coffee bar, which was really just an old vending machine that spat bizarrely foamy lattes into ten-ounce cups. I made a double for Mom, who still had sleep creases on the side of her face from her in-flight nap.

"How long do we have to drive now?" We'd left for the airport at ten a.m., and thanks to some delays we hadn't arrived until five p.m. I was ready to unpack my bag, take a shower, and eat something other than the canister of potato chips that I'd bought on the plane.

Mom absentmindedly ruffled my hair as she continued reading the rental-car agreement in front of her. "Not long, sprout. Under two hours."

"Ugh." I wandered back to the coffee thing to make myself a hot chocolate. I checked my phone to see if Dad had replied to the text I'd sent: We got to Norfolk okay. It's even more humid here than in our bathroom on a rainy day—and it's sunny outside. SOS. No response yet. Whenever I text, he usually replies right away. I squeezed my balled-up sweatshirt against my chest. No matter how much he tried to reassure me in his messages, I still felt unsettled by his absence.

"All set, Nell?" Mom stood behind me, jingling a set of rental-car keys. "Surprise, I splurged on the Jeep."

I rewarded her with a half smile. I wanted to hate my mom for dragging me away from New York, but she's pretty hard to hate. Even when she's totally keeping secrets from me. The night before, I'd overheard her call my aunt. "No," she'd said softly. "Not yet. Every time I try, I feel so guilty that I . . ." Then she had shut her door. I'd tiptoed over and pressed my ear against the heavy wood, but all I'd been able to make out was, "I want to wait until we've figured out what's next. You know?"

We drove slowly while Mom got used to the Jeep. It was weird to be in a non-Manhattan place and see so much open sky, trading pedestrians for cars, and city blocks of bodegas and bagel shops for strip malls with grocery stores and gardening supplies. It only took us a half hour to cross from Virginia into North Carolina and onto a road called the Caratoke Highway. The countryside around us was a rich green, dotted with farm stands, barbecue restaurants, and gas stations. Billboards enthusiastically detailed all the fun stuff ahead in the "OBX," which I knew meant the Outer Banks. I yawned and reclined in my seat, stretching my legs up and resting my feet on the dashboard.

"That's not safe." Mom swatted at my toes with her right hand. "Nice nail polish, though." Before I'd left, Jade and I had painted our nails the same shade, called "Alice Blue." It looked better against her skin than mine, but I wanted us to match. I wondered how I was ever going to have a fun summer without Jade.

"How are we doing, navigator?" my mom asked. I carefully unfolded the huge map the guy at the rental-car place gave us. Mom wanted to do a road trip the old-fashioned way, without a smartphone as a guide. Like the road trips she took as a kid. But just in case, I opened the map app on my phone. I watched our little blue dot creep down the unfamiliar road, farther from my home, my friends, my dad. Wherever he was.

"Fine. Like sixty-something miles to go." The blue dot continued to creep, and I thought maybe it was a good time to ask Mom again about the deal with Dad. Especially that missing passport.

But before I could find the words, she started talking. "Let me tell you why we're here, okay?"

I already knew the *real* answer—to escape our unsettlingly empty apartment. But I said, "The scupper-whatsit."

Mom seemed happy that I remembered at least part of its

name. "*Scuppernong.* It's a type of muscadine. I bet you never thought that grapes were native to the Southeast, right?"

My mom is so nerdy sometimes. Who knew plants could be so exciting? My dad jokes that she bleeds chlorophyll. *Yes, I like to sit and ponder whether grape species are native to various US regions.* But Mom gets so excited about her work that I can't be snarky about it. I nodded.

"Europeans didn't introduce grapes to North America— four species were already in this area, and muscadine is one of them. It has a big, round, *juicy* green fruit. They're beautiful. When explorers came to the coast way back in the fifteen hundreds, they wrote about how chock-full the place was with grapevines." She paused, brushing her hair off her face.

A message from Jade tempted me, but my mom has a rule about not texting when you're in conversation with people in real life. Dad is always pretty bad about that, and spending so much time gabbing with other writers online.

"Anyway, to make a long story longer, on Roanoke Island there's a vine called the 'Mother Vine.' People think it's the oldest cultivated grapevine in America. It's so old that the very first English colonists could have eaten from it."

So that was why "Roanoke" had sounded familiar. When we were studying Jamestown in history, the textbook had one little sidebar devoted to the colony that preceded it—the one that failed, on Roanoke Island. The colonists had gotten lost or been lost, or something. Because it was only a sidebar, it was light on details. I hadn't known that was the same Roanoke we were going to.

My mom was still talking. "Anyway, an archaeologist recently found *another* scuppernong in the woods, and we think it might be even older than the Mother Vine. We're calling it the 'Grandmother Vine,' for now." She chuckled at that. "I'm trying to figure out its exact age." She paused to take in a highway sign. "Time is of the essence."

"If it's hundreds of years old, what's the rush?"

"Because someone might build a golf course over it." My mom shook her head angrily and made the same exasperated noise she makes when people have thrown coffee cups in the flowers on our block.

"That's not cool." The afternoon light was fading to dusk. I hoped we got wherever we were going before dark. Arriving at a hotel at night feels creepy, like a scene out of a horror movie. It's better to check in to a room when it's sunny and fresh and you don't have to worry about anything scary lurking in the shadows. I punched on the radio and scrolled to find some good music. I settled on an oldies station, and Mom and I spent the rest of the drive singing along. I kept refreshing my phone, waiting to see if I'd hear back from Dad. I only got a text from Jade: Sofia & I r going 2 the movies & eatin at Ollie's after. Miss u. Ollie's has the best scallion pancakes in the city. I tried not to think about how long I'd have to go without them and cold sesame noodles. I tuned back in to Mom's rambling. She was talking about those colonists again, telling me that some were my age.

When the sun was almost set, we came to a low bridge. According to my phone, the Albemarle Sound glimmered in front of us. "This is the Wright Memorial Bridge," Mom said as she slowed the car down for the traffic. "Can you guess who it was named after? And don't cheat with that phone—I know you've peeked at the map."

I shook my head no.

"The Wright brothers," she explained. "First in powered flight. Kill Devil Hills is across the water, on that barrier island. See, this *is* a cool place. It's steeped in history. You might learn a lot this summer."

"I could learn a lot at your museum. Or up at the Cloisters." Every year we take a school field trip to the Cloisters, which is this medieval art museum way at the tippy top of Manhattan. It has armor and super-old books and stuff on display. But what's great are the gardens, which have all kinds of cool medieval plants. Mandrakes, just like in Harry Potter! I asked the docent one year if we could yank it up to see if it would scream, but she declined.

Mom took a deep breath and clutched the steering wheel a little tighter. I forgot that she hates driving across bridges.

Like, really *really* hates it. It's part of her open-water phobia. She had some kind of canoe incident when she was a kid, which she never got past. Whenever we leave the city, Dad has to drive over the George Washington Bridge while Mom shades her eyes and does deep-breathing exercises.

"It's okay, Mom," I tried to reassure her. "This looks like a very sturdy bridge. We're not up high, and people are driving slowly."

She gave me a grateful smile. "One of these days, we'll live in a place *not* surrounded by water."

"It would be okay if Dad were here." I regretted saying that immediately, as the smile on Mom's face crumpled.

We made it across and drove down the Croatan Highway, past the Wright Brothers National Memorial at Kitty Hawk. Mom got all excited when we went past a sign for Jockey's Ridge State Park, which she said has the tallest sand dune on the east coast. Then we came to another bridge heading in the direction of the marshy mainland. I noticed some sign about "Dare County."

"Hey, *Dare*! Like our last name." Although my mom kept hers. You can't expect a botanist to give up the name "Wood."

"That's a big name around here. The first English baby born in the New World was Virginia Dare. I wonder if she's related, some distant branch on your family tree."

"Neat." I turned my attention back to our driving. "Wait,

why are we heading away from the ocean? I thought we were staying at the beach."

Mom shrugged. "Roanoke's an island, but it's on the sound. Bodie Island is between it and the Atlantic."

We crossed onto Roanoke. Soft grasses, which looked like fox fur, dotted the side of the road in small clumps. Boats bobbed in the water, and houses hugged the shoreline to the right. Mom studied the clock on the dashboard. "I was hoping we'd have time to drive to the Grandmother Vine first thing, but that'll have to wait until morning. Better get our cottage set up first."

"We're not staying in a hotel?" I had been picturing a sunny beach resort, featuring a pool with lots of lounge chairs and a vending machine on every floor. I seriously love hotel vending machines. When I was little, vacations and hotel stays were the only times my mom would let me buy candy bars.

Mom laughed. "Not for a whole month, silly! Do you know how much that would cost? We're going to be in a nice little cottage in downtown Manteo. You'll love it."

I was doubtful. Cottages made me think of camp, and that made me think of daddy long legs and mosquitoes in the same environment as my bed. Not cool.

We inched along the main drag, Highway 64, while Mom peered over the steering wheel to read street signs in the waning light. "Budleigh! That's it. We're almost there, sprout."

Her tone was chirpy and bright again. We turned right, and drove past a bunch of houses and the Ye Olde Pioneer Theatre—seriously, that's what the sign above the marquee said. Mom stopped the car in front of a white cottage. It had a little front yard with the thickest green grass I've ever seen—thicker than the Great Lawn and the Sheep's Meadow in the park, for sure. The windows had bright pink awnings over them and flower-stuffed window boxes below them. Mom jumped out of the car and started stretching her legs.

"That drive was a killer!" She grinned at me. "But this place looks pretty sweet, right?"

I didn't want to like it. I felt like any ounce of enthusiasm for this place or this trip wasn't fair to my apartment and my life back in New York. But . . . the cottage was adorable. It looked like a doll's house. I'd never lived in anything but an apartment, and we've always had other people on the other side of the thin walls. I can smell Mrs. Kim's cooking and hear when Mr. Cohen has a hacking cough. Living in a place where you can't tap messages in Morse code to your neighbors might be kind of nice.

"It's pretty." I walked to the gate of the picket fence, pulled up the lock, and swung it open. "How do we get inside?"

"The keys should be in the mailbox," Mom said, skipping in front of me. She was almost giddy, like a kid on her way into Disneyland. "Look at all these beautiful flowers! Smell that grass!"

"They left the *keys* in the *mailbox*?" That I could not believe. People would never do that back home. They won't even hold the door so you can follow them into a building.

"Toto, we're not in Kansas anymore," Mom singsonged to me. It was nice to see her so excited about something, after the past week. But at the same time, I didn't want her to be *too* happy. She should be missing Dad, at least as much as I was. What did it mean if she wasn't? My stomach started to feel sick, and not from the vending-machine hot chocolate.

Mom pulled an envelope from the mailbox and ripped it open. Two shiny keys were inside, along with an information packet. She tucked the papers under her arm and shoved the key in the lock. The door popped open, and we stepped over the landing. It felt like a fairy house inside, all white and flowery. Even though the cottage was tiny, the vaulted ceiling made it feel spacious. I followed Mom around as she exclaimed over every detail. "You can pick which bedroom you want," she offered.

I peeked my head into both. One had a bright pink crocheted blanket as a bedspread and the other had a green comforter with embroidered leaves. "I'll take the green room." I dropped my messenger bag inside the door and stepped in. The floorboards creaked, making familiar sighing sounds as I walked over to the window. My view, once I parted the curtains, was of the back garden, which had four brightly painted Adirondack chairs on a little patio and a pergola above. Floral vines twined up and down both sides. My room was small and the ceiling slanted, but still fit a white dresser, a light teal nightstand, and an off-white vanity and mirror. There was even a small padded stool in front of the vanity. It reminded me of the one Jade had in her room. I wished I could show her this place. It would be an awesome space for a sleepover.

While Mom flopped down on the pink bed, I wandered into the bathroom, which had a creepy clawfoot tub and one of those ancient toilets that still uses a chain. I felt a certain relief to find something that I didn't like about this place, so if Dad called I wouldn't get all gushy about where we were staying and make him feel like he was left out. Every time I thought about how it had been more than a week since I'd heard his voice, I felt that stabby stomach feeling again. I'd never gone that long in my whole life without talking to my dad.

Next I scoped out the kitchen, which had checkered curtains and an old-fashioned sink—the kind with the rippled side for stacking dishes to dry. The fridge, small and rounded, was the kind my grandma would always call an "icebox." But at least it had a big freezer compartment, so I wouldn't have to give up sufficient Popsicle and ice-cream storage along with all the other sacrifices, big and small, I was making this summer. I unlocked the kitchen door and stepped out into the garden.

Even though we were right in town, all I could hear was the soft breeze blowing and some cicadas buzzing. No honking taxis, no chortling buses, no kids laughing or supers yelling on the street. Tipping my head back to look up, I could see stars peeking out from the twilight sky, more than I'd ever seen in Manhattan—other than at the planetarium at Mom's museum, of course. But those didn't count.

I sank into one of the Adirondack chairs, nestling into the cold, smooth wood. The light breeze smelled briny, tipped with pine and flowers.

Mom stood in the doorway to the kitchen. "Nell? I don't know about you, but I'm famished."

I turned toward her and smiled. "I'm only peckish."

"Ha-ha. Let's see if we can't get something delivered? I'm too wiped to go out and scavenge." I followed Mom inside the kitchen. She pulled out her laptop and started searching for delivery places nearby.

"Hmmm," she said after a minute. "We seem to be limited to pizza or barbecue. Or, wait: Chinese!"

"That's fine. Do they have scallion pancakes?" My stomach started growling at the thought. I waited for Mom to click on the menu.

"Bad news: no pancakes. And . . . let me see," she scrolled to read something else, then glanced at the top right of the screen. "Worse news. They stopped delivering already."

"What? That's crazy! It's not even nine." I only knew of two places in our neighborhood that quit delivering so early—the weird vegan restaurant and the after-school pizza place. Everywhere else delivers until late, late, late. At sleepovers, we've even called out for cookies after midnight. And they show up at your door, piping hot, in less than thirty minutes.

"Same for barbecue. On to plan C, pizza." Mom typed the number into her phone and hit call. I waited as she pressed the earpiece to her head. And waited. She pulled the phone away and pressed end. "They're not picking up. Maybe they're done for the night too."

I flopped onto the kitchen floor, sprawling out on the linoleum and making sad guttural noises. "I am *starving*. How do people *live* like this?"

"They make their own food." She bent to give me a sympathetic pat on the head. "Anyway, I bet there are places that *do* deliver—we just don't know about them yet, and Google is asleep on the job." Mom walked over to a brown grocery bag sitting on the counter and started pulling things out. "It looks like a dried mango with chile and sweet-and-salty trail mix night, sprout."

We ate the mango and mix out in the garden, silently listening to the cicada buzz and breeze. But the good feeling that I'd started to get pre-dinner was gone, and the sounds and smells and stars made me feel so very far from home. My thoughts turned to those colonists. I wondered how the ones my age had felt upon arriving at Roanoke, hundreds of years ago—when they hadn't traveled a half-dozen states south, but across a whole wide ocean.

October 1587

This is my tale.

The story of how I journeyed across the sea, for a life in a new world.

Our company set sail from Portsmouth on the twenty-sixth of April, in three ships. 'Twas a voyage most rough. Tempestuous seas. Quarrels constant between our fledgling colony's governor, John White, and the ship's pilot, Simon Fernandez. And even poisoning on the island of Santa Cruz. Arriving thither, we were most hungry and desperate for fresh food after weeks of chewing mouldy bread at sea, all our marmalade and butter devoured long ago. On the isle we found fruits most alluring and we did sup. But alas! They swelled our tongues so thick that we could speak nary a word. After, we kept unfamiliar green apples far from our bellies. My mother, she tasted my food before I took a bite, to keep me from harm.

Then we drank the water of a pond. But the water was most evil, and sick we fell again, with burning faces and eyes swollen shut for six days. Our three ships next sailed for Saint John and anchored in Mosquitoes Bay, whither blood-sucking pests did drain us. Fearing the water, we dared only to drink beer.

O, how I longed to be home.

On that isle, we were to replenish our stores of precious

salt, which would preserve food when we reached Virginia. But one of the men became convinced of danger most grave. "Beare up hard! Beare up hard!" Fernandez called. Before we could load the salt on board our ship, we were off again, tossed hither and thither and yon on the wide sea. We also had hoped to gather sprouts of pineapples and oranges to plant in Virginia, but that knave Fernandez denied us.

Next we passed by the island of Hispaniola but saw no preparation for landing. We left sight of it. Stopped on the island of Caicos, we hunted swans. How fresh the air smelled! Crowded in the streets, crowded in the pubs, crowded in the theatres—London was ripe with people. Our ship stank of its sogged passengers, but these islands on which we dallied did not. Sweet-smelling were they, like a newfound Eden.

We left with the goodly hope of next seeing Virginia. At long last, on the sixteenth of July, the first of our ships fell along with the mainland. We did intend to make our colony, under the charge given us by Sir Walter Raleigh, in a bay called the Chesapeake. 'Twas a fine place for a home—fertile land and good weather. We anchored near Roanoke only to join with the remaining fifteen Englishmen of Sir Richard Grenville's colony. We waited and watched, anxious and desirous of solid ground, as the men on the decks argued over some thing. At long last, we loaded into shore boats and rowed through the murk to the island called Roanoke.

As the oars cut through the water, I had a remembrance of England, and my grandfather and grandmother, who cried the day we bid them farewell. Should e'er again I lay mine eyes upon them? Mother clasped my hand, then rose to see after Eleanor Dare, who was very much with child. Young George, Thomas, and I sat most quiet and still, and even the little children were good. The land in the distance looked dark and dense. 'Twas a mystery what lay ahead of us. How would we e'er tame such wildness into a home? Father said we were to have all the riches of Virginia. Gold and pearls. We should be landowners, with five hundred acres belonging to e'ry family. Verily, we arrived with nothing. All our goods, we did sell before we set sail.

"My lad," Father said, clapping his sea-worn hand on my shoulder. His signet ring glinted in the sun—it bore the same family crest as the smaller circle that encloseth my finger. Father bended down to meet my eyes. His shone bright with pride. He pulled out his drinking flask and thrust it toward me. "Take thou a swig. Yea, thou art a lord in a new land." Mother smiled at me. I tipped my head and swallowed the bitter drink, with a cough. Though my father is brave, I was lily-livered. I gulped my fears away.

My family and I watched the shore skip e'er nearer to our ship, taking in our new home as it loomed closer, closer.

'Tis with a heavy soul I hold this remembrance now.

CHAPTER THREE

The sun streaming in through the curtains woke me, disoriented and hungry. First thing, I rolled over and pulled my phone off the nightstand. Dad had messaged me, but he didn't answer any of my questions. Instead, he wrote: "This [your] life, exempt from public haunt, finds tongues in trees, books in the running brooks, sermons in stones, and good in everything." That's from *As You Like It*. My translation: I know you want to be back in the city. But find the good in where you are. I hear it's lovely there, on Roanoke. Lots of trees and brooks. I wanted to reply that I'd have an easier time finding the "good in everything" if I wasn't worrying about his whereabouts. But my stomach was growling, so I heaved myself out of bed and padded into the kitchen. Mom sat at the white table, drinking a cup of coffee. A big plate of pancakes, some bacon, and scrambled eggs was sitting on the counter. "Morning, sunshine," she said.

"Did magical elves bring us food?" I asked, grabbing a plate and loading it up. I started gnawing on a piece of bacon immediately.

"Nope, I woke up early and found a grocery store. I needed to feed my sprout ASAP."

"Aye shmappreciate ish," I said, mouth full. The pancakes weren't the best, though. My dad has the magic touch. He makes them in the shape of Mickey Mouse and gets really creative with the chocolate-chip faces. He calls them Evan's Expressive Pancakes. Mom's were somewhat lumpy silver dollars.

After I stuffed my face, we got into the car to go find her scuppernong, in the fruit flesh. "Did I already tell you? I'm coauthoring a paper on bioarchaeology methods with a local researcher. If the Grandmother Vine is as old as we think, it's seen every generation of Europeans in the United States, and probably several generations of Native people prior. I'm wondering if some were caring for the vine, because it's survived against drought and invasive species and even development in the area." She was practically bouncing in the driver's seat.

We drove out of town, and I was surprised at how un-sandy it was everywhere. Roànoke was a very green place, thick with trees—as much a forest as an island. We took a couple of wrong turns, righted ourselves, and then bumped down a gravelly road, marked with a PRIVATE PROPERTY–NO TRESPASSING sign. Next to it, on the other side of a chain-link fence, was a big banner touting the future site of the Elizabethan Links golf course and luxury resort.

"Uh, Mom? Are we supposed to be taking this road?"

"It's fine. The property owner said he's happy to let me study the vine. It's the looky-loos he's trying to keep out."

I had a hard time imagining why people vacationing would want to drive around to look at an old grapevine. Mom continued, "Also the developers, I suppose. They're putting the pressure on him to sell his land. If he does . . . we might lose this piece of botanical history."

Suddenly, Mom let out a gasp and pulled the car onto the shoulder. She hopped out and speed-walked, arms swinging like a little kid's, over to this huge, gnarled plant thing at the edge of the woods. It looked like the cross between a tree and a branch-bare bush, with ropy gray-brown stalks intertwining around one another and toward the leafy ends. It dwarfed my mom as she knelt down and touched it. "Isn't this *awesome*?" To me, it looked like . . . a big plant, and not even with pretty buds.

She motioned for me to come over. I tiptoed around a few piles of deer poo, which I recognized thanks to the "How to Identify Animal Scat" exhibit at Mom's museum. When I joined her next to the vine, she had some dusty green circles cupped in her hand. They looked like bouncy balls, ones that were filthy from rolling under the fridge or something.

"Look at the grapes! They're huge."

I picked one up and rolled it between my thumb and fore-finger. "Are you sure you can eat them?" They were always scaring us about poisonous berries at sleepaway camp.

"Remember what I said in the car? You can, and people even make jelly, juice, and wine out of them." She dusted off one on the thigh of her cargo shorts and popped it into her mouth, chewing thoughtfully. "Not bad."

I circled the Grandmother Vine, careful not to trip over any roots. Mom pulled out her camera and snapped some pictures. I trailed my hand along the smooth surface of the vine as I walked, and a chill ran down my spine. It almost felt like someone was watching us—maybe the guy whose property we were on? The golf-course developers? I glanced around, but I didn't see anyone through the mess of trees. I pulled out my phone, thinking that maybe the shivery feeling was some kind of signal that I'd gotten a message, from Jade—or my dad. No messages, but I also had no bars. I started walking away from Mom to see if I could pick up a signal.

I wandered toward the woods, twigs and leaves crunching under my flimsy sandals. It was so quiet in the forest, damp and solemn. The air smelled like the best perfume I could imagine: flowery sweet and piney. Sunlight streamed through gaps in the treetops. I heard the faint noise of rippling water. My dad was right about there being lots of trees and brooks. Maybe

New York looked like this island once upon a time, when Native people—the Lenape, whom we studied in history—lived on it and it wasn't covered in concrete.

I heard a noise then, like a soft voice. A whisper light as the wind. *Something is here with me, in these woods.* I could feel eyes on me again. There is no mistaking that sense of being watched: The nape of my neck prickled, and I shivered despite the heat. I whirled around, heart pounding, eyes darting through the trees. There was a shape, a nontree shape, moving slowly toward me on my right. I froze, all my city-girl street smarts utterly failing me. I hadn't realized how far away I'd wandered from Mom and the vine. I wanted to cry out for help, but the words stuck in my throat.

A snapping branch broke the quiet as the shape moved forward. I blinked my eyes shut, not knowing what to do. Maybe if I couldn't see it—whatever *it* was—then it couldn't see *me.* Even though years of hide-and-go-seek should've taught me that's not how it works. I stood as still as possible, wishing really hard whatever it was would go away. Finally, I peeked one eye open and saw it clearly: a deer, a young buck with fuzzy antlers. I let out a shaky laugh as it stepped closer. It was pretty awesome.

"Nell! Where'd you go?" Mom startled the deer, who raised its tail and leapt off into the forest, away from me.

"Mom!" I crashed through the underbrush, wondering how I would've woven my way out of the woods if she hadn't started hollering for me, her voice leading me toward the road. I saw her just beyond the trees. "There was this cool deer. It had little antlers!" I'd only ever seen does at the petting zoo before.

"I must have scared it away—I didn't see anything."

I ran up next to her, panting. My flip-flops were cutting into my feet. They're great for hanging around the park in the summer and showing off nail polish, but I was going to need different shoes for running through forests on Roanoke. I hadn't followed Mom's packing instructions, except for all the tooth stuff.

"Ready to go? I have to get back for a meeting with that archaeologist. You can come with me if you want, or you can hang around the house."

A meeting sounded boring. I thought about the shops we'd seen while we were driving in town. "Could I go to that bookstore instead?"

"I guess. But only there, okay? We don't know this area well yet." She started up the Jeep.

I rolled my eyes. I had walked myself home from school every day since the fifth grade. The past year or two, sometimes I came home to an empty house if Dad was writing or researching at the library. Although the *building* wasn't empty, because Mrs. Kim was always around, in case I needed anything.

Mom dropped me off at the cottage so I could get my bag. "Text me when you are leaving and when you get home."

"Mom, really. I'll be fine." She leaned down to smooth my hair off my forehead and give me the lightest of kisses on my hairline, like she always does. I have a theory that all moms have a signature kiss, and that is mine's.

Once she left, I spent a half hour padding around the cottage, peeking into all the nooks and crannies that I hadn't had the energy to explore last night. It was the homiest non-home I could imagine. All it was missing were the framed photos, vacation souvenirs, and heirloom knickknacks that make people's houses theirs. When I'd opened every last closet door, I decided it was time to hit the bookstore.

I shuffled down the shady sidewalk, passing a few other friendly white cottages. The buildings and houses on the island were either very East-Coast-islandy—lots of shutters and porches—or English-village-looking, like the theater up the street. The beachy look made sense to me, but the "Ye Olde" one didn't really. I guessed it's because this used to be an English colony.

It was hotter out than I expected, at least walking in the sun, and it was a muggy heat. I passed a store with beautiful weaving on display in the windows, a place renting big kites, and a sandwich shop called Poor Richard's. When I saw the bookstore up ahead I felt relieved, already anticipating a blast of fresh, cold air-conditioning. The store was in a Ye Olde building, marked by dark brown wood that crisscrossed against white stucco. It had a front porch with a couple of rocking chairs on it, empty except for a sleepy golden retriever. I walked across, a little nervously. I don't know why; most of the bookstores I've been to have always been welcoming places. Still, it felt kind of like the first day of school. I hadn't talked to a single person on Roanoke yet.

I sucked in a deep breath and ventured inside. The screen door slammed shut behind me, letting out a clattering *smack*. Glancing back, I could see the poor dog on the porch startle. Inside, a few people looked up from their books and at me.

A blond woman leaned over the counter as I slouched away from the entrance. "Hi! Don't let the screen hit you on your way *in*!" She grinned, and I blushed. "Can I help you find something?"

"Thanks. Um, I'm just looking." I raced over to the first section of shelves I saw and immediately pulled out a book.

"Take your time!" I was intrigued by her accent—the way she said "hi" and "time" sounded more like "hoi" and "toime." She didn't sound like the Southern people I knew in New York. But the woman seemed nice enough. Maybe I'd wait a few minutes, then ask where to find the series that Jade kept insisting I read, the one about a foodie girl.

Before I could study the back cover of the book I'd grabbed, I almost tripped over a person next to me in the aisle. "Sorry!"

"No worries." A dark-haired girl, about my age, stood up

from her browsing crouch next to me. She glanced at the book in my hands. "That book has great research, but it's kind of boring." She tipped her head, like she was sizing me up. "What else have you read?"

Was she suggesting I looked like someone who didn't read a lot? "I've read a lot of books," I finally said. And it was true. I need to have a book at every meal, and when Mom makes me put it aside to "participate in the family dinner," I find myself skimming the can of Parmesan cheese or the edge of a newspaper visible on the floor. I bristled at this girl I didn't know acting like I might be the type of person who doesn't read. I mean, my dad's a writer! So what if his past couple of mysteries didn't sell. I turned back to the shelf, my face flushing.

She tapped my shoulder. "Sure, but have you read a lot about *Roanoke*?" Her scrunched eyebrows suggested she already knew the answer.

Oh. I looked down at the title I'd pulled: *Roanoke: The Search for the Truth.* I put the book back on the shelf and crossed my arms in front of my chest, hugging my elbows slightly. "I read a couple of travel guides."

She smiled at me like I smile at Mrs. Kim's tiny dog when it can't climb back up the steep hallway steps it jumped down. "Not the island, silly. The lost colony!" I shook my head, wishing that at some point I'd read beyond that sidebar. "Hoo boy. Where were you during history class?"

The way she was acting, like me not knowing all about this lost colony was *the most unbelievable thing ever*, was annoying. Maybe people in the city have better things to obsess over than long-gone colonies. "We were busy learning about Henry Hudson." I bet she didn't know a lot about him, seeing as he was important to New York's history.

"Right, the sea explorer. His story had a sad ending too. But not a mystery." Even though she was being kind of annoying, I was impressed. The girl grabbed my hand and led me to the door. "This is a story best told out in the heat, otherwise you'll get goose bumps times a thousand. Renée, I promise I'll bring the customer back, okay?"

The woman at the counter grinned and waved at us. The girl pulled me outside to the rocking chairs, the door ricocheting shut behind us. "I'm Lila, by the way. Lila Midgett. And you?"

"Nell Dare."

Her eyes widened. "Dare?"

Thanks to my mom mentioning the significance of *Dare* during our drive, this was something I knew. "Yes, as in *Virginia*."

Lila looked impressed. "At least that's ground we don't need to cover. You're not from around here, are you?" She climbed into a chair and sat cross-legged on the seat, managing to rock herself back and forth without her feet. I considered walking down the steps and away from her bossiness. But did

I want to spend my summer alone? The cottage was perfect for sleepovers, after all. Maybe we could be friends. I sat down in the chair across from her.

"No, I'm here from New York, just for the summer."

"Welcome. Let me tell you a little about 'here.'" She cleared her throat. "Roanoke. Picture this island, 1587. Wait, no. First picture it a couple of years earlier. People had been living here for, like, ages. Algonquian-speaking people, like the Roanoke tribe, and the Croatoans, too. But the Europeans only found the island in the fifteen hundreds. Pirates and explorers got shipwrecked off the coast all the time; the shallow waters and barrier islands are treacherous. They call this area the"—she paused for dramatic effect, lowering her voice and leaning toward me—"Graveyard of the Atlantic." Lila nodded slowly, letting her words sink in.

That was creepy, honestly. Pirates and shipwrecks and graveyards, oh my. There aren't that many cemeteries in New York City, which is something I like. I've wanted to avoid them ever since Jade told me that when you walk past one you have to hold your breath and say "Dray Evarg," or "graveyard" backward, in your head until you're away. Otherwise, she said, the ghosts of the people buried there could rise out of the earth and inhabit your body, forcing out your soul. I don't really believe her, but I do it now anyway, just in case.

Still, something about Lila's know-it-all tone made me

want to play it cool. "Hmm" was all I said. Although I was pretty interested in what she was telling me. I sent a quick text to Jade: Met this girl in the bookstore—might be kind of cool. Maybe now I wouldn't feel so bad about all the time Jade was spending with Sofia.

"Anyway, in 1585 a group of English guys, mostly soldiers and stuff, came over to establish a colony. But they didn't last long. They were clueless, especially about getting food. Some of the Native people helped them out at first, but things got really bad after the Englishmen killed the Roanoke's leader, Wingina, in 1586. Eventually a bunch of the colonists went back to England, leaving fifteen behind to literally hold down the fort. Those guys all pretty much died." I shuddered a little at that.

Lila sat back in her chair, still rocking. The way her eyes shined, I could tell she loved being a storyteller. "In 1587 the English tried a second colony. Sir Walter Raleigh was behind that one. Do you know about him?"

It was a familiar name but I wasn't sure why. I bit my lip and debated whether I should say yes. But what if she asked me questions about him I couldn't answer? Impatient, Lila slapped her thighs and whistled. "Here, Sir Walter!" The sleepy dog bounded over and, panting, plopped in front of Lila. "Sir Walter Raleigh is my dog. *Aren't you, good sir!*" She petted him on his graying nose and he gave us a doggy smile. "But this *good sir*'s namesake was an important English nobleman. He sent over the second colony, made up of families. They called themselves 'planters' and were people who wanted a fresh start in a new country. Well, new to *them*." Lila paused. "Not so much the people already here, you know? My dad always reminds me of that. He's an archaeologist—and he's studied the Carolina Algonquian people that lived here long before the English." That made sense—of course Lila would know everything about this place if her dad researched it. Like how I know a lot about cool plants. It made me feel a little better about seeming clueless in comparison.

Lila kept going. I was starting to feel like I'd stumbled into summer school. "But the second group of colonists still couldn't figure out how to gather enough food on their own. They depended on help from people like Manteo, a Croatoan man who had sailed back from England with them. This town, Manteo, is named after him, of course. Anyway, it got so bad that the leader of the colony, John White, decided to go back to England to get more supplies and stuff. He left all the colonists behind, including his daughter, Eleanor. Her baby girl, Virginia Dare, was the first European born in the United States."

"I wonder if I'm related to her," I blurted out. I don't know why, but I thought that might impress Lila.

She shook her head at me, kind of sadly. "Not likely. I'll get to that in a second." I frowned and leaned back in my seat.

She was totally lecturing me, but now I really wanted to hear the rest of the story. Also, while we'd been talking Sir Walter had shuffled over and plopped on my feet, and I was enjoying petting him.

Lila glanced to her left and her right, like she was making sure we were alone. Then she scooted her rocking chair even closer to me and Sir Walter, so near I could smell the bubble-gum on her breath as she talked. She spoke in a low, serious tone. "So John White set sail for England. He left one hundred and sixteen people behind, because although two babies had been born on the island, one guy had been *murdered* right before he left." I rolled my eyes a little. It takes a lot more than mentioning the word "murder" to faze me after living in New York City my whole life.

Lila continued, "There were all kinds of delays, so it took three whole years before he returned to Roanoke. Now, he had told the colonists that if they ever left the island, they should carve where they were going into a tree. That way he could find them. Also, if they were leaving because of danger, they should carve a special symbol, called a Maltese cross." Lila swished her index finger in the air, drawing the plus-sign shape. By then I actually was on the edge of my seat, in danger of falling onto Sir Walter.

"White arrived on his granddaughter's third birthday. I bet he brought her presents from England." I pictured a man on the shore, clutching a sea-damp doll. For some reason, it made me a little wistful to think of a grandfather—or a father—doing something thoughtful like that after being away for so long.

"The fort was totally deserted. The buildings they had put up were taken down. A few things were left, like cannons and some stuff that belonged to White. But everything else was gone. The colonists had disappeared without a trace. Then White found three letters, carved into a tree: *C-R-O*."

"What did that mean?"

Lila shrugged. "White thought it meant that the colonists went to Croatoan Island, which we call Hatteras today. Manteo's village was there. But White never found the colonists, and neither has anyone ever since. They simply vanished." She made a *poof* hand motion.

"But the crosses you mentioned—did they put one on a tree? To show there had been danger?" I shifted in my rocking chair. How could so many people disappear, without anyone finding them—ever? People don't vanish into thin air, even if they die. Watching police procedural TV shows with my dad has taught me that.

Lila shook her head. "Nope. At least, not that anyone has ever found. Some people think the colonists moved onto the mainland, up by the Chesapeake. Others think they joined up with tribes in the area, like the Croatoans. They might've died of illness or been killed in a conflict—maybe the Spanish found them. And a few people actually think it was something stranger, like alien abductions." She paused for dramatic effect. "We may never know the truth."

"Crazy" was all I could bring myself to say. I felt in my pocket for my phone and refreshed the screen to see if I had any messages. None. I felt a little sick to my stomach again. But maybe it was because I hadn't really eaten lunch. I sent a quick text to my dad, telling him that I may have stumbled upon a mystery here in Roanoke. I also asked if he knew anything about our Dare family background.

Lila started rocking again. "I like to think that they're still here, haunting the island. Because there are lots of ghostly things on Roanoke, like a spooky white doe that people see in the woods. You see, nobody knows exactly where the colonists lived on the island. But I have a theory about how to find them." She gave me a self-satisfied smile. "Wherever they settled is probably where their ghosts are now. Find the ghosts, find the lost colonists."

"But what if their ghosts are gone?" Like I was even sure ghosts existed.

Lila made a *duh* face. "If you had been missing for hundreds of years, don't you think you'd stick around to see if anyone ever finds out what happened to you? Anyway, people have been trying to use archaeology to find them for decades and that hasn't worked. So maybe paranormal investigation will. Even if my dad thinks that ghosts have nothing to do with science . . ." She trailed off, then cleared her throat. "Hey." She grabbed my arm. Her hand was cold and clammy, even though it was so hot out. "I know what. You'll be my assistant. I'll teach you *everything*." She grinned at me. "You are *so* lucky you stumbled on me here. This is a rare opportunity, to learn about both Roanoke and ghost hunting from the master."

The master? Please. Even though she had good stories, Lila was bugging me. I'd also be doing enough assisting for my mom, *thankyouverymuch*. I sent another quick text to Jade: Nevermind. The girl's kind of full of herself.

"Actually, my mother is here to do very important *scientific* research, so I'm pretty busy helping her. She's a botanist at the Natural History Museum in New York. It's where—"

"I know all about that museum!" Lila interrupted. *Ugh.* That's one of my biggest pet peeves. I stood up from my chair. Sir Walter made a sad *woof* as he moved out of my way. I gave him an apology pat.

"I should head home. My mom's probably wondering where I am." I offered a halfhearted wave good-bye. "Nice talking." Jade had replied with a frowny face. *Pretty much,* I thought.

"Where are you staying?" Lila called after me. "I'll take you out on a ghost tour some day. Gratis."

Gratis. Really? I pretended not to hear her. I hurried down the steps and in the direction of the cottage. Even if I didn't like Lila, she told a good story. Hers had stuck in my head and gave me goose bumps despite the muggy heat smothering me and everything else here. All those people, left stranded on this island. How long did they wait for White to come back? And how did they feel, not knowing where he was or if he'd return? I pictured the man standing on the shore again, clutching that doll for his three-year-old granddaughter. Virginia Dare. It made me so sad to think about how he never knew what had happened to her.

Even if I didn't want to hang out with Lila and her pretentiously named (but cute) dog again, I wanted to know more about the lost colony. I couldn't believe that nobody ever figured out the truth about the colonists. There must be answers somewhere, because people just don't let those they love vanish from their lives.

Because if people did do that—could my dad vanish from mine?

CHAPTER FOUR

I felt better when Mom got home that night and grilled us steaks and corn on the cob, dripping with honey butter and dusted with salt. She chided me for not calling her when I left the house or when I got back, but because my trip to the bookstore went totally fine she didn't push it. It was like both of us knew that despite the great food and cozy cottage and charming town, something was amiss; Dad wasn't there and we weren't really talking about *why* he wasn't there. One step in the argument direction and the whole façade of fun summer research trip would come crashing down on us. No, thanks.

Mom declared that for the weekend, we were going to be tourists in the Outer Banks. She pulled out the official guide-book and a highlighter. "We'll do anything you want, sprout."

"I don't even need to look at this to know what we're doing on Saturday," I said.

She raised an eyebrow. "Oh?"

"Beach day!"

Mom rolled her eyes but smiled. My dad and I love the beach; my mom always says that it's not her thing. First, there's her fear of open water. She'll swim in a pool but I've never seen her jump in an ocean or a lake. I don't think she even likes going out in boats, in case they'd spontaneously capsize and she'd get tossed overboard. Second, Mom's one true love is plants, and they grow on land. Seaweed, she says, is not enough to make her like the ocean. Especially when it washes up on shore and starts stinking as it breaks down in the sun.

"I said 'anything,' so I suppose I have to agree to this plan. Figure out which beach you want to hit. But pick something else for Sunday, okay?"

While Mom cleaned the grill, I curled up on top of the green comforter, struggling to find a position that felt right on the lumpy mattress. I opened the guidebook and flipped through the ads. I stuck in the highlighter to mark my place and pulled my phone off the nightstand. I sent Dad another text: We are going to the beach tomorrow. You are missing out! What I really wanted to write was, What is the deal with you and Mom? Why is she acting like everything's okay when it so clearly isn't? And where in the world are you? But the thought of writing out those words—making my feelings real—was too scary.

I almost picked a Hatteras beach because that's where Lila

said that the lost colonists might've gone, and I wanted to see what it was like there. If it was the sort of place that people would want to disappear to, and if it was the sort of place where it would be hard to be found. But then I read an article about wild horses on the beach at Corolla, which changed my mind.

As I was carefully highlighting a square around a minigolf listing, my phone rattled on the nightstand. I dropped the highlighter, getting a streak of yellow onto the one white part of the comforter, and grabbed my phone.

A mystery and a beach! I am most jealous. Reminds me of this, from *The Tempest:* "Be not afeard; the isle is full of noises, sounds, and sweet airs, that give delight and hurt not. Sometimes a thousand twangling instruments will hum about mine ears, and sometimes voices." Delight in the sweet airs on the beach this weekend, and be not afeard exploring such a special island. I can't wait to hear all about it. I'll look into the Dare family stuff. Miss you.

I texted back as fast as my fingers could type: Then come join us! Where are you? I knew he was by his phone; his message had just come in. But he didn't reply, even though I stayed up for an hour, waiting to see if he would.

The next day Mom coated us both in a lifetime supply of SPF 85 and dutifully drove over the bridge and up to Corolla. The barrier island looked so long and skinny on the map that I expected to be able to see the beach from everywhere, but it was full of grass and tall trees—live oaks and crape myrtles, according to Mom—and marshy areas like on Roanoke and the mainland. Driving through the town called Duck, I saw a sign for a doughnut shop.

"Mom?" I started.

"Say no more." She flipped the blinker on and turned into the parking lot. Minutes later, we found ourselves at a wooden picnic table, eating the freshest doughnuts I'd ever tasted in my life. They put the chain doughnut shop on our corner in New York to shame.

"This," Mom said, licking lemon glaze off her fingers, "is heaven."

Stuffed, we headed to the beach, and even Mom had to admit that it was pretty gorgeous. Miles of powdery white sand, fringed with beach grass and something my mom identified as sea oats. The mugginess disappeared once you crossed over the dunes, where the sea breeze and sun combined to create the perfect temperature. The water was clear and foamy, with waves great for swimming: Big enough that it was fun to dive under them, but not so big that it was scary. Of course we were at a spot with a lifeguard, just in case.

I ran back to Mom, shaking the water off me like a dog. She didn't flinch as the droplets hit her sunglasses and mottled her sun hat. "You should swim! Dip in your toes, at least."

"Sometimes I forget that sitting on a beach and reading can be an excellent way to spend time," she said, ignoring my suggestion.

"You should tell Dad that." I stretched out next to her on my towel.

Mom was quiet for a minute, smoothing the cover of her book. Finally, she said, "I know you miss him, and he misses you, too. I'm sure when we get back . . ." But as she trailed off, she didn't sound sure at all.

"What exactly *is* his project? Is there a reason why it takes him ages to respond to texts now? Have you talked to him on the phone since we left?" I'm not stupid. Jade's family might be perfect, but plenty of my other friends have divorced parents. I know what leads up to that. Sometimes it's a parent who totally flakes out and disappears.

"I don't want you to think he's ignoring you, sprout." Mom rubbed her temples. "He's actually . . . well, he went to London."

I almost dropped my soda. "I knew it! His passport was gone." I remembered another hushed phone call, one I'd overheard our first night in the cottage, when I'd walked past Mom's room on my way to use the creepy clawfoot tub. *"England! How exactly does that fit in the budget?"* I'd thought she was talking to my aunt again, who's always going on crazy trips. But maybe Mom had been talking to Dad. If so, how in the world wouldn't she have known beforehand that he was jetting off to another *country*? "For how long?"

Mom sighed and gazed at the waves, which reminded me of those colonists. Staring out into the sea, waiting for somebody to reappear. I wonder if the moms in the lost colony had to explain to their kids why they were left alone on a mosquito-rich island to fend for themselves while the head guy sailed back to Europe. They probably made a lot of exasperated sighs too.

"It's kind of up in the air, for now." Mom looked like she was about to say something more—her mouth was opening and closing slightly, like a fish's. But then she pressed her lips shut again.

Frustrated but not wanting to fight, I pushed myself up and walked to the water. Turning around, I watched my mom pick her book up again and start reading. But I noticed, as I doodled in the wet sand with the straw from my soda, that she didn't turn a page for a really long time.

We left at sunset, tanned and tired from the salt and the heat. On the drive, I announced where we were going the next day. "It was a tough call between the Elizabethan Gardens and the Festival Park, but the park won." To be honest, it wasn't that close of a call, but I thought she'd like hearing that I was interested in a place with plants.

We got a late start on Sunday morning, and it wasn't until early afternoon that we'd cleaned up breakfast dishes and gotten out of PJs. The Festival Park was right across the sound from the Manteo waterfront, so Mom suggested we try out the two rusty old bikes in the carport. We pedaled down Budleigh Street, headed left at the stop sign, then took a right at the inn to cross the cute bridge to the park. Mom didn't have to do her breathing exercises to bike over it because it was so tiny. A bunch of boys, a little older than me, were hooting and hollering as they jumped over the railing to the water below—and my mom didn't even tell them to be careful.

Somehow I hadn't gotten the right idea from the guidebook, and I'd been expecting an amusement park: roller coasters, cotton candy, et cetera. This "Festival Park" was more of a historic site, kind of like Colonial Williamsburg. Dad dragged us to that when I was in third grade, when he was writing a Revolutionary War story. We kept joking that he should get a job as one of the reenactors in order to "write what you know," but he didn't find the idea of becoming a blacksmith very funny. He did buy a fancy quill in the gift shop and attempt to write longhand with it for a while, though, to "get inside his characters' heads." I wore a tricorn hat around the apartment for encouragement.

We locked up the bikes and walked into the visitor center. While Mom paid our admission, I wandered around, looking at the brochures and letting the air-conditioning dry the sweat I'd worked up biking over.

Mom stuck an admission sticker on the strap of my tank

top. "These will get us into the museum, the American Indian village, the settlement site, and on the sailing ship *Elizabeth II*. Today and tomorrow—so if you're bored while I'm working, you can come back."

"Sweet," I said. "Let's head over to the ship." It would be cooler by the water. The ship was one of those old, wooden, brightly painted vessels, and some costumed guys were busy unfurling the sails as we boarded.

I stopped short. "Oh wait, you hate boats."

"Not landlocked ones like this," she said. "It's okay."

"Ahoy, there!" A teenage boy in a billowy shirt squinted at us from across the deck. "Welcome aboard the *Elizabeth II*!"

"Ahoy!" Mom enthusiastically waved back, and I cringed.

Another guy came up from behind us. "Aye, two lassies, and in time to help swab the decks!" He winked at me, and I blushed. Luckily, a bunch of hyperactive little kids ran out from belowdecks and started chasing one another in circles around him.

"I'm too old for swabbing, methinks." Mom grinned at the guy. Her dorky enthusiasm made me want to walk the plank. "But I'd love to check out the astrolabe."

"I'll see you above deck," I said, hurrying toward the stern. I leaned over the edge of the boat, staring at the murky water below. I turned around to face the rest of the park. Trees hid most of the structures in the settlement site, although I could see the tip of a roof and a red-and-white flag. A pier stretched over the grasses and into the water. One boy, older than me, stood at the end of it. He stared at the ship—was he watching me? I blushed and looked away. It was silly to think that. But when I sneaked another glance, he was still looking in my direction. He raised a hand for a tentative wave. I squinted for a closer look—he was wearing some of the colonial clothes. Maybe he was one of the reenactors? I waved back at him. A huge smile overtook his face.

"Nell? Whom are you waving at?"

I dropped my hand to my side. "Wasn't waving, just swatting a mosquito."

Mom came up behind me and put her hand on my shoulder. "Did you know they actually take this ship out on the ocean?" The boy moved back into the dense trees, probably onto the footpath.

"Seriously? That's pretty neat."

A big group of tourists was waiting to climb on board. "Are you ready to disembark? I'd love to see the museum," Mom said. I looked at my mother, with her cargo shorts and frizzy hair and slightly too-large T-shirt. I wanted to go see the settlement, and maybe say hello to that boy. With a pang of guilt, I realized that I'd rather not try to talk to him with my mom there. Also because the settlement featured a set of armor for visitors to try, and I just knew my mom would force me to put it all on.

"Did you say I could get in with this sticker tomorrow, too?"

"Yup, and that's a good thing because we won't have time to see everything today. Are you having fun?" Mom asked, with a hopeful smile.

"Mm-hmm. Let's go to the museum now." We clambered off the ship and onto the dock.

"Wonderful. I could use an hour of air-conditioning, before I melt. 'Oh, what a world, what a world.'" Mom grinned at me. I knew I'd made the right call in terms of not venturing near that boy with my *Wizard of Oz*–quoting mom in tow.

But as we walked toward the museum, I kept sneaking glances in the direction of the settlement area, to see if maybe he was still over there. Jade always talks about eye contact—most of her "relationships" so far have consisted of her staring at the boys she likes. She insists that she has amazing eye contact with them and it means that they like her back. *I* think it means that they probably think she has a major staring problem. But I started to understand what she was saying. There was something about the way in which that boy and I looked at each other; it wasn't how you accidentally catch someone's eye on the subway and then quickly glance away. It sounds super cheesy, but I felt like we made a connection. It made me want to talk to him, to see if we actually had. Or if the heat had simply melted my brain.

Mom left early the next morning to spend quality time

with her vine. As soon as the Jeep pulled out of the carport, I grabbed my bag and pedaled off on my bike, even though the park was close enough that I could have walked. This time, I went straight to the settlement village. I was nervous, but I kept thinking about Jade and Sofia hanging out with tennis boys, while I spent my whole summer with my mom and a grapevine. If I talked to the reenactor boy even just once, I could go home and tell Jade that I'd had more than eye contact. She and Sofia would be impressed.

A grinning man in Elizabethan work clothes approached me as soon as I stepped onto the woodchips. "Care to try on a suit of armor, sweet maid?"

"No, thanks. Just looking around." I slipped past him and headed behind the blacksmith's building. *Maybe I was foolish not to say hello to that boy yesterday. Maybe he doesn't work every day, and I missed my chance.* I walked the whole perimeter of the settlement, but I didn't see him anywhere. As I was leaving for the American Indian village, though, I heard a voice behind me.

"Good morrow."

I whirled around. It was him—same faded white colonial shirt, slightly baggy pants, and worn-out buckle shoes. His hair was dark brown and a little long and unkempt—the kind of style my mom would call a "mop." His blue eyes, staring at me both shyly and intently, were the brightest I'd ever seen. His voice had the slightest hint of an accent, or maybe it was the fact that he had said an old word like "morrow" throwing me off.

"Hi," I replied. "I mean, good *morrow* to you." I curtsied, and immediately after, I started to blush. The curtsy happened without thinking. The armor guy looked over at me funny, and internally I cringed. Already I could picture myself telling Jade that I had a chance to talk to a boy on Roanoke, but I blew it by acting like a weirdo.

But the boy laughed. "Aye, a most mannerly lass!" Relief.

When I saw him the day before, I thought he was older, maybe even in high school. Whatever age you have to be in North Carolina to get a summer work permit. Now that I was standing next to him, he looked a lot closer in age to me. He was only an inch or two taller than me, and thin in a way that didn't make him scrawny but did make his pale cheekbones stick out. I know I'm too young to work, so why was he at the park, sweating in colonial garb, in the middle of the summer? "Aren't you kind of young to work here?" I asked. "No offense."

Something flashed across his eyes, a seriousness that I wasn't used to seeing in someone my age. "None taken. I am certes—I mean, certainly—young." He blushed. "It's tough to stop speaking like a colonist." I admired his commitment to attempting period language. If my dad didn't text me Shakespeare all the time, I'd have been lost with all the olde talk. The boy pointed to a woman leaning against one of the settlement buildings, in the shade of the thatched roof. She was wearing a heavy woolen dress in a drab charcoal color, one so long I couldn't see her feet on the ground, and her hair was pinned back in a severe bun. Her eyes, the same bright blue as the boy's, were forlorn. I guess I would be sad too, if I had to wear that kind of an outfit every day during a North Carolina summer. "Anyway, my mother's over there. She barely lets me out of her sight." She looked pretty young to be his mom.

"My mom's super overprotective too. And I'm also helping mine at work for the summer. So, what's your name?" I wasn't normally capable of asking a boy I'd just met for his name, much less after establishing myself as a total dork by curtsying in front of him. Maybe it's because I had caught him staring at me the day before. That gave me some confidence.

His face flushed. "Where are my manners? I'm Ambrose Viccars Junior. My mother is Elizabeth Viccars. And you are?"

"Nell Dare, and my mom's Celia Wood." I stuck my hand out to shake his, but he didn't reach for it. I quickly pulled back and clasped my hands together. My palms were kind of sweaty, anyway, so maybe that was for the best.

"Dare!" His eyes lit up with excitement. *What is it with people around here and* Dare*? I get that it's a famous name, but it's not like I freak out about every Hudson or LaGuardia I meet.*

"I know, like this county."

His cheeks lost some of their paleness. "Er, right." He glanced over at his mom. "Excuse me for one minute? I'll ask my mother permission to take you on a tour of the grounds. If that's, um, *cool.*"

I nodded, and Ambrose raced over to his mom. She looked at me somewhat suspiciously at first, her mouth set in a tight frown. But he kept talking and suddenly she smiled. I could see her nod yes to Ambrose, then take his face in her hands and kiss his forehead. She disappeared around the side of the building as Ambrose walked back to me, turning once to wave, but she had already slipped away. It seemed kind of weird that he was such a mama's boy, but at the same time it was nice.

Ambrose and I strolled to the American Indian village. "The park is very accurate. It's almost as though the people who created it had been able to see John White's drawings. Or speak with Manteo themselves," Ambrose said.

John White—I remembered that name from Lila's lecture on the bookstore porch. "He was the governor of the colonists, right?"

Ambrose grinned at me. "Yes! So you know about him?"

"A little. I've started learning the history of this island—I figured I might as well, if I'm stuck here for the summer."

Ambrose nodded. "Me too."

"I thought you lived here all the time?"

He paused thoughtfully. "Well, I suppose I live here *and*

I'm stuck." His voice still had an accent. It wasn't unlike the one Renée at the bookstore had, and other people in the area, too. Maybe that was some kind of Southern drawl, although it sounded more like a brogue. I smiled at him, and we kept walking.

"Does your dad work here too?" I didn't know why I'd asked that. I wasn't normally so nosy, and I'd been trying to keep off the subject of dads as much as possible, so long as mine was MIA. But there was something about Ambrose—he was easy to talk to. Mellow. The opposite of Lila, who made me feel oddly competitive with someone I'd just met and never had to see again.

"My father left us," Ambrose said. "But he'll be back someday."

I felt like someone had punched me in the gut. I actually stopped midstride, and Ambrose took two steps ahead of me before he realized that I was standing still. "Nell?" he asked. "Are you all right?"

"Sorry," I said, a little dazed. Hearing Ambrose talk so matter-of-factly about his own dad leaving was a shock. I still hadn't even told Jade what was really going on with mine. "It's that, well, my dad is gone too, and I don't know when he's coming home." It felt good to say that out loud to someone. I let out a deep breath.

Ambrose's smile showed so much sympathy that I thought I

might cry. "Home to Roanoke?" Ambrose stood next to me, so close our arms were almost touching. It felt like we both wanted to reach out and give each other a hug, but neither of us had the guts to do it.

I shook my head. "New York City. Where I'm from. Apparently he went to London."

"London!" Ambrose said, grinning. "That's where I'm from."

"I knew it! I could hear it in your voice." It wasn't just the fake colonial speak, or that local twang, but traces of a British accent that hid in his vowels and certain words, like "over" and "never." "How long have you lived here? And why'd you move?"

He shrugged. "My parents wanted a new life, I suppose. We've been here a few years."

We'd walked past the village and were at the edge of the park, close to the shimmering Shallowbag Bay. "So if you work here, you must know a lot about the lost colonists," I said.

Ambrose was quiet. I hoped I sounded curious and not like an interrogator, as Lila had, even though Ambrose had brought John White up in the first place. Being near the water reminded me of the scene I had imagined, of the man on the coast with the doll for his granddaughter, Virginia. Even though I had made it up, I couldn't erase it from my brain. It was so painful to think of the friends and family of all those colonists, never knowing what became of them. "I can't get it out of my head. It's unbelievable that they still don't know the truth, after all these years."

Right then, I had a thought—one that should've occurred to me sooner. This island was the site of a massive, centuries-old mystery. My dad writes about those two very things: mysteries and histories. What if he could write about Roanoke? What if he—or *we*—could figure out what happened? Or find clues about where the colonists had lived. It would be the best kind of mystery to solve—a real one. "I want to find them," I said. "Or at least some clues that nobody has been able to uncover yet."

Ambrose turned slowly, letting the idea sink in. "Maybe you could. Exploring this island is practically all I do, and I know all the places they might have been—and gone."

"Really?" I asked. He nodded, biting his lip. "Then let's explore the island together." I felt a little flutter in my chest. As curious as I was about the lost colony, and excited about the idea of solving the mystery to help my dad, I have to admit that I also wanted to spend more time with Ambrose.

He grinned, his eyes shining. "Awestruck!"

"You mean 'awesome'?"

"Er, yes." He shrugged. "That's what we say around here." Ambrose was definitely a little odd, with his reenactor clothes and having to get permission from his mom to walk around with me. But there was something very charming about him. I'll admit it: He was super cute. Every time his floppy hair fell over his blue eyes, I had to restrain myself from reaching over to brush it away. I wanted to take his picture with my phone and send it to Jade. She would gush over how adorable he was. She'd probably get on the next plane to come visit me (and meet his friends).

Ambrose suggested we meet up at the Elizabethan Gardens the next morning at eleven. From there, we'd figure out how to start our investigation.

"Maybe we should exchange numbers, so we could text before meeting up."

He looked embarrassed. "I don't actually have a telephone."

I nodded. "It took years for me to convince my parents to put me on the family plan and get me my own phone." What finally made it happen was the day that Dad, on a deadline for some freelance thing, got caught up in his writing at the coffee shop and forgot to pick me up from school. I walked home, which was fine, but once I got there I was locked out of the apartment. Mrs. Kim found me sitting on the stoop and took me in for tea and cookies. She had me call Mom at work to let her know where I was, and Mom freaked. After that, I got my own phone. Also, Mr. Cohen had watched the whole thing unfold from inside his front-facing apartment, so he pulled an old manual on locksmithing from the depths of his bookshelves and gave it to me, along with a few lessons in lock picking. I wasn't a natural, which is to say I've never managed to get a lock open.

"Do you really think we could find something?" Maybe I

was being foolish, a city girl coming here and thinking she'd stomp around the woods and on the beach for a couple of weeks and solve the oldest mystery in America.

"As a colonist would've said, *perchance*," Ambrose said. "I really do."

Maybe this summer would be more exciting than I thought.

If the voyage were rough, our arrival was e'en more so. Once the last of the planters loaded into the boat for shore, the slippery and wicked Fernandez announced he would take us no farther. How absolute a snake was he for leaving us to find our way to the Chesapeake.

Until we could journey thither, Roanoke was our home. For not yet a week we had stood on its shores, when already one of our colony we lost: George Howe, assistant to Governor White and father to my friend George. The elder George we found dead in the shallow water whither he had gone to crab.

'Twas a murder!

When news reached the village that sixteen arrows had struck him, 'twas as though a cloud covered the whole island. Nary a soul knew what caused him to be killed. Mother and I stayed with his son, George, day and night, to console him as best we could. In light of that most wicked event, the island grew dark and eerie. How hopeful we all were, on the way to our new land. Upon his death, we all clearly saw the struggles that lay ahead.

Fortune had given us the assistance of Manteo, the Croatoan man returned from England with us. He was our friend and our guide. Two days after poor George was found, Manteo and some of the men sought answers on Croatoan Island. Thither they heard that George had been killed by Roanoac men, led by Wanchese—who still wanted to avenge

· 66 ·

the werowance Wingina's murder. The Croatoans, though, had shown much compassion in helping our group, so long as we agreed to ne'er take their grain. They would help us plant crops and gather for the coming winter. 'Twas a blessing, nothing less, to have their help—especially as, for lacking salt, we would struggle to store food for the cold weather.

Despite the danger that lapped at our settlement, like the waves upon the shore—Roanoke was a beautiful isle. The flowers and trees, most bountiful. The sandy ground smelled nothing like the mucky, malodorous dirt in London, but had a fresh and rich scent. 'Twas the goodliest soil any of us had e'er seen. We were most eager to set our plantings.

Upon us was the task of repairing the structures from the failed colony of 1585. When at long last we found the fort, 'twas filled not with Grenville's men, but with an overgrowth of melon vines—and bleached bones of those who had tried to settle the isle before. We were not to stay thither, among the fallen, for long. Mother was relieved—she was afeard whilst living among the ruins. Although I boasted to Thomas that I had no qualms to sleep in the old fort, in truth I was happy that we should leave. I still dreamt of the Chesapeake, full of riches: glittering gold and copper, fresh crabs and crops. And pearls as big as cherries.

Thomas and I (and sometimes young George) devised sport and merriment in the woods. We frolicked and explored, *enjoying majestic trees and quiet spaces unlike anything e'er seen at home. We gulped up the water from the streams, so fresh and clean. And we gorged on grapes—the island was thick with vines from which the largest, most juicy white grapes dropped like manna from heaven. Dare say I they were more delicious than anything I e'er ate in London? Explorers who had come hither before proclaimed that this island was "so full of grapes . . . in all the world, the like abundance is not to be found." My father fretted about drought, but I was not afeard: How possibly could we starve with so much bounty from nature, hither to take? 'Twas our good fortune that we 116 planters might feast upon it.*

CHAPTER FIVE

I had such a wonderful day today!" Mom burst through the kitchen door into the back garden, where I sprawled across a chair, reading about the lost colony. I'd stopped at the bookstore on my way home from the park. When Renée had recommended a title to me, she'd said, "I'm absolutely tickled that little Lila finally has a pal. You history-loving girls are peas in a pod." I just smiled and took my change. I hadn't *completely* given up on being pals, but I didn't think we'd be sharing a pea pod.

Mom flung herself into the chair next to mine. "Well, mostly wonderful. The construction for that golf course starts soon, so now I'm scrambling. Not to mention the archaeologists are concerned. For all they know, the secrets of the lost colony are one dig away from being uncovered—and a bulldozer coming into the picture could mean that they're never found."

I set my book down. "Wait. Hasn't most of the evidence been found near the historic site, not your vine?" The book mentioned some of the artifacts scientists had uncovered.

She shrugged. "The reconstructed fort there is from the 1585 colony—not necessarily the lost one. It was excavated way back in the nineteen fifties, when methods weren't as great, so parts could even be from the Civil War. Most people think the second colony's village was near the fort, or possibly along the edge of the island. There's nothing to suggest that the site was anywhere near Alder Branch—the stream where the Grandmother Vine is. But there's no evidence it *wasn't*, either."

Lila had said the English were super secretive about the colony's location, because they didn't want pirates or the Spanish to raid it. Too bad that meant we didn't have all the information four hundred years later. "Someone should figure out how to stop the construction." Maybe Ambrose and I could help.

Mom sighed, pulling her frizzy hair into a bun on the top of her head. "They're trying. Luke Midgett, the archaeologist helping me write my paper, filed a slew of requests and has been negotiating with the developer."

Midgett. I had a sinking feeling in my stomach. This was a small island, after all. "Does he have a daughter?"

"Who, Luke?" Mom asked. "Do you have ESP? I was about to tell you. Another reason why this was a wonderful day is that I found a friend for you."

I groaned and sank back into my chair, covering my face with my hands. "Lila?" I mumbled from beneath my palms.

"Now you're freaking me out, sprout. How did you know her name?"

"I ran into her at the bookstore," I said, still mumbling.

"What a coincidence. Anyway, they're coming over for dinner tomorrow, with Lila's mom. Kate's her name." Mom grinned. "I never like entertaining in our apartment because we don't have a dining room. But it might be kind of fun here. Like playing house."

It bothered me how thrilled my mom seemed with our new life on Roanoke. Sure, it was nice to live in the cottage and all. But didn't she feel like something—some*one*—was missing? Every time she grinned, I felt like yelling, *Why aren't you as upset as I am?* But I didn't say anything. Maybe Ambrose's sensitive mom-handling had rubbed off on me.

The Elizabethan Gardens didn't look that far from town—an easy bike ride. At least that's what I thought. But it turned into, as my dad would say, a comedy of errors.

While I was only a few blocks from the cottage, the pedals started to feel funny and then *thwack*! The bike's chain was off, and despite covering my hands with grease, I couldn't get it back on. *Great. So I can tell a coniferous from a deciduous tree, but I can't fix a bike.* I raced back to Budleigh Street, where I left the busted bike in the carport, taking the bigger one out.

It was already 10:54 a.m., and Ambrose had said to meet at eleven, so I biked as fast as I could. My hair underneath the helmet was sticky with sweat, and my legs burned. Like all New Yorkers, I was used to walking everywhere, but biking was a whole new ballgame. I didn't think I had the gears set right, because it felt like I was pedaling against nothing. My flimsy flip-flops were not helping the situation.

I panted my way down the highway leading north to the gardens. Occasionally a car or truck passed me from a comfortable distance, the driver waving or giving me a little salute. Then I heard a rumble behind me and turned around, wobbling a bit. A construction truck barreled down the road, taking up the full lane—heading straight toward me with no room to spare. Frantic, I swerved off the pavement and onto the shoulder. I almost toppled off the bike as I came to a stop, right before the truck whizzed by, honking angrily. Debris from its gravel load spewed off, pinging my bare legs and arms and making me cough. I wiped the grime off my face and sunglasses, glaring at its trail of dust. Why couldn't they leave this place like it was: a quaint town, a quiet island soaked in an old mystery? I biked with renewed energy, thinking of how important it was to look for clues *now.*

Finally, I saw a sign for Fort Raleigh National Historic Site and the Elizabethan Gardens next door. I took a deep breath, forcing my feet to keep moving. The wooded side road eventually led to a parking lot. I wheezed in, locked up my bike, and used what little strength I had left in my legs to dash over to the entrance, which was a stately brick building flanked by ornamental shrubs and flowers. The building looked English—at least like some of the ones I saw in photos in Mom and Dad's album from their honeymoon. They went all over Europe, but spent a full week in London. Dad still talks about how they saw a play at the Globe Theatre, where Shakespeare's plays were performed in his time. Mom still talks about the meal they had at a restaurant near the theater called the Arden. Dad's always promised me that he'd take me "across the pond," as he put it, and we could see a play at the Globe. But apparently he decided to go by himself.

Right then, I'd have settled for Shakespeare in Central Park—meaning we'd both be home.

Through the doorway, I entered a bright and cheerful space doubling as a gift shop and ticket counter. Inside, it smelled like my grandma's favorite soap: "English Rose," which made sense because of all the flowers and the scented candles. I pulled a sweaty five out of my shorts pocket and handed it to the lady behind the register. She thanked me, held out an admission sticker, and asked if I needed any help navigating the grounds.

"No, thanks. I'm meeting a friend here, and I'm late. Has a

boy"—I blushed saying that—"about my age come in yet? Maybe a half hour ago?"

She shook her head. "I'm afraid not. But I've only been taking admission for the last fifteen minutes—perhaps he got here early." She winked at me, which made my blush even deeper, and handed me a brochure. The tagline on the front read: A LIVING MEMORIAL TO OUR ENGLISH COLONISTS. Interesting. "There's a map inside. Feel free to ask a docent or employee if you need any help."

"Thanks," I said, slapping the sticker on my shirt. I hoped Ambrose hadn't waited long in the hot sun. Or worse: What if he'd thought I was standing him up, and had left? I hurried out of the entrance building. To my right, past a gurgling fountain, was some kind of herb garden. I opened up the brochure to figure out where it was on the map. *Shakespeare's Herb Garden!* I wished that my parents were with me, because it would be the perfect attraction for both of them: Shakespeare for Dad, plants for Mom. Even though I needed to get back to finding Ambrose, I pulled out my phone and whipped off a text to Dad: I am @ Shakespeare's Herb Garden! Come here & you can see it! (Also, you still haven't said why you are in England.)

I put my phone away, folded up the brochure, and hurried down the path. According to the map, I was on the Fragrance Walk, and it did smell like a perfume bottle had exploded, but in a good way. Yucca and sea-holly plants grew on either side of me.

I turned down another path and wound up in front of a big metal statue of Queen Elizabeth I. I stopped to take a quick picture to send to Jade. *New hairstyle for me?* I will never understand why people in the olden days thought certain things were attractive, like hairstyles that show off a high forehead or collars that spread out beyond your head like some hybrid of a halo and bat wings. I moved on, scanning the grounds for Ambrose. Seeing no one, I turned onto yet another wooded path. At the end, right in front of a tree, was a white statue, surrounded by worn stone benches. A boy sat cross-legged on the ground. Ambrose.

I raced down the pine-needle-dusted path toward him. "I'm so sorry I'm late!"

He turned to look at me, and his eyes lit up. "Nell! I thought you were lost!"

I collapsed next to him, leaning against a bench. Sweat had pooled on my back, and I wiped lines of it from my forehead. "My bike broke, and I had to go back to the cottage for the other one, and I don't think the gears were working right. Then this construction truck almost ran me off the road. Now I'm super late." *And super embarrassed*, I thought.

Ambrose pushed his hair back from his forehead. He didn't look sweaty or hot at all, and his skin was milky pale as ever. He leaned back onto his elbows and smiled, so I knew he wasn't too mad. "And despite all that, you made the journey. I'm so pleased to see you."

"Likewise." I shaded my eyes and looked up at the statue, which was a teenage girl, carved out of weathered marble. "Who's this we're looking at?" Figures a boy would be sitting and staring at a pretty marble girl, especially one not wearing much clothing. As I looked at it more closely, I felt my cheeks redden. I knew it was art and all, but the woman wasn't wearing *anything* up top except for a necklace and some upper-arm bracelets. She had only a shawl or something draped over her bottom half. She could've been a pop singer on a magazine cover. The huge oaks surrounding the statue cast shade over her exposed parts, making it seem a little more demure. But they didn't hide the fact that this was a very *naked* statue.

Ambrose hopped to his feet, looking embarrassed. "Your first lesson in Roanoke history. This sweet, um, girl is the famous Virginia Dare."

"Wait, that doesn't make sense. Virginia disappeared before she turned three." I scrunched my eyebrows as I thought more about Virginia versus the statue. "Plus why would she be wearing that? If the colonists were anything like the pilgrims, they weren't exactly known for skimpy clothing. I mean"—I made a little snort—"she should be wearing something like your mom's costume." As soon as I said it, I worried that maybe I came off as mean. "No offense," I added weakly. I scooted over to read the plaque and swallowed hard. Ambrose was telling the truth—the sculpture *was* of Virginia Dare. "Oh. I guess you're right." *I am such a jerkface.*

Ambrose shook his head at me. "Well, you've got a sharp tongue." He didn't seem upset, though. "It's supposed to show how Virginia would look if she'd survived on the island. Anyway, there's much more to see."

I was happy to move away from the statue and my embarrassment. "It said that this garden is a memorial to the colonists. Kind of like a grave?"

"Yes," Ambrose said, stepping over a root in the path. "But not so somber. I come here a lot, to nap in the thatched gazebo or play on the grass. It's very peaceful. I like thinking that there's a place created in memory of the colonists. It makes them seem less lost." He cleared his throat. "Anyhow, the first place we should look for clues is the sound," he said. "If anyone left the island by boat, that could be the spot. I've always wondered if perhaps others sailed for help, like John White did."

We made our way along the pine-shaded path. Ambrose seemed different from yesterday, quieter. Maybe he actually *was* annoyed that I showed up so late. Maybe I really had insulted his mom with that stupid comment about the dress they made her wear at the Festival Park. I sneaked my phone out of my pocket and refreshed the screen, hoping to see a text from Dad. I'd taken a picture of the sign for Shakespeare's garden too, and sent that to him. No word. My heart sank a little bit, and even though it was a perfectly sunny day, I felt cold and uneasy. How was I going to convince him that there was a story to write about Roanoke if he wasn't here to see this history for himself? But when I noticed that I no longer had any bars, I didn't feel so bad that he hadn't responded yet.

"Look!" Ambrose stopped in front of a tall and gnarled tree.

I gazed up at it. "That's a nice-looking tree."

Ambrose pointed at a plaque. "This is an ancient live oak. It's been here since before the colonists first arrived in 1585."

"Whoa!" I ran over and touched the bark, just because. "I had no idea trees could live that long."

"It's *super* interesting," Ambrose said. He looked kind of proud of himself when I nodded. We stared at it appreciatively for a few minutes, and I took a picture.

We emerged from the manicured gardens at the start of another walkway, lined with spiky saw palmettos and a few loblolly pines. I loved how that tree's name rolled off my tongue. The sign said we were on the Colony Walk, and at the end was a large wooden gate; beyond that, the blended edge of the island and the sea. Silvery calm water lapped at the patch of beach—it wasn't really a *beach* beach, like the one I'd been to at Corolla, but there was a sliver of rocky sand circling the marshy coast.

Once we were up at the gate, I saw that it was padlocked. "How are we supposed to get to the beach?"

Ambrose grinned. "Like this!" He shinnied up and over the gate fast as a squirrel scaling a tree. When I tried to follow his lead, it didn't work out as well.

"Can you give me a hand?" I was stopped precariously at the top, one leg on the beach side, one still dangling garden-side. Ambrose nervously spotted me as I heaved myself all the way over and down, dropping onto the dirt.

Overgrown with beach grasses and piled with fallen branches, it wasn't the easiest beach to walk on. Tufts of sharp plants popped up among the sandy pools of water and stone. I swatted away a pesky mosquito near my elbow. Thanks to all that soggy grass, it was bug heaven. Even the breeze wouldn't keep them all away.

"The weather was like this the day my father left," Ambrose said, kicking at a stone. "Windy." I noticed, for the first time, that today his feet were bare. Was that part of his reenacting thing? His clothes were still colonial-looking: a frayed white long-sleeve shirt and dark, rough-looking pants. Or maybe he was like the barefoot runners I sometimes saw in the park. Personally, I like shoes—especially out in nature, where there is plenty of scat and insects.

"You saw him off?" I didn't know whether it would be harder to miss someone if you saw him leave, or if he sneaked away at a time when he wouldn't have to say good-bye. "Did he take a ship?" There weren't many passenger boats in the area.

Mom's guidebook had said that many of the fishing tours left from Wanchese, the town on the southern half of the island.

Ambrose shaded his eyes and stared across the sound. "He left on a pinnace." I had no idea what a pinnace was, but I didn't want to sound like an idiot, so I simply nodded. "How I miss him," he added softly.

All this talk was starting to depress me, big-time, and I couldn't think of a thing to say to make Ambrose feel better, despite my similar situation. I leaned toward him, wanting to put my palm on his shoulder in a friendly squeeze. But as my outstretched arm moved closer to him, he shifted and bent to pick a blade of grass. I dropped my arm, both surprised that I'd had the guts to, literally, reach out and also kind of relieved that I hadn't succeeded. I was too shy to even stand next to most of the boys at my school, and they were a lot less cute than Ambrose, with his curls and bright eyes. I definitely had to get a picture of him, so Jade would believe me when I went back home and told her about his cuteness.

Clearing my throat, I said, "I'm going to look around." Slipping off my mucky flip-flops, I left them and my phone in the dry sand and scooted past Ambrose to the water's edge. I glanced down the coastline and, a few hundred feet away, saw a bunch of pilings and a sunken dock sticking out into the sound. A small, sturdy rowboat was at the end of it, tied up with a mossy green rope. *So I guess people do leave on boats around here.*

I waded to the dock, my toes curling into the pebbly sand to keep my balance. "Ouch!" I cried, my big toe stubbing on something round and hard sticking up from the soft floor of the sound. I pulled my leg out of the water and rested my foot against my bent knee, kind of like a flamingo, to examine it. No fresh cuts, at least. My toe throbbed.

"What happened?" Ambrose asked, standing behind me. He'd moved so quietly through the water, creating barely a ripple, that I hadn't heard him.

"I stubbed my toe on something buried in the sand." I lowered my foot back into the water. Then I bent down and felt around the muck, trying to find whatever had tripped me up. My fingers trailed through the silt and stone, searching until I brushed something oddly shaped, hard and heavy. I yanked at it, but it didn't budge. "Whatever I stepped on is stuck." It didn't feel like something natural, like a rock. I wondered . . . Could it be a clue?

The water was shallow enough that I could kneel down and the hem of my shorts wouldn't get wet, so I did. With both hands, I scooped at the heavy sand covering the sides of the object. It felt like some kind of pottery or glass, with rounded edges. I wrapped my hands around it and tugged harder. This time, it popped up out of the sand, sending me backward into the water with a splash. *"Argh!"*

"Nell! Are you all right? Oh, what a knave I am, letting you dig that out yourself." Ambrose moved frantically through the weeds and water, but I scrambled up without his help.

"I'm fine, really. I didn't realize how buried that thing was." Now where was it, floating somewhere in the water? My soaked shorts clung to my legs; even the back of my shirt was plastered to me. My wet ponytail slapped the back of my neck, and I squeezed out some of the water. There was no use in trying to wring my clothes. I took a deep breath, then crouched to run my hands against the bottom of the sound again. *I am going to find that thing. I did not just fall on my butt in front of Ambrose for nothing.* Whatever "knave" meant, I was the one to feel embarrassed.

"There!" He pointed to the left of my right foot. "I can see it." Sure enough, whatever I'd uncovered was lying there, already tucked under a soft blanket of silt. I yanked it out of the murk.

Ambrose grinned. "Huzzah! You found it."

At first I thought it was a vase, but as I turned the object right side up, I saw that the opening was too narrow. Some kind of bottle? The bottom part was round like a globe, but there was a spout that ended with a flared top, sealed in by more crusty goop. It looked almost like a flask—Mr. Cohen has a square metal one that he sips out of when he sits on the stoop, but since he doesn't drink anymore, he fills his with apple juice.

"I can't believe it! It's just a piece of trash. Litterbugs." I rolled it over in my hands. It wasn't made of glass but of some kind of reddish ceramic. That was hard to tell, though, because it was encrusted with sea gunk and all sorts of scratches. I rubbed off some crud on one side and rinsed the bottle in the water. "See?" I held it up for Ambrose. His eyes widened as he pointed at the object. "What is it?" I turned the thing back around so I could see what made him go pale and quiet. Was there something crawling on it? I tensed up, thinking maybe I'd picked up a sea creature or a bug.

He shook his head. "This—this isn't garbage. It's made of good stoneware." He let out a little gasp. "Wait—what marks are on that side?"

"Um." I held it right up to my face. I'd thought the markings were dings and scratches, not script. "It looks like maybe *A, V*? That might be an *E*—it's hard to tell."

"*A, V,* maybe *E*," Ambrose repeated.

"Looks like a monogram." I squinted some more at the marks. "Maybe this was somebody's special bottle."

Ambrose closed his eyes for a few seconds and raised his face to the sun. "Or a drinking flask. Nell, I think . . ." He opened his shining eyes and stepped closer to me. "It might be an artifact," he breathed. "From long ago."

"Are you serious? Here, take a look."

He peered at the flask while I held it out. "Do you know what this means?"

I shook my head no. The flask suddenly seemed both weightier and more fragile in my hands. I was holding a piece of history. "This is from the colony?"

Ambrose nodded. "I am sure of it. Totes."

I barely stifled a laugh. "Totes" sounded pretty funny in his accent. "Wait. Why are you so certain? How much do you know about this archaeology stuff?"

Ambrose's cheeks flushed. "Because I've seen ones *exactly* like this before. At the museum."

A wave lapped at my shins, and that reminded me of something my mom had said about the colony being close to the water. "Ambrose—unless this flask just happened to wash up here, do you think this means that the site of the colony was somewhere in this area? Maybe the settlement was along this shore." Maybe I was standing *right next* to the lost colony.

Ambrose bit his lip, kind of adorably, and then said, "I . . . People don't know where their settlement was. But I know this could be an important clue."

Something told me I should try to clean off more of the flask. Instinct, I guess. I scraped at the goo and rubbed with my fingers for a few seconds, gently, not wanting to hurt it. "Do you want to try?" Honestly, I didn't want to be responsible for scrubbing too hard and breaking it.

Ambrose lightly brushed the side with the edge of his shirt. "Er, give it another rinse," he said. I dipped it into the water, and it came out much cleaner. So clean that I could see there were even more scratches on the other side.

"Wait, is there something *written* on it?" I could recognize only a few words—like "shipp" and "mutinous," and "childe." "I think it's a message."

"What does it say?" Ambrose's voice rose to an almost-squeak. He hurried over, standing so close to me our cheeks were practically touching. In silence, we stared at the crude lines of old-fashioned, near-impossible-to-read handwriting. More like hand-scratches. The letters looked like those in the old manuscripts at the Cloisters, which the guide had said were in Gothic script. Regardless, it was Greek to me. Except for those few words and something near the top—a Maltese cross, like Lila had told me about. The colonists' symbol for danger.

"Could this be a message from one of the colonists?"

"Let me see," he whispered. He traced the lines of text. I couldn't make much sense of most of the writing, but one word was unmistakable: the year in the upper right-hand corner. 1587.

"Whoa. Just, whoa." Ambrose must have seen old-fashioned writing like that at the Festival Park. "Can you tell what it says?" I handed it to him.

His hands shook as he grasped it. "Take it, please," he said. "I can't keep it steady."

I cradled the flask, and Ambrose read quietly for a few long minutes. Then he swallowed hard, like he had a big lump in his throat. "I can't understand all of it. But it seems this *is* a message from a colonist—telling his whereabouts."

"Where did they go?" I practically shouted. Over four hundred years of mystery, and here we'd figured it out so quickly!

He coughed. "N-not all of them. It appears . . ." Ambrose paused. "A group of the colonists left Roanoke."

I gasped. "And does it say why they marked *C-R-O* on the tree? To tell people that they were going to Croatoan? What was the danger—there's a cross on it!"

He shook his head. "I'm afraid it doesn't say."

Then it hit me. If we knew the colonists had left, what would be on the island for us to find? "So now we don't have anything to search for here, huh?" The flask was amazing—but had I just lost a reason for us to go exploring together?

Ambrose shook his head. "It doesn't say that they *all* left. I think the writer was trying to reach someone still on the island."

"That doesn't make sense—why wouldn't the colonists stick together?"

Ambrose's face darkened. "Perhaps some went for help. Perhaps they thought they'd come right back. Perhaps the carving on the trees came later, or meant something different."

I nodded thoughtfully. "We need more evidence." The disappointment I'd felt, thinking we wouldn't have much else to look for, faded. Then I had an idea. "Can you see who scratched that message? If there's a name?"

"Hmm. That's difficult to make out."

"Let me try," I said, bending awkwardly to get it in the best light. "Hey, is that a letter *A*?" I swear Ambrose turned a shade paler.

He squinted at it. "Yes, and I think it reads . . . Archard, Thomas."

I stood back up. "Interesting. Maybe we should show it to someone. Like at the Festival Park. They might recognize the name." I wanted to do the right thing, but I kind of hoped Ambrose would say no. Now that we had an actual clue from the lost colony, the possibility that we could solve the mystery seemed real. If we told the museum, a lot of people would get involved—but I wanted this to be our thing. Because my hands were still gripping the flask, I crossed my toes that Ambrose wouldn't want to share it, at least not yet.

Ambrose shook his head. "It's better if we keep this to ourselves for now. Only until we know more." *Huzzah.*

Pesky mosquitoes or sand flies were swarming me, now that I was damp from falling on my butt. "I need to go home and change." I picked up my phone. Still no bars, but the clock worked. Somehow, it was already three thirty p.m. Mom would want me at the cottage when she got back, so I could help her make dinner. And I would need time to rinse off and hang my wet clothes on the line, so she didn't get overprotective on me and nosy about what I'd been doing all day. "Also, aren't you being eaten alive by mosquitoes?" I hadn't seen Ambrose swat a single one. "I guess you're more covered up than I am. Wearing long sleeves was smart."

Ambrose nodded. "Believe it or not, there are benefits to these old clothes."

We crunched down the garden paths, and I felt dizzy every time I glanced down at our treasure. *We really might figure this thing out. I can't wait to tell Dad.* I tucked the flask under my arm and shoved my wet hair off my face. I looked like a hot mess. The heat and humidity still hadn't fazed Ambrose—he must've adapted to it by now.

Before we got to the entrance building, Ambrose stopped on the path. "My house key." He patted the side of his pants, feeling an empty pocket. "I think I left it over by the statue. Go ahead, and I'll meet you on the other side."

"Okay." I yanked open the door. The air-conditioning of the entrance room was bracing. I stopped to take a deep, cool breath.

"Honey, look at you! Did you fall into the fountain?" The lady behind the counter did a double take when she saw me.

I startled, remembering that I was holding the flask and I didn't want her to see it. What if she recalled that I had been empty-handed this morning? I couldn't risk her taking it away. I tucked the flask under my shirt on my right side, opposite the admission lady, and pressed it tightly to my sweaty hip with my elbow. It made a large round bulge under my wet clothes. "Uh, no. I tripped when I was walking by the sound."

"Poor thing," she *tsk*ed. "Anyway, did you find your 'friend'?"

I nodded. "Yeah, he was already out there." She smiled like she didn't believe me. "Thanks for your help today. Bye!" I dashed out before she could notice the flask-shaped lump.

Ambrose was already waiting once I got outside, lurking behind a shrub. "How did you beat me out here?"

He shrugged. "You were busy talking to that woman." I *harrumph*ed at that—why did *I* have to sneak the artifact past the sticker lady? He continued, "So, when can we continue our adventures, Nell? Perhaps at Fort Raleigh?"

The historic site would be a good place to look for more clues and to compare our find to the items on display. But my mom and I had made a deal that to earn my "stipend," I'd help out with her research three days each week. I'd put it off, so Wednesday, Thursday, and Friday I had to work for her. It would be tough to slip away by myself during the weekend— Mom would want to go sightseeing. That meant I had to wait until next week to go exploring with Ambrose. "I have to help my mother with her work. The next time I'll be able to meet up is Monday. Sorry that's so far from now." We had walked over to where my bike was locked up.

"That's fine—I have to work with my mother too." I'd

forgotten that he actually had a job at the Festival Park. "But I'm good at waiting. It's not often I get to spend a day frolicking like this, with you."

My heart pounded in a rush of nervousness. *He likes* frolicking *with me. Whoa.* That was kind of a weird way of telling someone you liked hanging out with her. But I still felt a little burst of pride. I had tons to tell Jade, whenever I had enough bars to send a text.

"Till Monday, then?" he asked. "I'll find you at the fort, in the morning."

I nodded. "I'll be on time, too. I promise."

We stood awkwardly for a few minutes, neither of us saying good-bye first. Finally, not knowing whether I should try to give him a hug or just ride away, I spun the combo lock to unchain my bike. "See ya later, Ambrose." I swung my leg over and sat down. This was going to be one fun ride home: wet butt on a bike seat, precious artifact in the basket.

"Fare thee well, Nell." He smiled and waved as I carefully pedaled away.

CHAPTER SIX

The sun blazed down on me, stronger than it should have at almost four p.m., but it was a hotter-than-hot day and I *was* already sticky-sweaty. To make matters worse, whomping blisters on both feet screamed with every push of the pedal. I wobbled along the road as I biked with one hand on the handlebars, the other arm hugging the flask—I hadn't trusted it in the bike basket, where it could roll and bounce. *I have to take a break.* I pulled onto the shoulder and sat down cross-legged in the grass. I ran my fingertip over the etched letters. *A, V,* maybe *E.* I knew *AVE* could be "ave," like "Ave Maria." We used to have an opera-singer neighbor who sang that a lot.

Putting the flask aside, I flopped onto my back and stared up at the sky. I felt happier than I had in weeks. Kind of exhilarated, like I'd just finished running the mile in gym class. Ambrose had seemed excited about our find, but not as giddy as I felt. The sadness in his eyes never faded, even during excursions in the sunshine that made the dad-less pit in my stomach disappear, at least for a few hours. *Poor Ambrose.*

When I got back to the cottage, I dropped the bike on the lawn and raced into the kitchen, where I rinsed the outside of the flask (but not with soap because I was afraid that chemicals could hurt the markings) and carefully dabbed it dry with paper towels, then wrapped it up in a couple of dishcloths. In my room, I put the bundle of cloth and flask into a cabinet on the bottom the vanity, firmly shutting the door. Then I threw a load of my dirty clothes, including stiffly dried shorts and sand-covered shirt, in the washer. Before I hopped in the shower, I used the Notes function on my phone to start a log of the evidence so far. I wrote down what I'd learned about the colony from Ambrose and Lila. All this info would help my dad write his greatest mystery yet. I had just turned on the water when I heard the clatter of Mom coming in the front door.

She was standing in the kitchen, with a bunch of big paper bags lined up on the counter, when I wandered in, still toweling off my hair. Mom turned away quickly to fuss with something in the sink, and when she faced me I noticed her eyes were red and watery.

"Onions," she said, clearing her throat. Although the cutting board wasn't out. "You're in time to help me cook. Start unloading those bags, will you?"

I reached into the first one and pulled out a shrink-wrapped package of crabs. "Ew! Mom! You know I don't eat anything that swimmeth or creepeth upon the sea!" I dropped them onto the counter and hurried to the sink to wash my hands. Seafood is so gross.

Mom rolled her eyes. "Still, Nell? When's the last time you ate fish? If you try it again, I'm sure you'll feel much differently. I mean, you wouldn't even eat potatoes when you were little, and you've outgrown that, Miss French-fries-are-a-food-group."

"Doesn't matter. It's my right to be totally and completely disgusted by fish food! Just because I'm not an adult doesn't mean I can't have strong food preferences."

Mom sighed. "Well, I thought it might be rude to not serve it with the Midgetts coming over. Lila's mother is a fisherman, you know."

"Fisher*woman*, you mean?"

"My bad." Now it was my turn to roll my eyes.

The Midgetts didn't ring the bell like I expected, but bounded into the garden, where my mom was grilling. Specifically, it was Lila's mom, and Sir Walter, who did the bounding. "What in tarnation is that glorious smell?" She strode right over to my mom and poked at the sizzling fish with a huge smile across her tanned face. "This looks absolutely divine, Celia!"

My mom opened her mouth, to say hello or something. But Lila's mom kept on talking and waving her arms around, showing off her biceps. She was wearing a striped tank top underneath a very worn pair of overalls, which kind of made her seem like an overgrown kid, and maybe one on a sugar high. Sir Walter hustled over to me and nosed my hand to start petting him.

"I've forgotten my manners!" Lila's mom stuck out her hand for my mom to shake. I noticed right away that hers looked rough and weathered like, well, a fisherwoman's. "Kate Midgett. Very pleased to make your acquaintance." She turned to me next. "This darling little gal must be Nell. So nice to meet you, sweet thing! Why, I heard so much about you after Lila came home from the bookshop. Can't tell you how happy I am that she has a summer friend." Her handshake was so firm it almost stung.

Lila had told her parents about me? "Uh, thanks." Given Kate's big personality and even bigger smile, I could see where Lila got her confidence. Although that was no excuse for being a know-it-all.

"You know," Kate leaned closer to me, in a confiding way. "Lila, for some reason, has the hardest time making friends. Don't tell her I said that. We encouraged her to try out for the play so she'd have something to keep her occupied this summer—and stop obsessing about ghosts all the time. But her audition was a bit of a debacle. So I'm pleased as punch that you girls found each other." She gave my shoulder a squeeze before standing up straight. I felt mortified on behalf of Lila. Maybe one of the reasons why she had a hard time friendmaking and friendkeeping was because her *mom* was running around telling almost-strangers about her social woes. I also wondered what the "debacle" she mentioned meant.

"Mom? What were you saying about my audition?" Lila and her dad had walked into the garden while her mom was spilling the beans to me. The look on Lila's face was pure horror.

"Nothing, sweetie! Just that you wound up being free for the summer, that's all."

Lila sputtered to me, "It was not a *debacle*. I didn't have a choice about stopping in the middle of my number—my EMF detector started beeping. I had to investigate why! Anyway, I only wanted to be in the play so I could look for the backstage ghost," she huffed. "I didn't care about hanging out with the other kids in the cast." But the way she bit her lip suggested maybe she had.

Lila's dad, Luke, came over to introduce himself. He was much quieter than Kate and Lila, and seemed like the sort of person who would happily sit for long periods sifting through rocks and dirt to find tiny artifacts. Which is not a bad thing. "Nice to meet you, Nell," he said. "I'm delighted to work with your mom this summer."

Our parents chatted over by the grill, Kate waving her hands around and miming something that must have to do with her fishing adventures—making motions like she was reeling in a huge catch. Lila pulled another Adirondack chair up next to mine. Her smile stretched across her face and for the first time, I noticed the gap between her front teeth. Something about it, and the embarrassing audition story, made me feel like I should be a little nicer to her. Maybe I'd misjudged her. Maybe I'd simply been having a grumpy day when we met at the bookstore.

"Have you reconsidered?" She perched on the edge of her chair, bouncing her legs with eagerness, while I sprawled back in mine. Sir Walter flopped onto my feet again, which was apparently his thing. "Because I could use a helper. Someone to take notes for me, and carry some of my heavier equipment. My work is *important*, you know. No matter what my dad thinks, I'm not just 'messing around' and getting in the way. Why, I made a very interesting discovery today." Lila paused, waiting for me to ask her what the discovery was. It was *killing* me to say nothing—especially considering what Ambrose and I had uncovered. But I didn't want to encourage her. I shrugged.

"Nope, haven't reconsidered." I fiddled with a piece of wood that was splintering off the chair. It was hard work to look so relaxed when Lila was irritating me and my foot was falling asleep from Sir Walter's not-insignificant weight.

Lila sighed and pulled her hair back from her face, winding it into a knot. She lowered her voice conspiratorially. "I really shouldn't tell anyone what I found. I have a strict confidentiality policy." She reached into her purple backpack and pulled out a typed-up sheet of paper. "Will you sign it?" The title, in bold type, was CONFIDENTIALITY AGREEMENT. Was this girl for real? I shook my head no. She sighed and zipped it back up in her bag. "Since you don't seem to know anything about this stuff, or care one lick, it can't hurt to talk to you."

But now I cared quite a few licks, and the notes on my phone showed I knew something. I kept quiet.

Lila continued, "I was on my way to the old swimming hole, and of course I had my EMF detector with me—you know, a tool that picks up electromagnetic fields, sometimes from ghosts. It started picking up some crazy energy. I wandered off the road, away from the houses and deeper into the woods, near where they're building the golf course. Then it went crazier. Even Sir Walter seemed affected. Normally, he loves to scamper around, and sniff everything within a two-mile radius, but he kept close to my side and growled." I looked down at Sir Walter, smile-panting up at me. I couldn't imagine him ever growling. "This was by a specific grouping of trees. There must be something—or some*one*—there." Lila leaned in closer. "Maybe a lost colonist. Which means that haunted area might be where the village was. I'm a genius, right?"

It made sense, but if she had been by the golf-course construction—that was near my mom's vine. Not near the beach where Ambrose and I had found the flask. I knew I should keep that information to myself, but there was something about the condescending look Lila was giving me, and her calling herself a genius, that I could not stomach.

"Unfortunately, I made a recent discovery, and it suggests you're not on the right track."

Lila's eyes narrowed to slits. "What do you mean *you* made a *discovery*?"

"*I* have a strict confidentiality policy too." I raised my eyebrows at her. "You're not the only girl around here who wants to find the colony."

Lila's mouth dropped open slightly. "Why aren't you working with me, then?" There was a smidge of disappointment in her tone.

I shrugged. "Why did people come to America in the first place? *To be their own bosses.* Same reason."

She leaned even farther off her chair, so much so that I was afraid she would topple it. In fact, it wobbled enough that Lila dropped the scowl from her face for a second while she caught her balance.

"Girls! Come set the picnic table. Food's about ready," my mom hollered. She and Lila's parents stood around the grill, clutching sweating glasses, huge relaxed smiles on their faces. I welcomed the chance to escape Lila, so I nudged Sir Walter and then sprang out of my chair. Lila followed close behind me, practically hissing.

"Nell! What did you mean? Tell me now!"

I ignored her, grabbing the stack of melamine plates and tumblers. I arranged them on the checkered tablecloth, humming nonchalantly just to drive her that much crazier.

Kate called, "Lila, help me carry the food to the table." Lila stomped over to her mom. I tried to set the table such that I could sit next to mine, or maybe Lila's dad, who might have some useful information for me. But I was thwarted when my mom came over and pressed her palms onto my shoulders. "I thought you girls could sit next to each other. We'll put Kate, Luke, and me across the table." *Great.*

After we sat down to eat, I felt something nudging my leg under the table. I thought it was Sir Walter wanting table scraps, but it was actually Lila. *"You* have *to tell me what you were talking about."*

"None of your business," I hissed in between bites of biscuit and veggie burger. Even though the spices smelled delicious, I still couldn't bring myself to touch the fish. My mom had thrown a veggie patty on the grill for me before the rest of the food.

"Nell, what have you done so far on Roanoke?" Kate pulled a piece of the crab out, dipped it liberally in some melted butter, and popped it into her mouth. *"Mmm,* that is delicious."

"Yes, *tell us,"* Lila said, reaching for a napkin.

"Let me see—mostly tourist stuff. Mom and I went for a beach day at Corolla. I've gone to the Festival Park and the Elizabethan Gardens. Tomorrow, I'm going to start helping out at the vine."

Lila seemed to take note of where I'd been. I'm sure she was calculating what I possibly could've uncovered in those places.

"Have you gotten to Fort Raleigh yet?" her dad asked. He had a napkin tucked politely at the top of his shirt and ate his crab carefully with a fork. Lila was a hybrid of her parents, angrily cracking into her seafood and then spearing it daintily with silverware.

"No, but I'd love to visit soon."

"Let me know when you stop by—my office is there, and I can show you around. We have an excellent exhibition of maps right now."

"Cool. That sounds fascinating." Lila glared at me.

Mom, sensing the tension, changed the subject. "Lila, honey, what do you like to do?"

Lila sat up a little straighter. "Historical research. Like my father, except our methods aren't the same. He looks for artifacts, and I look for ghosts."

Her dad chuckled. Lila's mom added, "On the land and the water. We hunt shipwrecks together on the weekend."

"What a neat hobby." My mom sounded impressed, and it made me grit my teeth. "Do you need a lot of fancy equipment for that?"

"Not really," Lila said. "I mean, you'd be surprised what you'll find with an underwater metal detector."

"There's an old fisherman's trick," Lila's mom butted in, "that the best fishing spots are also the best shipwreck-hunting spots. Wrecks on a sandy bottom are where the fish looooove to hang out. Gives 'em a good place to hide."

Lila looked annoyed that her mom was changing the topic. "Anyway, I'm trying to prove that paranormal energy can teach us what happened to the lost colony."

"Although there's not much *solid* evidence," her dad joked. Lila stabbed at her crab in frustration—and I felt a little bad for her that her dad didn't consider ghost energy a real clue, even though I had to agree with him. Ghosts were good for sleepover stories, not science.

"Very funny. But this is important—when they start constructing the golf course, it's going to upset all the energy. That's why investigating is a way better use of my time than being in the background of a play."

"That's very interesting," my mom said. "Maybe Nell could tag along with you when she's not helping me out." It was all I could do not to drop my head onto my plate of salad.

Lila swallowed her bite. "Maybe."

After all the plates were clean, Mom asked me to bring out some ice cream for dessert. I was stacking up the dishes when Kate volunteered Lila to give me a hand in the kitchen. As she followed me, I "accidentally" let the screen door shut right in her face. "Oops!"

She yanked it open and stomped in. "Okay, now spill." I shook my head no. She scowled, dropping the forks into the sink. "What gives you the right to go poking into Roanoke's history on your own?"

I shrugged. "It's a free country. If I want to learn more about the lost colony, I can. After all, I'm a Dare."

She stuck her hands on her hips. "Yeah, but I'm *from* here. My family has lived on Roanoke Island as long as anybody can remember. There are streets named after my great-grandparents. I've grown up playing in these woods and swimming in the bay. This is my home, and it's *my* job to find the truth about it. You're a silly girl from New York City who's just here for the summer. You barely knew a thing about the lost colony until *I* told you! If anything, you'll probably mess up any evidence you come across and make it useless. I have something to prove here—this isn't just a lark for me."

My not knowing specifics about the colony before her lecture was kind of true. But that didn't mean I didn't have a right to learn. And it wasn't a lark for me; I needed this mystery to get my dad back. "There aren't rules about what a person can find interesting. You're just jealous because I've been around for, like, a week and I uncovered something already. Despite spending your whole life here, all you have to show for it is a quacky ghost-meter, some spooky stories, and a bunch of regurgitated facts." That wasn't very fair of me to say, and "quacky" wasn't a real word.

Lila looked stung for a few seconds before smacking a dish towel on the counter. "Tell me what you found," she demanded, although her voice had a pleading edge. "At least so I know where to look."

A small part of me felt she was right: Lila knew a lot more about the island than I ever would. But letting her in on Ambrose and my secret would mean our investigating duo would become a trio—and I definitely didn't want that. I liked afternoons alone with him, splashing around the sound or wandering the woods. I shook my head no. "You'll find out when I help my dad write a book on the secrets of Roanoke—and it'll be a bestseller."

I thought she'd turn into a living cartoon with steam coming out of her ears and a train-whistle sound blasting out of her head. Instead, my mom bustled into the kitchen and found me with an ice-cream scoop in my hand and a melty half gallon sitting between Lila and me on the counter.

"Nell! Ice-cream emergency." She stepped between us and took the scoop out of my hand. "But I like seeing how much you two have to chat about. We'll have dinners together often while we're here."

Lila and I both smiled through clenched teeth and nodded.

"I have to use the bathroom. Excuse me." Lila darted off to the one next to my room.

"New friend material?" my mom asked.

I shrugged, sad at disappointing her. "Maybe." Which really meant, *heck no*.

Mom took three bowls and went outside. My phone buzzed in my pocket. I pulled it out to see a message from my dad: "The wheel has come full circle, [you are there]." From *King Lear*. Translation: You're not the first in our Dare family to set foot on Roanoke Island. We're descended from cousins of the Dares who were part of that colony! I dropped my spoon on the counter with a clatter, then scrolled to keep reading. Later on, *our* relatives came to America. I'll try to look up more info if I can. Love, Dad.

I couldn't believe it. *Wait until I tell Ambrose!* What's more—what a way to beat Lila's I-grew-up-here-and-I-claim-the-island attitude. The whole county was actually named after *my* distant ancestors.

I took the remaining bowls of ice cream out to the table. Lila's portion was almost entirely melted by the time she emerged from the cottage. I sneaked a glance at her, and she looked a little disheveled. Had she been crying? Maybe I'd really upset her. I thought better of rubbing the Dare stuff in her face.

Eventually, Luke couldn't stifle his yawns and Kate

announced that they'd be on their way home. Lila woke up Sir Walter, who had been snoozing by my chair. I leaned down, ruffled his fur, and gave him a doggy kiss good night—the one bright spot of the evening.

Lila's mom hugged us with fish-bone-crushing strength, promising my mom a slew of recipes and some of her fresh catch, and promising me a trip out in her boat one of these days.

"You don't have an aversion to catching fish, do you?"

I shook my head. "Just eating them." Although catching them without plans to eat them seemed a little cruel.

Lila stood next to her dad, arms crossed tightly against her chest. Before they left, she whispered, "This is not over, Nell. From now on, I'll be watching you. If anyone is going to find the lost colony, it's me." With one last glare, she left.

If Lila started keeping tabs on me, she would probably interfere with Ambrose and my expeditions, and might piggyback on our clues to find her own. If we were right, and evidence of the lost colony's settlement was along the shoreline, Lila would have a much easier time searching for it than we would. What with her underwater gadgets and all.

I felt rattled after dinner. Maybe it was from fighting with Lila. Or maybe it was seeing someone else's family together while my dad was away. I wanted to try asking Mom again what was going on, but then I thought about her red eyes from "onions" in the kitchen. She looked so sad anytime we edged anywhere close to that topic.

I didn't feel like I could sleep, so I turned on my flashlight to read under the covers. I sent Jade a text, telling her how Lila came over for dinner and it was kind of a disaster. When I didn't hear back from her, I wondered if she was too busy hanging out with Sofia. Eventually I conked out with the flashlight still on, illuminating my shadow under the sheet pulled over my head.

I jolted awake in the middle of the night. *Why is it so bright?* Then I felt something heavy in my hand—the flashlight, which I was still clutching. I snapped it off. I pulled the sheet off my head and sat up in bed. The room around me, normally bathed in blue moonlight shining through the loose curtains, now was pitch-black. The kind of inky darkness a room gets late at night, right after you turn out the lights and your eyes haven't adjusted. *What was that?* I heard something, like a door softly shutting. The noise it makes when a cupboard has magnets to keep it closed— the click as they attract and connect. The sound wouldn't have been nearly loud enough to wake me on its own, but because my senses were on hyperalert, it sounded like it had gone through a megaphone. I heard the faintest footstep, followed by a tiny sigh from the floorboards.

I did not feel alone in my room. But strangely enough, I didn't feel frightened, either—at least at first. I opened my mouth, about to ask if my mom was there. Except I knew she wasn't—why would

Mom be lurking in my room in the total darkness? If she had wandered in to turn out my flashlight and tuck me into bed, then she would have said something when I woke up. So whatever, *whomever* I could feel in the room—he or she or it wasn't my mother. There were eyes on me, watching me. I *knew* it. Just like that first day in the woods by the Grandmother Vine—and that had turned out to be something, even if it had been only a deer.

My heart pounded, so hard I could feel it in my ears like a drum. I clenched the sheets in my fists, pulling them closer to me. I had a flash of the magical thinking I used to have as a little kid, that so long as nothing could see me (with a sheet over my head, with my hoodie pulled up and over my face, et cetera), I was safe. I strained to listen to the room around me. It was silent—even the floorboards now. I could only hear the rustle of the trees outside and the hum of someone's generator or air conditioner. I didn't understand how a person could be so quiet—whomever the intruder was.

This is stupid, I thought. *This is all because Lila was here, talking about her ghost hunts. I'm letting my imagination run away with me.*

I reached for my phone, just in case. When I woke up the screen, though, I saw that I had no service. My stomach dropped, as I realized that whatever was in the room with me now knew that I was awake, thanks to the phone's illumination. I held my breath until the light faded.

I sat still for what felt like hours, but probably was only seconds to minutes. Eventually, my eyes adjusted to the room around me. I didn't see anyone, not even a shadow. I tried to muster the courage to turn on my flashlight, quick. Shine it around the room and catch whomever was there. That scared me more than anything else—the not knowing what I would see once I turned it on. *I'm being ridiculous, just like a kindergartener afraid of monsters under the bed.*

I took a deep breath, pressed my index finger down on the flashlight's switch, and turned it on. I squinted as the light shone around and I saw . . . nothing. I mean, just the normal stuff in my cute cottage room. And when I shined it past the vanity mirror, there was no evil ghost reflection in it like a horror-story cliché. The room looked safe and empty, just my clothes draped over the chair and my glass of water untouched on the nightstand and me cowering in my bed. My heart stopped pounding a little. *I could've sworn . . .*

I sat still for another couple of minutes, trying to get to a point where I felt comfortable lying down and going back to sleep. I couldn't, though, not after feeling so convinced that someone was in there, watching me. For all I knew, if nobody was in the room then maybe some creeper was at the window. I shivered. I'd only ever lived on the third floor of a building or higher, and at that height no one can stand at street level and peer into your room. (Seeing into your neighbor's windows, well, that's another story. Jade and I sort of love to spy on the people in the apartments across from ours and make up stories about their lives.)

Finally, I gave up. I jumped out of bed, wrapped the comforter around me like an invisibility cloak, and ran into my mom's room. She actually was awake and sitting up against the headboard of her bed; I hadn't realized that she still wasn't sleeping well even now that we were in North Carolina. In fact, her eyes were red-rimmed and she sniffed and wiped her nose as I busted in, like she had maybe been crying again.

"Nell? Is everything okay?"

I was going to sound nuts if I told my mom I thought someone had been in my room, or at least watching me in there. That was the last thing she needed right now. "Um," I paused. "I had a bad dream. I feel so lame coming in here for that, but I'm not used to waking up in that room. . . ." I trailed off. Mom already looked so miserable, and I didn't want to make her feel bad about my being in an unfamiliar room in the first place. "Can I sleep in here with you for the night?"

She smiled at me, like she was really happy to hear that. "Sure, crawl in." She pulled back the sheets for me to slide inside. I hopped into her big bed and curled up next to her. Mom put her arm around me and kissed my forehead. "My little sprout," she said. "Sleep tight."

I tried not to think about how lonely she must feel most nights, in a big bed in a cottage not her own, on a strange island far from home. More important, though, being alone after all those years of always having my dad snoring next to her and accidentally kicking her with his restless legs.

When I woke up the next morning, I could hear Mom puttering around the kitchen. I slipped out of her bed and padded into my room. It looked as fresh and friendly as it did every morning, and I felt extra silly for acting like such a baby the night before. I grabbed my book and flashlight off the tangle of sheets and set them on my vanity. That's when I noticed it.

The door to the bottom cabinet was hanging slightly ajar—the compartment keeping the flask safe.

My heart fluttered. That door had those magnet thingies in the closure, so it would make that slight *click* when you opened or shut it. I hadn't left it open the day before—especially not after I put the flask inside.

I yanked the door fully open. The crumpled dishcloths were still there, but the rest of the cabinet was empty.

I sank down onto my heels, head in my hands. *I know I made sure it was safely inside.* The dishcloths proved it. There was no way I had done something else with the flask. And my mom definitely wouldn't have gone into my room and taken it without talking to me. I thought of hearing the *click* noise last night, and I shuddered. Had somebody been in my room that whole time? Stealing the flask? But who would know about it, or care?

But wait: Maybe the noise had been the door popping back

open, or fully shut, because *someone hadn't closed it properly earlier*. I remembered Lila's long trip to the bathroom during dinner. How she seemed a little rattled when she came back to the table—or perhaps guilty! Maybe, after I told her that I was investigating too, and that I had found a clue, she went into my room and poked around. My hand clenched the dishcloths. Lila probably found the flask. If anyone could recognize an artifact, it would be her—and I would not put it past her to steal my discovery.

It was the only explanation. I wanted to kick myself for not checking my room last night after she went to the bathroom. Also for bragging about my find—I should've kept that secret to myself. But it was too late, and the flask was gone. I wanted to cry. *How am I ever going to tell Ambrose about this?*

"Nell! Breakfast! We've got to get to the site by nine thirty," my mom called from the kitchen. I wanted to tell her what was going on—that Lila was a thief and had stolen something precious from my room while we were hosting her for dinner. But then my mom would want to know what she'd taken, and I'd have to tell her about the flask. She'd probably be mad that I hadn't told anyone official about it yet. So instead I sat down for some whole-grain toast and kept my mouth shut. The only thing that got me through it was picturing Ambrose and me eventually finding the site of the lost colony, and then getting to watch Lila's horror at not having done it first.

After George's murder, on the eighth of August, Governor White called for a meeting among all the local chiefs, whom the Croatoans promised to bring. 'Twas his aim to enter parley with them. But the werowances of Pomeiooc, Aquascogoc, Secoton, and Dasemunkepeuc ne'er responded. It riled the men of our group, and although some—including my father—urged against it, they became set on revenge. The next day, a secret attack White did lead on their dwelling place to avenge poor George. The miserable souls fled into the reeds, but our men followed.

'Twas a tragedy, a mistake most wretched. One that weighs my heart heavy with guilt and shame. Those our men killed in the village—including womenfolk!—were none of the tribe that murdered George. Instead, by a cruel twist of Fate, those we slaughtered were Croatoans—Manteo's people, the very tribe that had offered guidance since our arrival. They had gone yonder to gather corn and fruit, which our enemies had left when they fled. Mother cried for days when she heard of the cruelty we had done.

Fortune repaid us in kind. A drought most terrible befell the island, and even those who had lived thither for ages upon ages scrounged for food. After the attack, the Croatoans did refuse to help us gather more. We lacked sufficient supplies. The wicked drought made even this most goodly soil inhospitable. Aside from the luscious grapes, we struggled to gather plenty to eat. The sea still provided: fish and crabs. Yet catch-

ing enough to feed 116 hungry bellies morning, noon, and night was a challenge.

Fearful of being found by enemies, we did choose to raise new cottages to the west, and south, of the last colony's fort, which was on the northern tip of the island. We could follow a creek down to the bay; our homes nestled between it and the sea. They had two stories, built of wood, and grass-thatched roofs. O, the joy and comfort I did feel—once again having a roof o'er my head.

Father and I walked to the water e'ry morn, to watch the sun rise over the waves. We kept watch for Spanish ships that perchance might have found us, despite being hidden from the open sea—the shallow water surrounding the island, rife with shoals, does make it impassable for large ships. As we fished, Father did spin tales of our life hither years from now—when our colony would bustle like those in the Caribbean. "Lords of Virginia," we were to be. Better than being poor Londoners. Father had so much hope for our new life. But I dreamt often of mine in London, and my heart ached for its comforts. My shoes were worn near to shreds. We were desperate for more supplies—food, clothing, and building materials. Some of the planters did think Governor White ought to sail back to England before winter seas would make the voyage impossible. Yet he would not leave before he could see his grandchild born, the baby Dare.

CHAPTER SEVEN

I had to wait for five whole days to see Ambrose again. I helped my mom, and I spent some of my earnings on another book about the lost colony and one with Shakespeare quotations. Maybe I'd start sending them to Dad. But the first one I opened it to was "We have seen better days" from *As You Like It*, and that was a little too on the nose.

I'd sworn to be on time to meet Ambrose at Fort Raleigh; the only problem was, we hadn't actually *set* a specific time. If only I had Ambrose's phone number, or even his e-mail address. Instead, I biked to the Festival Park around closing on Sunday evening. Maybe I'd run into Ambrose, or at least his mom. But even though I sat in the grass next to my bike and watched all the visitors and employees shuffle out to their cars and head home, neither emerged. I *did* see Lila walk Sir Walter across the bridge to the park, kind of conspicuously, although she pretended not to see me. Was she actually following me now? That was the last thing I needed: Lila becoming my shadow.

Birds had barely started to chirp when Mom got up on Monday. We had been waking extra early to make the most of the cool morning hours. "Nell, are you sure you don't want to come with me today? It would mean more allowance for books." Mom stood in the doorway of my room. I was still in my bed, in pajamas. I didn't want her to know that I had someplace to be. I sort of hadn't mentioned Ambrose to her yet, and I didn't know how she'd feel about me running around Roanoke with a local boy she'd never met. I could guess that she would not exactly be thrilled. I decided to wait until she could meet him—better yet, with his mom. I'd ask Ambrose if they wanted to stop by our cottage sometime soon. *I should probably remind him to wear shoes*, I thought, since he hadn't at the gardens.

Mom continued, "I need to estimate the number of fruit on the vine. Yesterday, I noticed that in one area, it looks sparse. I could kick myself for not calculating earlier how many grapes were on it, because now I can't tell if it's losing them at an abnormal rate."

"Maybe a deer got hungry?"

"Or an alligator," she said offhandedly.

"What?"

Mom gave me a *duh* look. "Didn't you know we're right across the water from the Alligator River wildlife refuge? It's not like the Everglades—but they're here."

Great—another thing to worry about while tramping around in search of clues.

Mom shrugged. "Anyway, somebody—or some*thing*—had a scuppernong feast. I could use your help counting."

"No, thanks. Threat of alligators aside, I'm kinda tired. Maybe I got too much sun yesterday." We had gone to the beach again on Sunday morning. This time we saw a few horses, and I took pictures and sent them to Dad, along with one of Mom finally dipping her toes in the Atlantic. I wrote, This is what you are missing across the pond. He replied: "I like [that] place and willingly could waste my time in it." (*As You Like It*)—plus a smiley face. It made me so happy to read that—maybe I *was* convincing him to come back. I also sent him an e-mail with my Roanoke clues so far, and he replied to say that he was really intrigued.

Mom put her hand on my forehead to check my temp. Satisfied that I wasn't burning up, she shouldered her tote bag. "Suit yourself. If you're feeling peaked, hydrate well today, and stay in the air-conditioning. Maybe you should call Lila and meet her at the bookstore."

I pulled the sheet up and over my mouth. "Maybe. Bye."

"Later, gator." Mom halfway shut my door. I waited to hear the Jeep's slam, then I hopped up out of bed immediately and threw on some clean shorts and a T-shirt. I had a brand-new pair of outdoorsy hiking sandals to wear, thank goodness. The blisters I'd gotten the first week still hadn't fully healed.

After checking the chain and the tires on my bike, I took a circuitous route out of Manteo to avoid any known Lila hang-outs. Last thing I wanted was her tagging along and spoiling my day with Ambrose, or stealing any more artifacts. Rather than demanding she unhand the flask, I decided it would be better to act like I didn't know that she'd snatched it, until I could figure out how to get it back. You know, keep under the Lila radar.

As I biked, I realized how used to this very different island I'd gotten in the twelve days I'd been on Roanoke. At home I almost always woke up to street noise, like the shrieks and groans of trash trucks, or cabbies honking at people double-parked in front of the school across the street. The quieter sounds of Manteo had become normal to me. Sometimes the loudest thing was the strong breeze rustling the trees. This was probably the longest I'd ever gone without taking the subway, in my whole life. And the most bike riding I'd ever done, since Mom and Dad will only let me ride in Central Park on the week-ends, and I don't even do that very often because it's a lot of effort to haul my bike up from the storage room. The tires have a magical ability to be low on air every single time I try to take it out.

One particular adaptation bothered me, though: How I was getting used to life without my dad. I swallowed the lump in my throat. I didn't expect him to wake me up in the morning anymore; I didn't look for his toothbrush in the holder. I didn't check to make sure I wasn't going to trip over his laptop cord when walking around, or expect to clear a slew of notebooks and pens off the couch cushions. Maybe it was simply because I was adjusting to a new space, one he'd never shared with Mom and me. But part of me worried that we were moving on from his being a part of our home. It made me feel both insanely angry at him for running off to London and creating this situation, and incredibly ashamed with myself for not missing him all the time. Was I letting him down by allowing life to move along? I didn't understand how my mom could forge ahead like we weren't hurting.

I pushed that out of my mind and focused on the scenery along the winding road. The trees were tall and mysterious. Lila's theory about using ghostly energy as a way to find the lost colony made sense—if you believed in ghosts. I'd never thought about them too much, other than on Halloween and when Jade and I sneaked scary movies on her computer. But why would a ghost want to stay where he or she got stranded? Couldn't a ghost decide to go haunt the place he or she liked best in life? That made more sense—or haunting where a ghost's loved ones still were. If I weren't locked into a feud with Lila, I'd talk to her about that.

Fort Raleigh was on the same land as the Elizabethan Gardens, but I hadn't seen it the week before. After the fork in their shared road, I came upon a woodsy area with a visitor center and a bunch of administrative and research buildings. I had expected a big military-looking thing, like a medieval fortress, but Fort Raleigh looked like a state park. A sign showed where people could park for *The Lost Colony* drama, which was performed in something called the Waterside Theatre. I'd forgotten about Lila's audition debacle. I decided that watching the play would be my next weekend tourist excursion with Mom.

Not seeing Ambrose, I started to wander. Beyond the visitor center was the reconstructed fort. I ran into the center of it, hoping to feel *something*. Even if it wasn't where the lost colonists' village had been, it was still a spot where a whole lot of history happened. I wanted the weight of time to press on my shoulders. But all I felt was the breeze and a mosquito biting my ankle. The Grandmother Vine, frankly, had more of an energy. I walked onto a path called the Thomas Hariot Nature Trail. The air smelled woodsy and floral-sweet, almost like Jade's mom's favorite perfume. Patterns of sunlight danced on the piney path as I crunched along. The soothing sound of waves crashing on the shore, punctuated by songbirds, was the only noise. I stopped to read some of the placards telling me what the plants were: more loblolly pines, a type of persimmon the Thomas Hariot guy called "medlar." Suddenly, I heard a rustling in the woods, to my left. I peered into the brush.

"What is up, Nell?" Only one person could be botching slang like that.

Ambrose hurried toward me, waving his hand. "Where are you coming from?" I asked. It didn't even look like he was walking on an actual trail.

"I was taking a stroll."

I gave him a funny look. "More like taking a *hike.* I hope you're careful about ticks."

He stopped next to me, panting a little, although his face was sweat-free and not even a bit red. I don't know how someone who works in an outdoor park and spends so much time in the sun can be that pale, but he was. *His mom probably is a sunscreen freak too.* But he kind of had that post-stomach-flu look—perhaps he'd gotten sick. "It's good to see you again, Nell."

I blushed. "You too." I cleared my throat. "Let's head inside. I could use a drink. I should've brought the flask." I winced, almost clamping my hand over my mouth. *Why did I say that?!* I still hadn't figured out how to tell Ambrose that it was gone. Grasping for a quick way to change the subject, I remembered what my dad had told me about my Dare lineage. "Oh! I found out something cool. Apparently I'm distantly related to Virginia Dare's family, because my ancestors were their cousins. My dad's looking into it. Neat, huh?"

"That is very neat!" He looked impressed, but he didn't sound as surprised as I'd expected. "The world is tiny."

I frowned. "I think you mean 'small world.'" It was like he'd never heard of the Disneyland ride.

I wrestled with the visitor center's heavy door. Ambrose slipped in behind me, so close he almost bumped into me as it quickly shut. *What a gentleman.* My mom would chide me for thinking that—she'd tell me that I can handle a door by myself, *thankyouverymuch.* Even so, it would've been nice of Ambrose to help me hold it open as I flailed. Weren't Southern, and British, boys supposedly known for their chivalry and good manners?

Inside, the visitor center had a darkened movie-screening room, a small exhibition room with ornate wood paneling, and a larger exhibition room. Glass cases full of artifacts filled the hushed space, with illustrations, maps, and educational panels mounted above them. Looking at shards of pottery, glass beads, and other items in the cases, I felt a guilty pang. How much would the clue we'd found help the researchers at Fort Raleigh? *Assuming we get it back from Lila, Ambrose and I will definitely turn the flask over to the people here,* I thought. *When we know the truth.*

"Where do we even start?" I asked after gulping mouthfuls of water from the fountain.

Ambrose scanned the lobby. "Let's split up to look around."

"What exactly are we looking for?"

But he had already flitted off to examine something in the

room with all the carved wood panels. I walked to the center of the lobby, stopping in front of a big display. The label read: CARTOGRAPHY: A KEY TO THE MISSING COLONY? I leaned in to get a good look at a picture of an old map, titled "The Englishmen in Virginia." I tried to find Roanoke among the shaded areas I took to be land. The labels didn't make much sense to me: WEAPEMEOC, TRINETY HARBOR, PASQUENOKE. Next to it was another map: "The Modern Area." I recognized the Albemarle Sound on that one.

"Need some help interpreting?" I whirled around to see Lila's dad walking past the gift shop. He slipped a pair of wire-rimmed glasses out of his front shirt pocket and set them on the bridge of his nose.

"Hi, Mr. Midgett," I said. "I'd love help, if you're not busy."

"Not at all. It's been quiet here today." Luke stopped beside me and peered at the display. "Can you tell what these two maps have in common?"

"Hmm . . ." I squinted back and forth at the two. "Both have something called 'Weapemeoc' marked."

"Excellent! That's a village on the mainland, across the water from Roanoke Island. It's where the Weapemeoc people lived."

"Okay." I nodded my head. "Why's it on both maps? Is it because . . ." I thought about the labels for each. "One shows what places were called in the sixteenth century, and one shows today?"

Luke smiled. "You're right! This map is made from John White's drawings of the area in 1585. It's remarkably accurate. The other shows the same area today. But it's not just the names of places that have changed—the land has too. A lot of these inlets"—he pointed at breaks in the little islands sketched on the old map—"have disappeared. Roanoke Island itself is smaller by almost a quarter mile along the shoreline. Places that were safely on land at the time of the colonists are now underwater. That's because of erosion. Entire islands that were south of Roanoke in White's time are now gone."

"So the lost colony could actually be underwater?" *Like the knee-deep spot where I stubbed my toe on the flask.*

He nodded. "It's possible. That's why in addition to searching for archaeological evidence on land, we search in the sound, too."

"How?" I could only picture archaeologists working in dirt and dust.

"Same tools—just plastic, because that's waterproof. Things that divers use—like scuba gear—help us access sites."

I wished Ambrose were around to hear this information. I scanned the lobby, but I didn't see him anywhere. Looking back at the map, I thought about what the flask's scratches said—that some of the colonists had left Roanoke. "Could the colonists have fled to the islands that are now underwater? Maybe that's why we've never found clues they left behind."

"Perhaps. There are lots of theories." He pointed to the tribe labels on the map. "We can use what we know about the history of Native people living in this area to figure out what happened to the colonists. If they moved, they might have assimilated with tribes in other places, becoming part of those communities. There are stories of European explorers meeting Native people with typically European features, like gray-blue eyes or light hair. The research your mother is doing interests me—because the colonists and the local tribes had different methods of cultivating plants."

"Cool." I thought about the old map. "If White made maps, then why didn't he draw one showing where he left the colonists?"

"The colonists faced a lot of threats. White wouldn't have wanted some people—their enemies—to be able to find them. Here." Luke motioned me over to a small map, locked a big glass case. He pulled a key chain out of his pocket and undid the lock, then removed the paper. He carefully set it on the glass in front of us.

"Is it very old?" The paper looked crumbly and thin. The whole map was covered in little patches and almost worn through in places. The writing was so faded, it was hard to read.

He nodded. "This is a map Sir Walter Raleigh actually used." I assumed he didn't mean his dog, but the other one.

"Are you serious?" I breathed. "Don't you need gloves to touch that?"

He shook his head, laughing a little. "Honestly, those gloves are mostly for show. Using them on parchment this delicate might actually cause more harm, because it can make it difficult to handle the paper gently. When we use gloves, it's partly to remind others not to touch." He pointed to one of the patches stuck on the paper. "See that? For a long time, we thought that the patches were here simply to preserve the map, or correct errors. But"—he carefully tapped the square—"now we've discovered that they actually *conceal* portions of it. Perhaps because it was so important that the English keep their location secret from Spanish spies."

"Maybe they *were* hiding the location of the colony!" I whirled around again. What was taking Ambrose so long? He was totally missing this!

"We can see that the shape of the island underneath has changed. Whether it was drawn that way to confuse people, whether the mapmaker made a mistake, or whether it's simply because of geographical changes like erosion, we don't know."

"Interesting. So have you found any evidence in the water?" I was thinking of the flask. Who knew what researchers had already discovered, or what else was waiting below the waves.

He nodded. "Most of my finds have been on land, but others have discovered artifacts in the sound. Sonar can find a lot of stuff, and so can some underwater metal detectors. You should talk to Lila about that."

I frowned. Lila had access to all this museum stuff, and everything her dad knew, all the time. If I told him what I was interested in, it might get back to her.

"Anyway, I was just about to add new information cards to our exhibit in the next room. Do you want to help me?"

"Sure!"

He locked up the map. "Excellent. I'm going to grab them from my office. I'll be right back."

I just needed to wrangle Ambrose. I found him in the doorway of the smaller exhibition room, tracing the carved wood with his fingertips.

"These walls tell a story," he said, dreamily. "The wood panels are from an Elizabethan estate in England. It reminds me of home. I mean," he added quickly, "what I remember of it."

"They're beautiful," I said. "But there's something else you should see. I've been looking at the maps with Mr. Midgett." Ambrose gave me a blank look. I added, "Lila's dad?" When he shook his head, I realized that I'd never mentioned her to him. "She's a girl I met at the bookstore. She's kind of a frenemy." He gave me a third blank look, like he didn't know what "frenemy" meant. "You know, a friend who's not really very friendly."

"Frenemy," he said. "Like the colonists were to those already on Roanoke."

That was one way to put it. "Kind of, but that was definitely a lot more serious. Anyway, Mr. Midgett is a researcher here, and he's working in that room over there. Want to go talk with him?"

He looked unsure. Just then, Lila's dad stuck his head into the room. "Coming, Nell?" Ambrose's face brightened a little when he saw him. "*Okay*," he whispered to me.

"Hi there," Luke said to Ambrose. "Didn't I see you out by the theater the other day? Taking a break from *The Lost Colony*?"

"Yep," Ambrose said. "It was time for one."

Lila's dad smiled. "You must work really hard. I know my daughter wanted to be a part of the show—you're lucky! Who are you this year?"

"Just a villager," Ambrose replied. "A small part."

"Well, congrats," Lila's dad said. "Now, you two follow me."

"*You didn't tell me you were in the show!*" I whispered.

"Er . . . it's a long story," he said, blushing.

The other room held a hodgepodge of artifacts, documents, paintings, and displays. Ambrose darted over to a glass case in the far corner. Nobody else was in the room, not even a security guard. Mom's museum had security everywhere, and if they had even the tiniest inkling that you were about to touch—or even think about touching—the dinosaurs or another artifact on display, they were all over you. "You would be amazed at what people try to do in a museum," Mom once told me.

Luke stopped at the cases along the wall. "Shoot. I printed the wrong cards," he said, pointing to the thick card stock printed with curatorial notes on top of the box he was carrying. "I'll be back."

Alone in the room, Ambrose and I strolled around, examining the bits and pieces on display. All of a sudden, he let out a yelp, and I asked, "What are you looking at?" I scooted next to him and practically pressed my nose against the glass. He did the same. His face was so close to mine that my breathing got a little shallower. After a few seconds Ambrose straightened up. He looked excited, maybe, but not happy. Distressed, I guess, was the right word. "Are you okay?"

Ambrose swallowed hard and took a long blink. Was he holding back tears? I glanced away for a few seconds. Maybe he wouldn't want me to see him cry, if he was on the verge after all. "I'm fine," he said eventually. He sighed and pointed at the third row of items behind the glass. "It's that." His voice cracked a little.

I followed his finger to a ring. The tag below it read: ELIZABETHAN-STYLE SIGNET RING, 10-CARAT GOLD. RECOVERED: 2004, FROM ALBEMARLE SOUND. "It's a . . . very nice ring," I said.

Ambrose faced me. His eyes were brighter than ever, but red-rimmed. "It shouldn't be here," he said. "There must've been some mistake. It belongs in my family."

"Wait." I tried to wrap my head around this. "That's from

Elizabethan England. How can it be from your family?"

"A relative." He paused, pressing his palm to the glass. "A distant relative must've lost it. See the crest?"

I looked closer at it. Even though it was worn away by age and salt water, there was a pattern, and I could see a shape that looked like a shield. "I think so."

"That's a crest that my family has used for ages. Since the time of the colonies, and earlier! That ring *has* to belong to a Viccars." Ambrose pulled his hands away from the glass and held them out to me. On his left hand was a signet ring that looked almost identical, except his was shiny and unscuffed. "You see? I'm telling the truth. And I need that one back."

"That's incredible!" I took a step closer to inspect the ring on his pale hand. "I'm sure if you explain this to the people who work here, they'll look into it. Mr. Midgett could help—"

"No!" Ambrose practically shouted, and I startled. He began sniffling, even though he tried to hide it. I hated seeing him like that. Quieter, he said, "It's better if we simply take back what's rightfully mine."

My mouth dropped open. "Um, Ambrose, that's *stealing.*" I shook my head. "That's not the way to deal with this."

"Nell, trust me," he begged. "That ring belongs to me, and I *must* have it. Pray, please help me." I couldn't turn away from his pleading eyes. "Look, I promise—we'll show it to my mother. If she tells me I'm wrong, we'll return it immediately."

Then, quieter still, "But I know I could never be wrong about this. I swear on my father's life."

I shuddered. "You shouldn't say things like that."

"I'm desperate," he said. "Please."

Ambrose missed his dad, just like I did. If I came across some kind of family heirloom—in my dad's case, it would probably be vintage 1980s toys, based on the contents of his "heirloom" boxes in our storage bin—I would probably go nuts trying to recover it too. I swallowed hard and, against my better judgment, scanned the room, looking for security cameras. I saw one, pointing the other way from where we were standing. Lila's dad still hadn't come back from his office. There was nobody else around. "Maybe we should come back to get it," I suggested. "Wearing disguises or something. People have already seen us here today. If it goes missing, they'll know who to blame."

Ambrose ignored that, studying the glass case. "Hmm. How might we open this?"

I stared at the tiny silver lock pressed in the slightest gap between two thick pieces of glass. *I can't believe I'm even considering this.* But if the ring honestly did belong to Ambrose's family, wasn't it right to let him take it back? Mom has talked about the long process her museum goes through when groups contest keeping something on display. It can take *years* before stuff gets returned, if ever. Ambrose did say that if he was wrong, he'd return it immediately.

I took another look at the lock, and then I remembered Mr. Cohen's wrinkled face. "I have an idea." I rifled around my messenger bag for something slim, like a bobby pin. I never use bobby pins in my hair, but Jade's always needing them to deal with her bangs, which are in a constant state of growing in or growing out. She spends so much time fretting about them that I don't understand why she cuts them in the first place. My fingertips grazed a familiar metal stick at the bottom of my bag. "Perfect," I said, pulling it out. Luckily for Ambrose and me, I'm Jade's bobby-pin packhorse.

"I'm afraid I don't follow," Ambrose said. "A . . . hairpin?"

I rolled it between my thumb and index finger. "You can use them to pick a lock." I bent closer to the glass case. "I've never actually gotten a bobby pin to work for that before, but I've had a lot of practice trying." I pictured Mr. Cohen's shaky hands twisting a pin just so into the lock on a wooden box, and popping it open. I'd tried it after him and failed. *Listen for the clicks, Nell,* he'd said. *You can feel them depress on the way to unlocking it.*

As Ambrose watched, I put my head right up next to the lock, so close my ear almost suctioned to the glass. My hand trembled, either from too much concentration or from nerves. "I think . . ." I paused, straining to see if I could hear any clicks from inside the lock. I did hear something, faintly. *Click.* "I think I've *almost* got it."

"Got what?" The voice had a slight accent. But it wasn't a boy's. Meaning: It was not Ambrose.

We're caught.

I dropped the bobby pin on the surface as I jolted upright. The pin somehow managed to slide directly into the crack between the panes of glass, then through them, and finally bounce off the ring to land inside the case.

Slowly I turned to look at my witness. Although I was pretty sure I knew who it was. Because even though the person asked me a question, the tone was that of someone who knew it all.

Lila, red-faced and hands on her hips, stood in the doorway. Sir Walter Raleigh was next to her, leaning against her left leg. Panting with a huge, eager dog smile.

Oh, scat. Times one thousand.

My face flushed, and I felt the beginnings of sweat trickles running down my back and forming along the edge of my forehead. I turned to Ambrose, thinking he could talk us out of this. It had been his idea and his insistence, anyway, that got us into this catastrophic mess.

Or got *me* into this mess, because Ambrose was gone. Somehow, in between me putting my head down on the exhibition case and Lila coming in to catch me, he'd fled the room entirely. Maybe he'd heard or seen her coming. *But why didn't he warn me?* I let out a deep, shaky breath.

"Aren't you even going to try to explain yourself?" Lila

asked, smirking now that she knew I was caught. Sir Walter continued to pant and smile, and even tried to lumber over to me for some attention. But Lila held firm to his collar, keeping him back.

"I—I know this looks bad," I stammered. "But I wasn't doing this for me. There's an item in there that belongs to my friend. Ambrose. He really needs it back." I glanced around the room, wondering how he'd managed to get away. There was only one entrance, and Lila was standing in front of it. *How could he desert me like this? What kind of friend is he?* I wanted to find Ambrose and throttle him.

"Sure," Lila said, sarcasm dripping off her words. "Your *friend* made you do this. 'Ambrose,'" she said, making quotation marks with her fingers.

"He'll explain it to you." I moved to walk past her, betting that once outside I'd find Ambrose cowering somewhere behind the visitor center, or crouched in the reconstructed fort.

"Whoa, whoa—hold up. You can't just walk out of here after trying to pick a lock." Lila crossed her arms and blocked me like a bouncer. Sir Walter lazily followed her. Then he plunked down on his favorite spot, the tops of my feet, like he was about to take a nap. Lila ignored him. "What artifact were you going to snatch? Because even if you aren't lying about your friend, I can assure you that everything in these cases is an archaeological object. Nobody 'misplaced' anything in here." She pointed to the case. "What's the real reason you wanted it? Does it have to do with your clue? Or are you just a *thief*?"

But Lila already knew what I'd found, right? She'd taken the flask out of my room. Now it was my turn to narrow my eyes. "Speaking of thieves—you have my clue, and I want it back."

"I have no idea what you're talking about. Don't try to change the subject."

"You took it!" I spat back at her. "You took it after you went to the bathroom at my house! I know you did."

Lila gasped. "I did no such thing, and I will not be accused of theft, especially by an attempted thief!"

"Girls? Is everything okay in here?" Lila's dad appeared in the doorway.

Lila put on a fake grin. "Everything's fine, Dad." She actually threw her arm around my shoulders roughly, in an awkward half hug.

He walked over to us. "I thought I heard yelling," he said, scratching his head.

"*Play along*," Lila hissed in my ear.

"Not yelling," I answered, gritting my teeth thanks to Lila's death grip on me. "Debating, maybe."

"Yeah! Nell was telling me how the Natural History Museum writes the curator's notes and it's pretty different from the placards you guys make."

"Really," he said. I don't think he believed her. "I was

beginning to think it was foolish of me to mention on the phone that Nell was here, if you two are just going to argue."

Lila flinched. *Aha.* She'd been tipped off to my being here. I'd wondered how she'd wound up in the visitor center at the same time as us. "Whatever, Dad. We're going outside."

"Take Sir Walter with you, Lila. He's really not supposed to be in here, remember?" He turned to me. "No dogs allowed."

Lila yanked me toward the door with one hand, urging Sir Walter up off the floor with the other.

"Nell, come back anytime," her dad said as we hustled out the door. "Same to your friend."

"Thanks, Mr. Midgett!" I smiled halfheartedly, flush with guilt that I'd been trying to lift something from his museum. If he knew that, he sure wouldn't be telling me to come back whenever.

Lila led me to a bench across from the grassy reconstructed fort. Sir Walter bounded toward it and then stopped, tensing up. He hunched and growled, which I'd never seen him do. After a few seconds, he actually started barking.

"Sir Walter! Stop it!" Lila pulled him back to us. "Stop. *It.*" He quit barking, but wouldn't let his guard down. He probably saw a squirrel or something.

"Why didn't you rat me out if what I was doing was so heinous?" I asked.

"Because now you owe me something. To pay me back for

not telling on you, you can tell me what you know. *And* help me with a ghost hunt, as my assistant."

I shook my head. "That's blackmail. Plus, I don't have anything to share with you, because you already took it."

Lila stomped her foot like a kid having a tantrum. "No. I. Didn't," she said, her voice rising with exasperation. "I have no idea what you're talking about, and I haven't stolen a thing."

What a committed liar. I wasn't going to give up anything else. I shrugged and shoved my hands into the pockets of my shorts. I traced a shape into the dirt with my toe, a circle kind of like the signet ring.

Lila sighed. "You're forcing me to go this route. If you don't want me to turn you in—and that bobby pin in the case is proof, you know—then stop looking for the lost colony. Don't snoop around my island anymore. If I find you back here or anywhere else but the ice-cream store, and you're looking for clues, then I'm going to tell my dad what you were doing. I'll tell your mom, too."

My mom would kill me if she knew that I'd done something wrong in a museum, of all places. Seriously: That would be a grounded-for-life event, with a Mrs.-Kim-will-homeschool-you-and-you'll-never-leave-the-apartment-not-even-for-the-dentist's-office sentence.

"Fine." Which I didn't mean at all—Lila was not going to stop me from doing anything. Nor would she stop Ambrose. A flash of anger hit as I remembered how he bailed on me. Where was Ambrose, anyway? There was no sign of him by the fort or outside the visitor center. Did he run home? Escape to the Waterside Theatre, where he apparently performed? Or was he what Sir Walter had been barking at in the woods? Either way, my blood boiled. If he was still hiding out around here, he should come out and help me. If he'd fled, he was a selfish coward. I didn't know if he'd be in shape to search for any Roanoke clues after I was done with him, whenever I found him.

"I'm going home now," I announced. "By the way, this is my family's home too. Because I *am* related to the first Dares *ever here*. So much for this being your island!" I turned and stalked away from Lila, sputtering on the bench with a still-snarling Sir Walter next to her. "For all you know, those artifacts could be my inheritance!"

"I don't care!" she finally called after me. "Roanoke is my territory. I'll be watching you!"

Any lingering questions about why Lila didn't have a ton of friends had been answered. She was a competitive tattletale. A know-it-all nark. I swore I could still hear her *harrumph*ing from the parking lot.

I didn't bother to look for Ambrose on my way out. I didn't care where he was; I didn't want to see his wide, crooked smile. It stung that he'd left me to get caught. I'd considered him a friend, and I'd thought he felt the same about me. Maybe I was wrong. A friend had never treated me like this before. Even when, in third grade, Jade and I borrowed some of her mom's jewelry and got caught wearing it home from school, we stuck together. Same thing when we broke my parents' rule about walking to the east side without telling them, and my dad happened to be walking the opposite direction from a reading at the library on East Seventy-Ninth. It's not like when Jade saw him before I did, she ran off into the park and left me alone to get scolded. Because, obviously, true friends don't do that.

Can we talk tonight? I texted her. You won't believe what happened today.

I hopped on my bike, happy to be leaving the fort. The canopy of trees offered welcome shade, but I shivered in the gloom. This was not how I expected today to go: Ambrose abandoning me, Lila catching me and then blackmailing me. Is it blackmail if you *were* doing something wrong? In any case, it was enough to make me want to close my eyes, click my heels, and find myself back on a New York City subway, heading home to my apartment and my real friend Jade. And hopefully my dad, too.

CHAPTER EIGHT

Something wrong, Nell?" Mom eyed me slyly from the side, one hand on the wheel and the other reaching for her iced coffee in the cup holder. "You're awfully quiet." I frowned and sank deeper into my uncomfortable seat. Jeeps might be cool, but they aren't especially comfy. Every bump on the road felt like it would leave a bruise. "And perhaps a smidge sullen," she added.

"It's nothing." I pulled my sunglasses out of my bag and popped them on my face. Despite a sympathetic phone call with Jade, a full night's sleep, a delicious breakfast (Mom made cinnamon rolls—something about this cottage was making her more domestic than she has ever been before, cooking and baking and even buying a cross-stitch kit at a shop on Budleigh Street), and the beautiful sunshiny weather, I was in a foul mood.

"Ah, the sunglasses treatment. So you *really* don't want to talk about it."

My instinct was to roll my eyes, but halfway through I realized Mom couldn't see that behind the oversize frames.

"Have you talked to Dad lately?" she asked, her voice a little softer.

I pulled off the sunglasses. "No. What's going on? Have you? Where is he now?"

Mom sighed. "I didn't say that to upset you, but I'm guessing the barrage of questions means you already are. Yes, I did talk to him." She took another sip of her coffee and cleared her throat. "Briefly. He said he tried to call you."

That was true. I'd missed a call while I was at Fort Raleigh—although I never felt my phone buzz in my bag. Once I had gotten back to the cottage, I'd seen that I had a new voice mail. *Hi, Nelly. Thanks for keeping me up-to-date on your and your mom's goings-on. Here's my quote for you: "The approaching tide will shortly fill the reasonable shores that now lie foul and muddy." From* The Tempest, *again. That one has a lot to unpack, but basically: Think about a tide of reason washing away what makes the shore muddy—or hard to understand. You're thinking a lot about mysteries these days, big ones and small ones, and trying to solve them. Anyway, well, um . . . I'm sorry I'm not there with you right now. London's great, and I can't wait to tell you all about it. We'll talk soon, and I promise I'll help unmuddy the shores. Love you lots. Dad.* He always says "Dad" at the end of a message, too—like I'm not going to recognize my own father's voice or phone number. *Although maybe right now that fear is a little more valid than it used to be.*

I'd almost deleted the voice mail as soon as I listened to it because I was angry. I wanted an answer to the simplest of questions: Why? Why did he abandon ship the week before Mom and I left? Why did he leave the country without first telling his kid? If he was so sorry, why didn't he just get on a plane and come join us? It was his fault, after all, that I was on a "muddy shore" in the first place. I felt angry with Mom, too, for being so vague, and trying to seem unworried. This was something to freak out about!

"Nell?" I jolted back to the present. Mom was no longer eyeing me from the side but turning her whole head to look at me, then snapping it back to watch her driving. With a lot of tourists on the road, that was not the best idea. "Sprout, are you upset?" It wasn't a question, the way she phrased it.

"I guess so," I said. "Not just about Dad or whatever." *Ambrose, my untrustworthy pseudo-friend.* "I think I'm kind of homesick." It wasn't an untrue statement. When I'd talked to Jade the night before, I could hear Sofia giggling in the background the whole time. Hearing about their sleepovers put a pit in my stomach. I felt kind of like my life was a snow globe that someone had shaken up really, really hard. Only it wasn't raining glitter flakes on me, that's for sure.

Mom reached over to ruffle my hair. "The good news, along those lines, is that we only need another week or so here. I'm almost done with field research, and Luke Midgett can help me if I realize I forgot something after we head back."

A little less than two weeks ago, I would've wanted to be on the next flight out of Norfolk. Heck, I'd even have been willing to travel home on one of those rickety First Flight airplanes from Kitty Hawk. But now . . . I needed to know what had happened on Roanoke. The mystery had even wound its way into my subconscious. The night before, I'd dreamt that I wandered into the lost colony's village on my way home from the fudge-and-ice-cream shop. The sad-faced colonists begged me to stay. "Don't give up on us," a woman pleaded. I can't remember her face, but she seemed familiar somehow. I woke with a start, worried for all those lost people. I wanted them to be found. But without Ambrose, would I even keep searching the island?

"Nell?"

There was another reason why I was hesitant about going home, as much as I missed it. "Is Dad planning on being there when we get back?"

Mom was silent for long enough for me to know that she was weighing out some part of her answer. "I don't know, sprout. Maybe. We'll see." *We'll see.* Historically, that has been Mom-speak for *no,* or *I don't really want to get into this complicated thing right now, so I will be super vague in my answer.*

We rode in silence the rest of the way to the vine. Mom turned on the radio to cover up my pouting and her frustration. Thank goodness for car radios. Whoever designed them must've understood a lot about family dynamics.

Once we got to the Grandmother Vine, I helped my mom collect samples for testing. She and Lila's dad had found some evidence that people had cared for the vine in the past. The only thing was, nobody on the island had been crashing around the woods to prune or fertilize it for the past couple of decades. The fact that it was thriving now, after a few bad drought years and a hurricane, too, was a mystery. (Considering all the deer poop scattered around the forest floor, I wondered if scat might be the secret to the vine's success.) As Mom took notes and prepared clippings, I carefully labeled her soil samples and also helped transcribe an interview she'd done with Lila's dad. He said that the colonists used fruit from the scuppernongs to make fermented beverages. With a sigh, I thought of the flask Ambrose and I had found, and lost.

Mom wouldn't stop pestering me about it, so I finally tried one of the enormous grapes—after dumping half the contents of my water bottle over it to make sure it wasn't dirty. The fruit was sweeter than I'd expected, but very pulpy. I savored it, imagining people four hundred years ago eating from the same plant.

After lunch, Mom didn't have any more tasks for me, so I tightened my hiking sandals, slapped on some bug spray, and headed into the woods. There wasn't a path, so I clomped through the underbrush without a plan. Even my hiking sandals weren't exactly great for the conditions—I stepped in a wet, marshy patch of mud at one point and it splattered all over my toes. I had to be careful of the sticks and twigs along the ground to make sure I didn't stab my feet through the sandals' loose netting. It was also hard to tread softly, which I was trying to do. I wanted to be stealthy so I could see one of the deer again, maybe that same buck. Or the ghostly white doe Lila mentioned people seeing. But with all the crashing and crackling noises I made, there was little chance of me surprising anything in the forest, no matter how deep I got. *At least I'll scare away any alligators,* I thought.

I didn't want to wander so far that I got lost and worried Mom, so I pulled out my phone to use its compass. It was fun to walk around the woods alone. Even deep in the Ramble of Central Park, you always come across other people. Not that I'm ever allowed to wander in there by myself. The freedom to explore the Roanoke woods was thrilling. The quiet was like nothing I'd ever experienced in the city. It wasn't silent; the hum of nature meant there were as many sounds as I was used to hearing on Columbus Avenue. Just different. The wind moving branches, insects chirping, distant and surprisingly near birdcalls. If I closed my eyes and listened to it all at once, it was like a symphony.

The longer I listened to my surroundings, the more I started to hear things. Things that almost sounded like low voices, whispers, words. The air moving through the trees, probably. I got that watched feeling again, like when the deer was near me. But it was stronger, so much so that the beginnings of a nervous tickle formed in my throat. I peeked one eye open, and then the other. I looked around me slowly. Nothing. But the hairs on my arms were standing up, and I felt tense. Surrounding me were old-growth trees, tall and strong. I was dwarfed by them, a tiny thing alone in the big woods.

Or was I alone?

I glanced at my phone's screen. The compass, which had been pointing due north, was spinning. Not quite wildly, but in fast and steady circles despite my holding the phone absolutely still. "*What the,*" I murmured. It had to be some kind of glitch. I closed out of the compass app, then reopened it. Same thing, spinning round and round and round. My phone didn't have any bars, either, and the clock had been displaying 12:43 p.m. for way longer than a minute. *One-Mississippi, two-Mississippi.* I counted all the way to sixty Mississippis, but the numbers didn't budge.

The battery must've died. Or my phone got a virus or something. But the whole no-longer-having-a-compass thing was a big problem, because I wasn't sure which way I'd walked in the woods. Give me the NYC subway system and I could make my way anywhere. But tracking my way out of the forest using broken twigs and smushed leaves and lacelike patterns of afternoon sunshine through the trees as clues? Forget it. I wiped the sweat from my face and ran in my best guess of the direction I'd come. *Did I walk past that gnarled tree before? Maybe?*

The only sound I heard was my heart thumping, at a pace slightly below mild panic, and my ragged breathing as I stepped over rocks and tree roots. I tried not to think of the episodes of that survival show Dad and I used to watch all the time, the one about people who got trapped unexpectedly in nature and beat the odds to survive. He said it was good fodder for his writing because the episodes were always so tense. I could almost hear the narrator telling the audience my situation: *Nell was just going to take a walk in the peaceful woods. But when her compass stops working, she finds herself hopelessly lost, with no way to get home. Nell struggles to survive, eating grubs and drinking rainwater collected on slimy leaves. But will she—*

"Hey-ho, Nell! Is that you?"

Startled, I spun around. Ambrose dashed through the trees toward me. Whether he was coming from the road or somewhere deeper in the woods, I had no idea. After all, I was completely and utterly lost. Part of me was relieved to see him—I wasn't alone, and judging by the lightning speed with which he ran through the forest, he probably knew his way out of here. Nobody would narrate a TV show about my demise. Plus, this meant I couldn't have gotten *that* far from civilization, if another person was around. Running into someone I knew in the woods showed me that, strangely enough, this place wasn't *that* different from Central Park, after all.

Still, the other part of me continued to be livid about Fort Raleigh, the ring, and Lila. So what if Ambrose saved me by finding me here? I didn't want his stupid help. I'd rather get eaten alive by mosquitoes than accept a favor from Ambrose, my traitor.

I ignored him and kept crashing along in the same direction, faster than before. Mud streaked up past my ankles, I almost impaled a toe on a twig, and perhaps mosquitoes are attracted to fuming girls because I swear there were more buzzing around my ears than ever before *in my life.* And my cabin at summer camp had holes in all the screens.

"Where in the world are you headed? Stay—you're going straight into the bog." The bog—that explained the uptick in the bloodsuckers. I kept moving, clenching my fists as I pumped my arms to power myself along. *I've had it with people leaving me behind. I don't need another person in my life who walks away when it gets tough or whatever.*

"Nell!" Ambrose's voice was closer, and almost pleading. "Tell me what you are running from!"

I whirled around. Ambrose was close behind me, his hand hovering above my sweaty shoulder. My messenger bag spun on a trajectory out past my hip and almost smacked him, but he dodged at the last second. His face fell from happy to crushed as he studied mine.

"You *really* don't know why I might not want to talk to you right now?"

"Aye—no, but why wouldn't you want help navigating yourself out of these woods? You're awfully far from the road, and not heading in any sort of direction in which you might care to go."

I rolled my eyes. "I'm taking a walk. The whole point is to be out in nature and wandering. *Alone.* Anyway—let me enlighten you as to why I'm mad." I thrust out my hand and started counting the reasons off on my fingers. "One: You totally abandoned me at Fort Raleigh yesterday! You convinced me to try to steal an artifact for you—and yeah, it *was* an artifact. Not something belonging to your family that's there by mistake, and I'm not sure why I was dumb enough to believe you in the first place." I paused for a breath, but when he started to open his mouth to explain himself I launched into my rant again. "Then, while I was in the midst of *actually trying to take it for you*, you ran off! Leaving me to get caught by Lila, my nemesis and the daughter of the guy in charge of the museum. Do you know how much trouble

I could've gotten into?" I realized that I'd stopped counting at some point, so I dropped my hand to my hip.

Ambrose opened his mouth to speak again, but I shushed him. "I think you *did* know how much trouble. If you hadn't, then you probably wouldn't have bailed on me. You got to avoid Lila's wrath, but I didn't." I paused, staring at the ground and my muddy feet. Letting out my emotions, even those angry ones, felt excellent. It was like I had released a steam valve of all the bad feelings that had been building up in me for the past day. Now that the worst of my anger had subsided, I peeked at Ambrose's face. His lower lip and chin were quivering ever so slightly, like he might be trying not to cry. His wide eyes brimmed with disappointment. In himself, maybe? My stomach dropped, with the first, tiniest hint of empathy.

"It's not a fun feeling, to think that someone—a friend— let you down like that," I said quietly. I kicked at a rock with my mud-caked right foot. "I was enjoying exploring with you, learning about this place, uncovering its secrets. I still want to know what happened here—I *need* to know it. Maybe now all that is a lost cause."

"Oh, Nell. Never give up." Ambrose's voice cracked with those words. "What you think is lost may still be found. But I truly didn't mean to hurt you. Nor see you accused of being a cutpurse. I only thought—that it would be better if they saw you, and not me."

"Cutpurse"? What does that even mean? Is that some weird British slang? "Do you want a shovel? Because it seems like you're trying to dig yourself even deeper." I crossed my arms over my chest. That is actually a comeback my mom used on my dad once. It seemed pretty effective.

"Huh? I'm not digging. . . ." Now he gave me a weird look. "It was too late by the time I heard Lila entering the room. That girl knows you, not me, and so I thought she'd be more understanding if you were alone. You left with such alacrity that I didn't have a chance of finding you afterward."

"Alacrity"? Either he meant anger or speed, because I'd stormed away from Fort Raleigh like someone chasing a crosstown bus that skipped their stop. I studied Ambrose's face to see if he was telling the truth. "You were hiding somewhere outside, waiting for me?" Knowing that made me feel an ounce better. I'd imagined Ambrose traipsing down the road and leaving me there, dangling like a fish on one of Lila's mom's hooks. (Actually, she said she uses a trawler, which has big nets.)

He nodded. "But I didn't follow when you left. She would have seen me. Believe me: I feel terrible about what happened. It is"—he paused dramatically—"my *bad*."

I couldn't help but smile. "I guess I believe you."

"Will you allow me to escort you back to civilization, then? You *were* lost, right?"

"In my defense, I *was* using my compass. But once I got into the woods it stopped working. My whole phone did. I have no idea what's wrong with it." I pulled it out again and turned it on.

"I'm not missing much after all, not having one of those," Ambrose said, laughing.

The compass wasn't acting crazy anymore, but now I didn't have any bars. "I think it's coming back to life." I waved the screen at him, realizing it was the perfect time to snap a picture of Ambrose on the sly. Now that I wasn't so mad, I could see that he looked awfully cute today. Jade kept bugging me for a photo, ASAP. She'd also said that she and Sofia hadn't had any luck meeting boys in their tennis lessons, which was a relief.

When Ambrose glanced up at a tree, I held out my phone and snapped. But he moved at the last second, and one of my fingertips was in the way of the lens. The photo was too blurry to be good. Maybe I'd have to work up the nerve to ask if we could take a picture together.

We walked through the woods, which felt peaceful and lovely, like when I'd started walking, and not ominous and creepy like when I'd figured out I was lost. Ambrose could step quietly, while I moved like a herd of wildebeests on the run. "Do you come here a lot? You know how to walk without carving a path of destruction through the forest."

Ambrose shrugged. "I'm light on my feet, I suppose. Always have been. I do spend a lot of time in the woods."

"Don't you ever hang out in town? The bookstore is fun, and the food is delicious. You know, fudge and ice cream and stuff. I suppose you get enough of the tourists, though, at the Festival Park."

Ambrose nodded. "I don't mind the visitors. I like to see people—who are happy to have traveled here."

I remembered a question that had gotten lost in my anger. "Oh! I forgot to ask—why did you tell Mr. Midgett that you were in that play? *Are* you in it?"

"That's a long story. I was in *The Lost Colony*," Ambrose said, "but some stuff came up."

"Like working at the Festival Park?"

Ambrose nodded. "It's okay, though. Now I get to hang out with you."

I blushed for the millionth time. "Lila auditioned for that." I thought for a minute. "Wait, why don't you know her? This is a small town, after all. I looked it up, and there's only one middle school in Manteo."

He shook his head. "I do school at home. My mother teaches me."

That could explain a lot about Ambrose's weird vocabulary, if his British mom was his teacher. "I have some friends who are homeschooled, and they like it. But I think I might get lonely."

"Sometimes I do." After a minute, he added, "Less so now that you're here."

My heart just about stopped beating. *Come on, Nell, it's not like Ambrose said he* liked *you or something. You're friends. Be cool.* I plucked a leaf from a bush and twirled the stem between my thumb and forefinger to distract my nerves.

"My mom says we might leave pretty soon," I blurted out.

"What? I thought you were here to stay." Ambrose stopped walking.

I turned to face him, shading my eyes from the now-afternoon sun. "No, we're only here for this month. Didn't I tell you that?"

Ambrose shook his head. "It must've been wishful thinking on my part. How much time do you have left?" There was an urgency in his voice that I found unsettling, but also kind of . . . exciting? Flattering, maybe? Even my best friend, when I'd told her I was going away for a huge chunk of the summer, responded by lining up a reserve friend via text. Ambrose sounded like my leaving was going to be a terrible thing for him.

"Mom is finishing her research this week, and then it's a matter of whether we want to spend the rest of the month here as a vacation."

"This means we must hurry if we want to find answers to Roanoke's mysteries," Ambrose said. He met up with me in two silent strides. "If I had known . . ." He trailed off. *Oh.* So it was all about the mystery, not me.

"I was thinking it would be a good idea to search along the

coastline to look for clues. Based on some stuff that Lila's dad told me at the museum."

"I know a way to get onto the water," Ambrose said. "Remember where we found the flask?"

I winced. Maybe part of why I wasn't holding a grudge with Ambrose was because I knew that I held a big, fat secret: that I'd lost our super important artifact. "Um, yes?"

"There was a boat, tied up to a dock. Only a skiff, but it was big enough for the two of us. We could paddle around the island, make a day of it."

Going out in a boat with Ambrose sounded really fun, but also hard. "Do you know a lot about looking for clues underwater? I doubt we can get fancy tools, like sonar." What we really needed was a metal detector.

"I can dive under the sea and look."

"You have all the gear?" I asked, skeptical. If Ambrose didn't have a cell phone and always wore his work uniform for regular clothes, how would he have the money for an expensive hobby like scuba diving? Or even snorkeling?

He shook his head. "I'll dive by myself—I don't need tools."

"Like free diving." I'd seen a documentary on that once— these people can take a deep breath and dive practically to the bottom of the ocean.

"Sure. The ocean in these parts is very shallow, especially near the shoreline. There are lots of shoals—sandbars."

"Okay." I had another idea then. A mischievous one, maybe, but it was too perfect to pass up.

"We could use your telephone's compass," Ambrose suggested.

That was true, but not quite what I was thinking. "Sure. But I could get some shipwreck-hunting gear to help us. Perhaps from Lila."

Ambrose raised an eyebrow. "Your sworn frenemy?"

"I have a plan." By now the trees were thinning out, and I saw the road ahead. My mother would be over at the Grandmother Vine, a few hundred feet away through the trees. "Looks like we're almost back. Do you want to finally meet my mom?" If I squinted, I could see her sitting in the distance, scribbling something in her field notebook.

"No!" Ambrose stopped me before I started waving and calling for her attention. "Beg pardon, it's that– Do you have the time?"

I refreshed my phone. Still no bars, but the clock worked. "A little past three." I couldn't believe it had gotten so late.

"Zounds!" Ambrose said. "I have to get home immediately. My mother will be worried sick."

"Let us drive you," I said. "Anywhere on the island takes minutes in the Jeep. It's not a problem."

"I couldn't ask that of you. Plus, I know a shortcut that will be faster. Another time I'll meet your mother." Ambrose gave me a sheepish grin. "Friday, shall we say? That gives you a chance to snag whatever tools we need."

I nodded. "Sounds good. I'll meet you at the Elizabethan Gardens, at the part by the sound. The Watergate, I think it's called." Ambrose was already dashing off through the woods. I called after him, "I'll be there at eight thirty!" Maybe for once, I'd be on time.

Ambrose turned to give me a thumbs-up but kept running away. I watched flashes of him fade through the trees.

I looked to the vine and saw my mom stand up and wave. I started to jog to her, but I was too exhausted to run. I'd been out in the hot woods for hours, and I hadn't been drinking water. Another survival fail, I guess.

"Nell! Were you calling for me?" Mom asked as I practically collapsed at her feet.

I shook my head. "Nope." I didn't know how she'd react if I told her I'd been talking to Ambrose. What if she got mad that I was hanging out in the woods with a boy, and then forbade me to spend time alone with him? If I didn't give her that chance, going out in the boat with Ambrose wouldn't be disobeying her. It would simply be a little omission. Plus, I felt bad that Ambrose hadn't wanted to meet her today.

Mom frowned. "Hmm. I could've sworn I heard you yelling. That's why I looked up and saw you flailing through the trees. And thank goodness, because I was getting ready to call a search party." She held out her water bottle for me, and I chugged from it. "Have you not eaten or had anything to drink this whole time?"

"I was taking a nice walk. I got turned around, though. The compass on my phone went on the fritz."

She *tsk*ed. "You need to be more careful, sprout. Let's get you into some air-conditioning."

I inhaled a granola bar before helping her pack up her things. I must've been near heat-exhausted because while driving home, I fought sleep, despite the bumps of the road. Each time my eyes almost closed, I pictured Ambrose leaning against the trees, smiling at me.

A blessed arrival and a bittersweet departure from our struggling colony. First the arrival: a child, born on the eighteenth of August. Ananias and Eleanor Dare did name their daughter Virginia, after the place of her birth, and she holds the distinction of being the very first English child born in the New World. (I dare say the green-eyed monster did bite Margery Harvie—her child was born thereafter.) Virginia was a healthy and bright babe. Her birth gave new hope to the whole company. 'Twas a difficult summer in the Roanoke colony—the drought worsened day by day, and our food stores became perilously low. We did not enter parley, and relations with the Roanoke people did sour like the rotten grapes that hath fallen from the vine. Even our few allies offered bare assistance as we struggled to stay fed. With autumn and winter looming, we were all most afeard. With so few crops planted, what would we harvest?

That leads to the afore-written departure of John White. The governor stayed for the wee babe's baptism the Sunday following her birth. But on the twenty-seventh of August, he set sail for England. The planters and assistants determined that although we may survive the winter with what little we possess, we would need supplies by spring's end. With one voice, they requested his departure. At first, White refused. He fretted it would be abandonment of his colony, and he would be slandered. He would be leaving all his things, he said, such as his decorations for the future governor's manse, and his pieces of armor. He could not expect for them to be kept for his return if we ventured into the main.

The next day, all the planters and assistants made the request of him again. This time, the women begged him too—including his own daughter, Eleanor. Verily, she told her father 'twas his duty to go. What hope for survival could sweet little Virginia have, if he did not procure the help our company so desperately needed? Standing near to them, I overheard him say again that his duty was hither, with the colony of which he is governor. But Eleanor persisted. "Prithee, do not let England forget us." We, the company, delivered him a testimony to prove our wishes. Eventually, White was convinced.

We all stood on the shore as he departed. Eleanor, cradling baby Virginia in her arms, did shed salty tears as he boarded the boat. "Fear thou not," he called to her. "I shall return, bearing goods for the company and gifts for my Virginia." Yea, we did hope for his safe return. Yet as I watched the boat fade into the horizon, I did wonder when e'er we would lay eyes on him again. Or if. Our voyage hither was rife with dangers. 'Twas a miracle we found this island, and 'twould be a miracle if our colony was joined by its governor once again. Until then, we faded back into the darkness of the forest, and we did wait.

CHAPTER NINE

*J*first heard about the storm on Wednesday night.
While drying the dishes, I asked Mom if I could have a
reduction in my hours. "I wouldn't mind going back to
the gardens or the Festival Park. You said we might be leaving
next week. This is my last chance."

Mom pursed her lips, thinking it over. "I guess that's fine.
Honestly, I'm running out of research-assistant work for you to
do." She rinsed a plate and handed it to me. "But don't forget
our ground rules, sprout. You check in on your phone whenever you leave the cottage."

"I know, I know."

"Especially if you go near the water. Only swim where
there are lifeguards. That's important this week: The first big
storm of the season is brewing off the coast. It's early for it."

"We're getting hit by a hurricane?" I asked. "Won't we
need to evacuate?" When I was little, hurricanes didn't scare

me at all. They were something that happened far away, to people who lived in oceanfront houses. New York City doesn't exactly feel like a beach town. But then we had *our* hurricanes, and now they terrify me. My parents, too—tucked in the back of our hall closet is a huge plastic tub filled with emergency water, food that won't spoil, flashlights and batteries, and a wireless radio. Mom bought Dad a cell phone charger that you crank by hand, which I thought was really funny. "It's for the new olden times," she said. "Thank you, climate change. NOT." A classic example of Mom's "NOT" jokes.

"More like an out-of-season nor'easter, according to the weather guy," she said, handing me another plate to dry. I missed our dishwasher. "Don't worry—it should stay out at sea. But it might bring rain."

That was a relief. If we got hit by a hurricane, there would be no way that Ambrose and I could sneak off on a skiff. But a faraway storm wouldn't stop us. The bay was calm as a bathtub, anyway. Except for the wind.

After Mom headed out on Thursday morning, I had the whole day to take care of business. The cottage's old-fashioned rotary phone sat on a little chest in the front hall, and tucked into one of the drawers was the Outer Banks/Albemarle Area phone book. I could hardly believe that the numbers and addresses for all the people and places on Roanoke and the surrounding area were contained in the slim volume. The Manhattan phone book was so thick, I used it as a booster seat when I was little. Roanoke's was so small in comparison that I almost felt like I could count the residents on my fingers and toes. First, I flipped to *V* for "Viccars," but Ambrose and his mom were unlisted. Then I looked up the entry for Lila's family: "Midgett, Luke and Kate." Their address was helpfully printed next to the number. They lived outside of town in the Mother Vineyard neighborhood—close to the water and the actual Mother Vine. It would be a short trip on my bike, once I made sure that Lila wasn't home.

If I borrowed her metal detector, Lila and her parents probably wouldn't even notice, right? All I had to do was return it first thing on Saturday, or even slip it into the garage late tomorrow, after Ambrose and I got back. The Midgetts would never know the difference. Asking them for permission wasn't an option—not if I didn't want Lila to know what I was up to. Desperate times call for desperate measures.

Slowly circling past the bookstore on my bike, I saw the familiar reddish-yellow fur of Sir Walter Raleigh, collapsed in a lazy heap on the porch. *Excellent.* Lila must be inside, chatting up Renée or doing research. This was my chance.

I pedaled as fast as I could to the Midgetts' address, arriving at a cheerful white house with bright green shutters and a tidy yard. I had expected their home to look a little ramshackle or something, maybe because Lila's dad was busy with his artifacts and her mom didn't seem like the landscaping type.

But like all the other houses on Mother Vineyard Road, the Midgett house was nice-looking. There weren't any cars in the driveway and inside the windows, everything looked still. I hid my bike in some bushes near the road and tiptoed across the yard, glancing behind me every two seconds like a truly paranoid person. I hurried around the house to the garage, which was a barnlike structure. The water of the sound glistened right behind it.

A few boats leaned against the side of the garage: a dingy yellow kayak, a shiny red rowboat, and a tattered Sunfish sailboat. I peered into the belly of the rowboat. I'm not even sure what I was looking for—something for shipwreck hunting, I guess. Sonar equipment? Magnetometer? I didn't even know what the tools I needed looked like, other than the Ping-Pong paddles Luke had said maritime archaeologists use to brush sand away from objects buried underwater. Maybe this was kind of a dumb plan, hunting through Lila's stuff without a clear idea of what I wanted to find. Anyway, wouldn't all their special equipment be on her mom's big fishing boat?

The door to the garage was slightly ajar. As I pushed it wider to let me into the darkened space, something fell over with a loud clatter. "Jeez!" I exclaimed, tripping all over myself. I bent down to pick up whatever I'd knocked over, and that's when I realized what it was: a metal detector. Judging from the label, it could be used in the water.

I'd seen people using them at the beach when Mom and I went—a potbellied old man slowly scanning the *bleep*ing wand over white mounds of sand. I watched him for a while, until I realized that steady noise of *pings* didn't lead him to any treasure. But if that detector could find metal buried deep under the sand, couldn't it find metal buried in the shallow water along the shore? Wherever the colonists had made their village, there had to be some metal artifacts: silverware, drinking cups, tools. Even if they took almost everything with them when they vanished, surely some things got left behind and buried by time. This was what Ambrose and I needed to find them.

I grabbed the metal detector, sneaked out of the garage, and hurried down the gravel path back to the street—the detector was compact but cumbersome, so I couldn't hustle that fast. *Now,* this *is dangerous,* I thought. It was one thing to trespass on the Midgetts' property to poke around. It was another to steal, I mean *borrow,* something of theirs. Lila and Sir Walter could come ambling up the path at any moment. I couldn't wait to be safe on Budleigh Street.

That's when I heard painfully off-key singing. It sounded like it was coming down Mother Vineyard Road. And getting closer.

I stopped in the middle of the yard, wondering what to do. *That warbling might not be Lila—but then again, she did have an "audition debacle."* My stomach dropped when I heard Sir Walter's bark through the trees. He was yowling at something, maybe a squirrel. Perhaps he didn't like Lila's singing. Or maybe he could sense me, terrified and standing as still as that deer in the Grandmother Vine woods.

I took off running as fast as my battered-from-the-forest-floor feet would allow and while clutching the clunky detector. I sped toward the dense brush bordering the Midgetts' yard and threw myself into it. Brambles and leaves tugged at my hair and my exposed skin, but I plunged in as deep as I could to hide myself. I crouched low to the ground, panting, hoping that I'd made it to safety before Lila and Sir Walter had rounded the corner.

Lila trotted up the walkway to her house. She was reading a book, singing, and walking simultaneously, so Sir Walter nudged her back to the center of the path whenever she drifted. I started to breathe easier. I watched her stop halfway to the front door and slowly turn a page. All I needed was for her to go into the house, and then I could make a mad dash to my bike. Home free.

Doot doot-doot-doot doot-doot-dah! That's when my phone decided to play backup for Lila. It blared the British-sounding fanfare music that I'd assigned to be the special ringtone for my dad's calls. Of all the times for him to make himself unlost to me.

I fumbled to hit silent, but it was too late: Lila had stopped in her tracks. The hand holding her book fell to her side, the pages fanning out as they moved through the air. She quit singing, and her eyes narrowed to a squint. I could see the concentration on her face as she listened, trying to pinpoint where the sound had come from. She slowly turned around and around, scanning the edges of her yard. My heart pounded; the sound of blood pumping through my ears was deafening. I didn't dare breathe. I clasped the cold metal of the detector, and prayed that she wouldn't look over to these bushes and see part of me sticking out.

Sir Walter barked in my direction, his tail wagging happily. *"Shush."* Lila pressed a finger to his wet nose. "Be quiet," she said softly. She took a few tentative, tiptoeing steps in my direction. I closed my eyes. I couldn't bear to see her approach me, knowing with each step the very deep depth of the trouble I was in. My sweaty hands struggled to hold tight to the detector.

I peeked one eye open. Lila had stopped again, listening. Slowly, she raised the hand holding the book. She fumbled to stuff it into the tote bag slung across her shoulder, her gaze never breaking from the bush in which I was hidden. She grabbed hold of Sir Walter's collar and paused again. Did she see me? Could she hear me, struggling not to hyperventilate? Was part of my shorts showing through the brush, or was the metal detector glinting in the midday sun?

It felt like years passed in those moments until Sir Walter started whining at Lila and she grudgingly let go of his collar. And then he dashed—or as close to *dashed* as a slightly overweight old dog can do—across the yard, on a beeline to me.

Frantically, I tried to slither farther into the bushes. I couldn't squirm away faster than Sir Walter could speed-lumber, and soon enough his wet nose was pushed up into my muddy, scratched hand. *"Not now, good sir!"* I hissed. *"You're blowing my cover!"* He panted happily at me. I'm sure if I could've seen his butt, which was still outside of the bushes, I'd have seen his tail wagging with joy.

I heard Lila running across the yard. In seconds, I would be caught. And then, a miracle in the form of a squeaky frog toy. My elbow found it, actually, pressing down hard enough that the resulting squeak made both me and Sir Walter startle. Lightning fast, I snatched the frog and gave it a more powerful squeeze before chucking it out of the bushes. It arced across the yard, and Sir Walter speed-lumbered after it. From within the bushes, I saw him almost knock Lila over like a bowling pin.

"Your froggy!" Lila exclaimed. "You finally found it, good sir!" Sir Walter proudly ran circles around Lila, squeaking frog clamped in his grin. The trespasser in the bushes was forgotten, for now. I watched through the brambles as Lila petted him. After what felt like an eternity, she stood up, taking the toy from Sir Walter's mouth. She tossed it to the front door, and after one final glance in my direction, headed after dog and toy. She was even caterwauling again. Now I could totally understand why her audition had gone so poorly.

I didn't shift, not even to swat at the flies and mosquitoes having a party on my bare arms and legs. I let the trickle of blood from a scratch drip down my thigh. I held my breath, waiting for Lila to disappear inside the house. By some miracle, maybe just maybe, I was going to be able to escape her.

Finally, Lila reached her green front door, pulled a key from her pocket, and slipped inside with Sir Walter. The screen bounced back open from the impact of her slamming shut the heavy inside door, and then everything in the yard was still again.

I wanted to collapse onto the dirt below me as all the adrenaline flooded out of my body. I knew, though, that if I did Lila might come bustling out of her house the minute I eventually picked myself up to leave. I had a small window of opportunity now—those minutes when you first get home, when you're preoccupied with checking the mail or pouring a glass of water from the pitcher in the fridge. That's not the time when you stand at the window and watch your yard for trespassers and thieves. (Or stand in the hallway and watch through the peephole, for city dwellers like me.) So I clutched the metal detector with one hand and pushed up from my crouch with the other. My legs burned from squatting for so long, and I got the world's worst head rush. That plus the heat was almost enough to make me pass out. As soon as the edges of my vision stopped twinkling, I scrambled through the scratchy bushes and ran along their perimeter to the road. I never glanced back, not wanting to slow myself down and being afraid that the act of looking would somehow make Lila catch me.

At the cottage, I hid the detector under my bed and recovered by making lunch. Mom had totally relaxed her grocery-shopping rules for this trip, possibly in another attempt to avoid conflict, and so our cupboards had stuff like marshmallow fluff and sugar cereal. As I chewed my fluff-and-puffs sandwich, I checked my phone to see if Dad had left another message, but it only showed a missed call. I sat and watched the cat clock on the kitchen wall tick-tock in time with the moving tail while I tried to work up the nerve to call him back. I hadn't talked to Dad in so long, and my current feelings toward him had been colored by worry and hurt. I didn't know whether I wanted to—or could be—happy and excited if I finally reached him. Maybe I'd still be mad and confused. What had he quoted in his last message? *"The approaching tide will shortly fill the reasonable shores that now lie foul and muddy."* Maybe I didn't want to clear things up. Finally, I dialed his number and waited. The phone rang four times before I was sent to voice mail.

I shoved my phone across the table and put my head down on the surface for a few minutes. *Ambrose understands how this feels*, I thought. If nothing else this summer, I'd found someone who made me feel a little less alone. I wasn't the only kid whose father had wandered off. Whether temporarily or permanently—who knew.

As murky as the situation with my parents was, at least it felt like the truth about the colony had a chance of becoming clearer. The stakes felt really high now—with us leaving soon, and more construction signs popping up along the road to the Grandmother Vine. I decided to do a little last-minute research on how to check the shoreline for clues. Leaving my bike at home, I hurried down the quiet Manteo streets toward the bookstore. A sleepy Sir Walter wasn't waiting on the porch as I walked up the steps, but I knew that already: Lila had made her visit for the day, while I'd pilfered her metal detector. I shook off the wave of guilt I felt, reminding myself that I was *borrowing* it, and breezed inside the store.

"Can I help you, sweetheart?" Renée asked, pausing her dusting work behind the counter.

"Yes, actually. I'm looking for books on how to search for stuff underwater."

"Stuff like what? Shells?"

"No, artifacts."

That didn't seem to faze Renée. "Oh, you mean from ship-wrecks?"

I tipped my head back and forth in a *sorta* motion. "More like stuff people lost—or left behind."

"The explorers. Or pirates?" Renée's eyes lit up when she mentioned pirates. I realized right then that there were an awful lot of pirate knickknacks behind the counter: a ship in a bottle; a clock with Blackbeard's face as the face; an impressively realistic stuffed parrot wearing a mini hat. I guess pirates were Renée's thing, like cows were Mrs. Kim's. Her apartment is full of cow stuff, right down to her Holstein welcome mat.

"Like the colonists. Is there a how-to book for finding artifacts in sand or shallow water? Or a manual?" I pressed my lips together as I thought hard. "Maybe a book on maritime archaeology."

"Believe it or not, a good person to ask is right behind you," Renée said.

I expected to see Lila's dad, or maybe a dive captain, when I turned. Or even the potbellied metal-detector guy Mom and I had seen on our beach day. They would all be "good people" to ask. I did *not* expect to see Lila Midgett, tanned arms crossed against her chest, glowering at me.

"Hi, *Nell*," she spat. "Let's take this outside and I can fill you in." She linked my arm with hers, then steered me out the door. I looked helplessly back at Renée, begging with my eyes: *No! Hand-sell me a book or something! Don't let Lila drag me out of the store.* I should've planted my feet on the area rug in front of the counter and refused to move. But I didn't want to make a scene, and it was embarrassing to show Renée that in the short time I'd been in Manteo I'd managed to turn a frenemy into my first-ever *enemy*. Renée, oblivious to my plight, smiled and waved at us, going back to dusting off her pirate tchotchkes.

Outside, Lila didn't let go of my arm. "You're still poking around in this stuff! Unbelievable. No, inconceivable!"

The shock of seeing her wore off. "Lila, you're not the boss of me." I wrenched my arm free and took a few steps back. "So if you'll excuse me, I'm going back into the store to read. It's a free country." I pulled open the screen door and pressed the handle of the heavy wooden one.

"It won't be so free if I tell my dad that you were trying to *steal* an artifact."

I let go of the handle. There was only one thing to do: call her bluff. "You don't have any proof. A bobby pin could fall into the case by accident. Anyway, I didn't take a thing." I added, "You're the one who's unbelievable. I mean, *inconceivable*." I started to stomp inside.

"I bet I could tell him about our metal detector, though."

Picturing it hiding under my bed at the cottage, I felt like I was going to be sick. Had she seen me running through the yard with it? I imagined Lila standing at the window of her house, watching as I raced away, and I cringed. *Try to play it cool, Nell.* Reading all the mystery books that Dad has lying around the apartment has taught me that the bad guys are often caught when they accidentally implicate themselves during questioning. No matter what, I couldn't admit I'd taken it. "What metal detector?"

"Don't play dumb. You know exactly what I'm talking

about." Lila leaned forward, like the prosecutors always do during the dramatic courtroom scene. Lila was good. I bet she read those kinds of books too. "You found an even better way to spite me—steal *my* stuff to do your totally amateur investigation, right?"

"I honestly don't know what you're referring to." I smoothed a piece of hair off my forehead. "You lost your metal detector or something? That's what this is all about?" My head throbbed. I could almost hear a telltale *blip-blip-blipp*ing from beneath my bed, all the way at the store.

Lila stamped her foot. "It's *missing* from our garage. I went out to get something an hour ago, and it was gone. I saw footprints, too. And when I was coming home, I heard a phone ring—from over near the bushes. Right before Sir Walter went nutso in them." She narrowed her eyes at me. "You were out there hiding."

The most genius idea ever hit me. "What did the phone sound like?" I asked innocently.

"A bunch of horns tooting." She added, "It was really annoying."

"Call me." I pulled out my phone. "Call my number right now and see what happens when my phone rings."

Lila watched me carefully as she pulled her scratched-up flip phone out of her bag. "Don't touch anything on yours."

"I won't." I even set my phone on the arm of the rocking

chair and raised my hands like people do when the police ask them to drop their weapons.

I told Lila my number, and she dialed it. A few seconds later, my phone rang. The noise it made was ducks quacking loudly. They woke up Sir Walter, who had been snoozing on the steps. Confused, he barked and stared up at Lila. When he saw me, he got that doggy grin on his face again and shuffled over to flop down on my feet.

"That's not exactly fanfare, is it?" I crossed my fingers on my right hand and my left toes, too, hoping that she wouldn't think of the ability to assign different ringtones for different people. Didn't her parents and even Renée strongly suggest that Lila doesn't have a ton of friends? If I only called a couple of people regularly, I wouldn't bother to assign different rings.

"I guess . . . it wasn't your phone." She gazed slightly beyond me, like she was concentrating very hard on how to match up these puzzle pieces: me giving off a guilty vibe, her metal detector mysteriously disappearing, but her only (and largely circumstantial) clue failing to tie me to the crime. Even Sir Walter's enthusiastic trip to the bushes could be explained by his long-lost froggy. Lila looked back at me and blinked. "Although I'm not convinced it wasn't you."

I shrugged, trying not to let my relief show. If she couldn't pin the theft on me, then she couldn't use it to prevent Ambrose and me from going searching tomorrow.

"You better be careful, though. I'm still watching you."

"Isn't that taking away from your precious time to hunt ghosts and find the colony?" I pointed out. "You're just mad that I might solve the mystery first."

Lila made an exasperated noise and angrily untied Sir Walter's leash from the railing. "You're absolutely right, for once. I don't have time for you. Construction for the Elizabethan Links is going to start in a matter of weeks and who knows how that will upset the paranormal hot spots on this island." She tugged Sir Walter up from the ground, then stomped away.

I watched her turn the corner, feeling an uncomfortable mix of frustration and guilt. I wanted to go back inside the bookstore, but I didn't want to risk another run-in with Lila if she came back. Instead, I shuffled home.

We turned on the news after dinner, to hear the weather report. "Some pretty gnarly weather heading into the weekend," the meteorologist said. Mom laughed at his surfer lingo. "'Gnarly'? Didn't that go out with Gidget?" I had no idea what she was talking about, so I just shook my head no. The weatherman went on about how a front from the west was going to meet with the tropical system or something, and push high winds and rain toward the Outer Banks.

"This weekend won't be a good time for a trip over to Nags Head to hike on those dunes. It's too bad," Mom said. "They're incredibly tall, like mountains of white sand—but not safe when there's a chance of lightning. Have I told you about dune vegetation?"

"Hmm," I said, trying to concentrate on what the weather guy was saying. I might've missed part, but I definitely heard him say that the bad weather would intensify Friday night. That was good. If Ambrose and I were off the water by mid-afternoon, which we would need to be, anyway, based on what time my mom usually came home, then we should be fine.

I stayed up late, working on an epic e-mail to my dad with everything I'd learned so far. I hinted that tomorrow I might have even more juicy stuff for him to write about. *Am I getting my hopes up too much?* I wondered what two kids with barely any equipment could possibly find. Then again, we had already found the flask, using just my big toe.

When I finally clicked off the light at midnight, I tossed and turned. Partly, it was the good kind of nerves. I don't know what made me more excited: possibly finding the long-buried secrets of the lost colony, or spending a day out on the water with Ambrose. Wait until I told Jade about that. I hadn't heard from her since she sent me a picture of her and Sofia hugging in their zookeeper gear, and she hadn't replied to my last text, which bugged me.

But truthfully, I had been having a hard time sleeping ever since the night the flask went missing. Even though I was positive that Lila took it during dinner, I couldn't forget that uncanny feeling of being watched in my dark room, the sense that someone or something was in the small, quiet space with me. I had debated buying a night-light at the Festival Park's souvenir shop, in case I ever got that sensation again, but ultimately that felt too childish. I still kept the flashlight in bed with me, curling my arm around it as I slept.

Once I finally fell asleep, I had more weird dreams. I was on the water with Ambrose, in a big old-fashioned boat, kind of like the *Elizabeth II* at the Festival Park. We ran across the wet deck, trying to find someone in between getting splashed by big, salty waves. Finally, I rounded a corner and saw the person we'd been looking for: Ambrose's dad. He was wearing reenactor clothes, like Ambrose and his mom—that's how I knew it was him. I pulled on his shoulder to make him turn and face us. But when he did, it wasn't Ambrose's father anymore. It was *my* dad. Feeling confused and relieved at the same time, I woke up.

The clock on my bedside table read 3:17 a.m. I rolled over and put my pillow over my head to block out the moonlight coming in through my curtains. I counted back from one hundred to fall asleep, like I used to do when I was little. It took at least three rounds before I conked out. The last thing I remembered thinking before I succumbed was that everything would be okay if we found something this summer. But in my half-asleep state, I mixed up "something" with "someone."

CHAPTER TEN

My mom came into my room at seven thirty a.m. to give me a quick kiss good-bye. I had set my phone to wake me up at the crack of dawn, and I'd very quietly gotten dressed and packed a bag while listening to Mom moving around the kitchen and preparing to leave. When I heard her padding down the hall to my room, I jumped back into bed and pulled the comforter up to my neck so she wouldn't see that I'd been awake. She'd know that I was up to something if she saw me up so early.

"You're on your own until dinnertime. I'm touring a winery on the mainland—they're showing me the scuppernong fermentation process. It's going to take a few hours, and then I need to finish my field notes at the vine." She smoothed my hair back from my forehead. "Are you feeling okay? You're awfully bundled up in here. It's warm out, you know. I hope you're not coming down with something."

It was already toasty in my room. I let one of my bare arms slide out from under my covers. "I'm fine. I just felt like snuggling in this morning."

Mom glanced out the window. There was one patch of blue in the sky, the rest overtaken by thick clouds the color of milky tea. "It *is* a gloomy, stay-in-bed day. But if you venture out, remember—you need to give me a call if you're leaving the cottage."

I nodded. "Have fun with the tour."

She stopped in the doorway. The way she stood reminded me of how Sir Walter's ears pricked up at Fort Raleigh, when he was barking at some unseen thing in the woods. My mom could sense that something was up. "Sure you don't want to come with me? The fermentation process is pretty interesting. You see, the sugar in the scuppernong grapes—"

"Mom," I interrupted. "No offense, but grapes and vines are your things, not mine. I'll be fine hanging out here today. Reading in the garden."

She smiled at me, and I felt a twinge of guilt for lying. Telling her that I planned to spend the day reading was a flat-out lie, not even a little white one. "If you say so. Bye, sprout."

"Fare thee well," I said. I listened to her footsteps to the front hall, the jangle of her car keys falling into her purse, the rattling *slam* of the door, and the *thunk* of the lock turning. Then the engine starting up, and Mom honking as she pulled out of the driveway. I leapt out of bed and stood at my window, watching her go. Time to move.

I looted the bins in the carport, finding goggles among water noodles. I added them and one last item to my overstuffed bag: a thin rain poncho I found in the hall closet, next to an out-of-batteries flashlight. My fingers were perma-crossed that we'd miss the coming storm, but it couldn't hurt to bring it anyway. I spread thick knifefuls of peanut butter and fluff onto two bagels in the kitchen, wrapping them up in tinfoil. I pulled a baggie of scuppernong grapes out from the fridge—their taste was growing on me. Then I filled my water bottle and headed out the door. It was cumbersome to get going on my bike, having to balance the metal detector in the front basket.

The air felt even more humid than usual as I pedaled toward the Elizabethan Gardens. I scanned the sky above me. Even that patch of blue was gone, and the clouds looked thicker and bumpier. Something about the quality of the air or the gloominess of the light made my stomach knot up a little. Maybe it was nervousness, too—about going out on the water. I'd been in a canoe once at camp and on a rowboat a handful of times, but always on the lake in Central Park. You really wouldn't want to fall into the slightly sludgy water there—it has an alarmingly oily sheen—but nothing truly bad would happen if you did. Shallowbag Bay surrounding Manteo seemed quiet and clean, and the sound was calm for the most part, but they were connected to the ocean and the thought of a little wooden skiff in the big waves by Corolla was scary. I reminded myself, *We're not going to* be *out in the ocean.* The plan was to skim the coastline of Roanoke, looking for signs of where the settlement might have been.

After locking up my bike at the edge of the parking lot, I hurried to the entrance building. I felt like a huge dork, carrying the metal detector in with me. What if they weren't allowed? I stopped to pull the poncho out of my bag and drape it over the detector. It hid it, but now I was carrying an oddly shaped poncho lump. I took a deep breath and walked inside, standing really close to the pamphlet-laden counter in hopes that the admission lady wouldn't be able to see below my belly button.

"I remember you! The girl who accidentally took a dip in the sound."

I blushed. "Yup, that's me. One sticker, please."

"Just one? You're all by your lonesome?" She gave me a pitying look.

"No, I'm meeting my friend. Again," I said, frowning. The lady was nice, but she did not know the meaning of MYOB.

"Ah, that's right. Your *friend.*" She smiled at me in a way that meant she thought I was meeting a made-up boyfriend. "Well, I hope you and your *friend* have fun. Let me know if you *all* have any questions."

"Thanks." I grabbed my sticker.

"We have some lockers, you know," she called after me. "If you're feeling weighed down by all that stuff."

"I'm fine, thanks," I called over my shoulder, hurrying outside. Once past Shakespeare's garden, I stopped to readjust my poncho/detector bundle so I'd look less like a bag lady when I met up with Ambrose. I checked my phone to make sure Mom hadn't called or anything while I was biking over. My stomach knotted up even more when I thought about lying to her. That's when I had the excellent idea to text Dad and tell him my whereabouts. If Mom found out and got mad, I could always say that I'd let one of my parents know—just the one who wasn't around. I wrote: Hi, Dad. I am going out on a boat with a friend today. Like I told you in that e-mail—we're hoping to unmuddy the shores. I'll let you know what we find. Vague enough, but still honest.

As I stood waiting for my message to send, the hairs on the back of my neck started to prickle. I felt watched. I turned, wondering if nosy sticker lady was snooping on me. I didn't see her or any other staffers around. The gardens were peaceful and quiet, except for the tinkle of fountains. Yet I couldn't shake the feeling that somebody was paying awfully close attention to me. *It can't be Lila, right? How would she know that I'm here?* I shook off the feeling and headed for the Colony Walk to the sound. Passing the Virginia Dare statue, I remembered Ambrose's blah reaction to my distant family connection. I was kind of bummed he wasn't more shocked and excited about that.

I managed to climb over the Watergate on my own. It was windy, and all the tall sea grasses whipped at my legs as I walked along the rocky sand, stepping over puddles. I shaded my eyes with my free hand to see if Ambrose was there yet. I didn't find him, but I spotted the skiff tied up at the little pier. I wondered to whom it belonged—on my way to the Elizabethan Gardens, I'd watched for a road or even an unpaved path from the highway toward the sound. There were none until the park's driveway. Looking inland, I didn't see a house or anything. The only building nearby was the Waterside Theatre. If there had been a path leading from the dilapidated dock somewhere, it was long overgrown. Weeds curled up the rusted metal poles that stuck deep in the sand, and the wooden planks were old and covered in green fuzz. Some were even broken or bowing in such a way that I wouldn't dare step on them. I set my things up on a relatively stable-looking section of the dock and peeked inside the skiff. It was dry and clean, with one oar lying on the bottom. Next to it was a single life vest, much newer than the rest of the boat. I sat down at the edge of the pier, carefully.

"Nell!" Ambrose ran to me along the shoreline, from the direction opposite of the theater. "Pardon me for being so late!"

"How did you get here?" I asked as he stopped next to me. Even though he'd trudged through a few feet of sandy water and sloppy seagrass, there were no stains on him. His pants were rolled up almost to his knees, and his long shirtsleeves past his elbows. Below the crystal-clear surface, I could see that his feet were bare again. "No shoes?"

"You don't need shoes if you're on the water," he pointed out.

"Is there a road to this spot? I looked for a path from the highway, but I didn't see one."

"Er, I know a shortcut." I wished he had shared it so I could've avoided paying admission and awkwardly parading in front of the sticker lady.

"Maybe I'll take that to get home." I glanced across the water, noticing that the clouds out at sea were even more dramatic than the last time I'd checked—far off in the distance they had turned a charcoal color and carved into huge banks. High cirrus clouds coming from the other direction swirled into them. The wind continued to blow, and there were even a few whitecaps on the surface of the sound. I'd never seen it this choppy. "I don't know about this," I said. What was off in the distance looked like more weather than my thin rain poncho could handle.

"Worry not," Ambrose assured me. He examined the mossy rope tethering the skiff to the dock, to see how he could untie it. "We won't venture too far."

"If you say so." I set my stuff down in the bottom of the boat. "Oh! I brought some things that might help us—a pair of goggles I found at the cottage, and a metal detector."

"Oh, summer's day!" Ambrose grinned as he watched me unpack the tools. "That is *super* helpful."

"I swear, you have the weirdest sayings. 'Oh, summer's day'? I've never heard that before." Ambrose blushed.

He used one arm on the dock's piling to vault himself from the sandy water over the skiff's edge. It barely shifted as he plopped inside. "Come on!" he encouraged me. "Time's a-wasting!"

I gripped the dock with one hand and held the edge of the boat steady with the other. Taking a deep breath, I lowered one foot onto the seat inside the skiff, then the other. I let go of the dock and the boat started pitching back and forth. "Ambrose!" I shouted, struggling to steady myself, and the skiff, before it capsized. "Balance me out!" Jade and I used to try sitting on the same side of a Central Park rowboat, testing to see how much we could make it dip toward the water before our parents or the guy in charge of the boats yelled at us to stop. Ambrose was sitting on the opposite side from me. He was bigger than me, but not so much that the boat should have been so unbalanced. I braced my hands on opposite sides of the skiff, and it slowly stopped rocking.

"Okay over there?" He giggled.

"You're not impressed with my graceful boarding?" I asked, rolling my eyes. Ambrose went back to untying the boat. I turned on the metal detector, holding it a few inches below the top of the water. I slid the attached headphones over my ears. No *bleep*s, so far.

"I'm ready to set sail if you are." He tossed the rope back onto the top of the dock. "Push us out to sea, Nell."

"Bon voyage!" I shoved the dock away from us, and the boat cut through the water. It was exciting to be moving, on our way to adventure. The possibility of finding something—something significant—felt so strong it was almost tangible, like a scent carried on the breeze. The *increasingly strong* breeze: The wind had picked up to a strength beyond gusty. I pulled out the oar. "Do you want to steer us, or should I?"

"You can steer, and I will scan the depths." Ambrose's head stuck out past the edge of the boat, his eyes searching for something below the surface. I hefted up the oar and took a few tentative paddles. I balanced the metal detector by squeezing it with my knees, hoping that the steady sound of *ping*s would speed up from a discovery. After all, we were near where we'd found the flask.

After a few minutes, I pulled off the headphones. "Want a sandwich?" I hadn't eaten much for breakfast. I dropped the oar and rummaged in my bag to pull out the PB-and-fluff bagels. I took a big swig from my water bottle. Even though I definitely didn't want to wear my swimsuit in front of Ambrose, I wished I had it on. The water, although rough, looked inviting. Despite the heavy cloud cover, the air was hot and prestorm sticky.

Ambrose eyed my gooey bagel hungrily, but when I tried to hand him his own, he shook his head. "I'm quite all right. I couldn't eat a bite."

I shrugged. "Suit yourself." I reached into my bag for the grapes. "Not even a scuppernong?"

Ambrose's eyes lit up. "From that vine?"

I nodded, popping one into my mouth. "Yup. But I washed them and everything." Ambrose held out his pale hand and I dropped a few into it. He ate them greedily, which seemed odd considering he'd said he couldn't eat a bite.

"Steer us out a bit?" he called from the bow. The island rounded to our left, and he pointed to the right. That would lead us into the open water.

"Are you sure?" Erosion of a quarter mile couldn't have put the site of the colony smack in the middle of the sound, after all. "I thought we weren't going to head away from the shoreline." A gust of wind battered us, rocking our skiff from side to side. At least *I* didn't want to stray from the island, especially as the sky and water darkened. But it wasn't raining yet, or anything.

"Trust me!" Ambrose called back to me. The wind carried his voice in an odd way, so it sounded like he was much farther from me than the front of our boat. Dutifully, I stuck the oar in the water to turn us and then paddled for the skiff to move out from the reedy, shallow water. Already I could see that the Waterside Theatre and adjacent patch of rocky sand were far behind us. We moved fast for a skiff with only one oar. Another gust of wind powered us from behind, sending us into the waves. The lurching motion made me slide off the bench, and I banged my knee against the hard side of the boat. "Ow!"

"Are you all right?" Ambrose looked back at me with concern.

I rubbed at my knee, which was already turning bright red. A rainbow of bruising was sure to follow. "I don't know," I said. "I mean, my knee is fine. But the weather is freaking me out, Ambrose. Honestly, I'm not sure this is such a good idea anymore. Maybe we should head in and call it a day." I swallowed hard. "I want to find the clues to the lost colony just as much as you do, but this doesn't seem very smart."

No sooner had I said that than the first crack of lightning lit up the sky, far off in the distance. I listened for a clap of thunder, but even after ten seconds I didn't hear one. "Did you see that?" I yelled to Ambrose. "There was lightning!" I scrambled to pull the detector back into the skiff and turn it off so we wouldn't have a big piece of equipment hanging off our boat like an electrical-charge bull's-eye.

"Fie on this weather!" The wind tousled Ambrose's hair and he struggled to brush tendrils off his face. "Perhaps you're right. . . ."

I'd been so busy listening for thunder, and making sure the lightning didn't flash any closer, that I didn't notice how far we'd drifted. I could still see the theater, but it was approaching speck-size. "We're really getting far from shore," I said, my voice wavering a little, but I wasn't sure Ambrose heard me. The farther into the sound we got, the more the skiff rocked in the waves. I took another sip of my water and tried to focus on the horizon so I didn't get seasick. I thought about my mom and the canoe accident she'd had as a kid. She'd told me so many times that if she hadn't had a life jacket, she could've drowned. I picked up the one we had and hugged it tight. I stuck the paddle in the water and tried to move us back toward the shoreline, which was fading even more into the distance, and fast. "Ambrose," I struggled to keep panic out of my voice. "We're moving too far away." He was looking the other direction and didn't seem to hear me over the wind. I set the oar in the boat and tried to climb over the junk in the bottom and the seats to talk to him, but moving only made the shakiness of the skiff worse. "Ambrose!" I finally screamed. I squeezed my eyes shut for a second, both embarrassed that I was stressing out so much and too anxious to care.

"Nell?" he turned around, looking scared. His hair waved wildly in the wind and the loose sleeves of his white work shirt billowed with the gusts, like sails.

"We're too far from shore! And we only have one oar." I clutched at the sides of the skiff. "How are we going to get back? In these waves, and in bad weather?" I looked out at the whitecaps. I'm an okay swimmer, but honestly I never go in over my head in the ocean. If the boat capsized, if we fell in—I couldn't finish the thought.

"I know it's frightening, Nell. But I've been in seas far rougher than these. I've spent *days* in storms, when everyone on board was sick and terrified. The water is shallow here, and there are other islands all around. Put on the life vest, please. You should wear it. I think we will be safe—but I don't want you to be so afraid. I won't be upset if you want to paddle back."

"I—I don't know." I did not find the possibility that we might not make it back to Roanoke and would have to take refuge on a random mini island in the middle of the sound very reassuring. What if we drifted through an inlet and went out into the ocean? I snapped on the jacket.

"'Tis an adventure?" Ambrose smiled, but it was wobbly with fear. I tried to repeat his words in my head, like a mantra. *Adventure, adventure, adventure.* I hadn't wanted a boring summer, right? *Adventure, adventure, adventure.* Well, I definitely didn't have one anymore.

Time passed most slow after Governor White left Roanoke. The hope brought by Virginia's birth—and Margery Harvie's new babe—we ne'er again found. We were hungry—so hungry. As the weather turned brisk, the remaining riches of the island shriveled. What little stores of food we held ran out. There were grapes on the vine, but with the days e'er colder, we knew not how much longer they might sustain us all.

The planters and assistants argued about what our colony ought to do. Some did want to abandon our homes and venture fifty miles into the main. Mayhap we could find our way to the Chesapeake. Some argued we ought to join the Croatoan in their village, if they would be e'er so merciful to allow us. Yet more thought we should sail the pinnace from the safety of this hidden isle, to flag a passing English ship for supplies. Of course, we were all afeard that we might encounter a Spanish vessel instead, and England's hiding spot would be found.

Young George, Thomas, and I still wandered the isle, looking always for goodly things to eat. Perhaps we would stumble upon some morsels, and the threat of starvation would fade. My mother worried e'ry time we ventured from the village—fearing revenge for the innocents our men had slain. What if our enemies returned? But even as my belly cried for food, I sought to be as brave as my father.

"Yea, in time, we shall find our way," said he. "Hope, my lad." I closed my eyes and imagined our colony bustling with life. It would be thanks to those in our company, and our struggles.

But hither we shall struggle no longer. Days ago, I returned from the forest to learn that our colony seeks a new home. First, some men of the company shall make their way to the Chesapeake. As I write, they leave on the morrow, in the pinnace. It shall take many trips for them to carry all our possessions away. A second group, with the women and children, shall wait on the island. We shall hide ourselves well—a passing Spanish ship may have seen smoke from our fires. If threatened, we shall flee to Croatoan.

My brave father is needed aboard the pinnace. But my mother and I, we shall stay.

This morn we watched Father and the other men load the pinnace with as many supplies as it could bear, so much that the wood near bulged. My mother shed nary a tear before they departed. But she clasped my father's hand so tightly, the signet ring near branded her palm.

A hug from my father most gruff. "Good cheer, I promise I shall come back for thou, my son," he did say to me. "Not the last words thou hear from me shall these ones be." Then he swung himself on board and set to work, manning the pinnace sails. Mother and I stood on the shore, among *the weeds and marshes, and watched as the ship floated toward points unknown. The weather mourned with us, dark clouds above a roiling sea and bleak grayness blanketing the sun.*

As I write, we wait for him hither. And nothing shall move us until he returns.

CHAPTER ELEVEN

Eventually, despite the wild wind and the salt brine stinging my eyes, I spotted a spit of land to our left. The boat pitched back and forth like a bathtub toy. We started to take on water—only enough that it sloshed my ankles, but it still worried me. Ambrose crouched at the bow, exclaiming with each shudder and roll of the boat. I stayed huddled by the stern. At one point, I leaned over the side and heaved my sandwich and scuppernongs into the depths. I hoped barf didn't attract sharks.

"Ambrose," I said weakly. I cleared my throat and called his name a little louder. He turned and shaded his eyes to look at me.

"Alas, poor Nell! You look green around the gills." He scooted closer to me.

"Let's try to get over there. I need to be on land again." I also really, *really* needed to pee, but I was too embarrassed to tell him that.

"Good idea. Try to steer us o'er there." He gestured to the oar.

I stuck it in the water. Luckily, the wind helped by pushing us in the direction of the land. Couldn't Ambrose try to paddle for once? I was the one who had been puking her guts out. I felt weak and scared. And, I guess, increasingly crankypants. "Can't you take the oar for a while? I'm not feeling well, and I have blisters on my palms."

"Er, okay," Ambrose said tentatively, taking it from me. But as I sank back onto the wet bottom of the skiff, I noticed that he barely attempted to move it through the water. The wind did all the work for him.

A few minutes later, the skiff slammed into something hard, sending both of us tumbling from our perches. *Land.* I stepped onto the wet sand with relief, taking a minute to dig my toes in. Then I dragged the boat far up onto the beach. No way did I want to leave it near the waves and watch it drift out to sea without us. I unsnapped the life jacket and left it on a dry spot of sand.

Ambrose scrambled out behind me. "I'll see if there's a place to tie up the skiff." But there wasn't—if what we were on was an island, it was totally deserted. No trees or anything, just patchy dune grass, sea lavender and sea oats, rocks, and shells surrounded by pebbly caramel-brown sand. At least it was a relatively dry place, where we could wait out the rough weather.

But I needed to figure out the logistics of peeing, without any trees or shrubs or anything to hide behind.

I pulled out my phone to see what time it was—my sense of that had skewed, and we could've been at sea for minutes or hours. The roiling sky hid any time clues based on the sun. But my phone must've gotten wet either when I was on the bottom of the skiff or when one of those big waves smacked us. I kept trying to refresh the screen, but it stayed blank. I pressed and depressed the power button repeatedly. Nothing. *This is not good.*

No matter how weird or bad or *whatever* things got, my cell phone meant that Mom was only a call away. Mom *and* Dad, once upon a time, although I wasn't sure whether that held true anymore, even in an emergency. And this was turning into an emergency, fast.

"Do you have a watch?" I asked hopefully.

Ambrose shook his head.

"My phone is dead. I think it got wet or something. Any idea what time it is?"

"It can't be much past midday," he said. "We were at sea for not very long at all."

It hadn't *felt* like "not very long at all." But I had to trust Ambrose on this one. He was, literally now, all I had.

I plopped onto the sand and put my head in my hands.

"Nell, you should have some water." A worried pause. "Are you okay?"

I shook my head, blinking back tears. I was afraid to open my mouth, afraid that vocalizing how I felt right then would mean that I would start bawling. And when I cry, I look like a red-faced, snotty-nosed baby. Even if I was frustrated with Ambrose, I didn't want him to see me that way. I grabbed my water bottle and took a big swig, even though I still hadn't figured out how to solve the bathroom problem. I nervously tapped my fingers along the bottle's metal sides.

Finally, Ambrose pushed himself up from the ground. "While we're here, let's see if your contraption will find anything."

I supposed he was right—it would be silly to have gone through all this to sit on the sand and sulk while waiting out a storm. We were out here to find clues, so even if I was wet, scared, and in truly desperate need of a toothbrush or at least a stick of gum, we might as well make the epic trip worth our while. Although I wasn't sure what we could find this far from Roanoke. I had gotten so turned around, I didn't know if we were in the sound, the bay, or even near the inlet to the ocean. "Okay."

Standing up made my head spin. I took another sip of water, then reached into my bag to grab the other sandwich. "Are you sure you don't want—" I stopped when I found the bagel, which like everything else in my bag was thoroughly soaked with seawater. "Never mind." So now we were on a desert island, in a storm, with no means of communication, no food, and limited fresh water. Once again, I found myself in what sounded like the beginning of a survival TV show, and I didn't like it one bit. I sighed and grabbed the metal detector.

Ambrose and I walked side by side along the sand, the waves crashing against our feet and breaking above my calves. Even though it was the height of summer, it was cold out here in the wind and drizzly rain. I couldn't stop shivering. Goose bumps covered my skin. Only my ears were warm, because I had on the detector's headphones. I listened carefully to the *bleep*s and *blip*s of the detector, hoping that I'd hear them accelerate and this whole thing would turn out to be something other than the Stupidest Idea Ever.

I had opened my mouth to suggest we give up when *bleep . . . bleep . . . bleep* turned into *bleep! bleep! bleep!* Which then turned into *blipblipblipblipblipblipblip!* Eyes wide, I turned to Ambrose.

"We've got something!" we exclaimed at the exact same time. Although Ambrose added a "Zounds!" In spite of myself, I grinned. Maybe the currents and winds of this storm had stirred up the bottom of the sea and found something for us.

"*Onetwothreefourfive* jinx!"

Ambrose tipped his head in a way that said *I'm confused.* "'Jinx'?"

"We said the same thing at the same time." Maybe saying "jinx" was a New York thing.

Ambrose bounced on his toes. "Let us see what it is!" We waded into the water, the *blip*s intensifying with every wet step. When we were up to our knees, I stopped. The waves and the current were so strong, we were in danger of being knocked out to sea with one big swell. There could be a sharp drop-off from the sloping beach. Who knew how deep it got out there; we could be in over our heads in seconds.

"Wait," I said. "I don't want to go out any farther."

"Good idea—keep a lookout on shore." Ambrose forged ahead, the waves crashing higher onto his thighs. "I see something!" he shouted.

A gust of wind, combined with the sea swirling around my ankles, almost knocked me over. "How can you tell?" I looked down at the foamy water. I could barely see my freezing toes through it. What could Ambrose possibly be seeing? Fish? Seaweed? He didn't even have my goggles.

"Verily, I can feel it. Over there!" The wind carried his voice away from me, and the headphones muffled all sounds. He turned and cupped his hands around his mouth like a megaphone. "I'm going to swim out for a better look."

I pulled the headphones off my ears. "Ambrose!" Ignoring the huge, dark clouds gathering over our heads, I splashed closer toward him. "Are you crazy? You don't have any equipment. We're in the middle of a storm! There are probably rip currents. You're going to get killed!"

"Nell! Please stay back where it's safe!" There was a longing in his face, a terrible sadness, which rattled me more than the skiff had. I shuddered as I watched him wave good-bye. "I'll be fine, Nell—nothing will hurt me." Then he dove underneath an incoming wave.

"Ambrose!" I shouted into the howling wind. I backed up a few feet and sank into the sand, burying my head into my crossed arms. The water sucked at my legs from the strong undertow. I felt like when I had realized that my dad was gone—this desperate need to be *not here*. In my room that night, I'd covered my ears and pretended that while I was blocking out all noise, Dad had actually come home. The key had scraped in our lock, he had noisily dropped his laptop bag and kicked off his shoes in the front hall, then he had wandered into the kitchen and slammed the cupboard doors. My mom had probably chided him for it, pointing out that our cupboards were already in rough shape and it wasn't like we had the money to get new ones anytime soon. But maybe their voices had softened and eventually they'd hunkered down in front of the TV, watching one of their boring shows about wealthy British people or real estate in exotic places.

I'd tried to convince myself that all those sounds had really happened while I had my ears plugged. But when I'd removed my hands, the silence in our apartment had been deafening.

As I sat on the beach, I put the headphones back over my ears, squeezing my eyes shut, too. *Ambrose is coming out of the water right now. He's walking up the sand, shivering, and he's about to plop down next to me. We'll look at each other and laugh about what a crazy idea this was, and then as soon as the wind dies down we'll hop in the skiff to go back to Roanoke. The wind will push us right to the beach with no effort. Then we'll go to the ice-cream shop. I am definitely getting extra sprinkles.* I opened my eyes and gazed out to sea, in time to see Ambrose's head—his tangle of hair, really—bob up from the water. I jumped to my feet, waving my arms around wildly. "Ambrose! Come back!"

I don't know whether he heard me, but he dove under again. This time I watched for him, willing myself to not blink as I stared at the surface, waiting for him to emerge. I don't know much about free diving, but I know enough to guess that people typically don't do it during conditions as rough as these. Or alone. I counted the seconds to see how long he was staying under. *One-Mississippi, two-Mississippi, three.*

I got all the way to *one-hundred-Mississippi* before I saw him surface again. How was that even possible? I was counting slowly. *I must've missed him bobbing up at some point; it's the only explanation.* You'd have to be some kind of world-record holder to hold your breath that long underwater.

The waves pounded the sand with even more force, and the sky had darkened so much that it looked like night was falling. Rain pelted me, cold and stinging on my bare arms. I remembered the poncho in my bag. I tore my eyes away from the patch of sea where I'd last seen Ambrose and turned toward the skiff. Just in time to see a wave coax it from its sandy cushion back into the water.

CHAPTER TWELVE

S creaming, I dropped the detector and ran after the boat, pushing myself through the waves until my feet couldn't stay on the sandy bottom anymore. Then I swam, fighting terror with each kick and stroke. I was so close to catching up with the bobbing skiff. *Just keep moving.* Finally, after swallowing a big gulp of seawater, I reached the boat. I clung to the side as it drifted farther out to sea. It took all my strength to heave myself over the edge, and then I half fell, half collapsed inside. I realized then that the life jacket was still in the sand.

At first, I curled up in the bottom of the skiff and sobbed. It wasn't just possibly-lost-to-the-sea Ambrose, and the raging storm, that made me cry. It was *everything.* Missing New York, and missing the summer I'd planned with Jade, whose texts had grown farther apart and always mentioned Sofia. Missing my father, and missing the kind of relationship with my mom in which she didn't keep huge secrets from me. I'd felt lost ever since the day he'd disappeared. I'd wanted so badly for something—anything—to be found. But it looked like I'd only worsened things. Now, trapped in a rickety boat in the middle of the Graveyard of the Atlantic, I was in danger of losing not only Ambrose but myself.

The skiff rocked me as my tears started to slow. A lot of my problems had just happened to me—I didn't do anything to make my dad go away or my mom bring me here. I also hadn't done much to *solve* my problems, although how I could solve my dad sneaking off to England was beyond me. But *I* was the one who'd put myself in the boat. I couldn't blame anyone else for that choice—even Ambrose. *Maybe right now*, I thought, *I need to stop letting stuff happen to me.* It was time for me to paddle my own way home, or die trying.

I seriously hoped that last part wouldn't be literal.

Sniffling, I sat up and grabbed the oar. I tried to steer, but the waves had other plans for me. The boat drifted toward the area where Ambrose and I had stood with the metal detector, which was still lying on the sand, probably getting ruined by the beating waves—not that I'd be able to recover it. Returning it undamaged to Lila's garage should have been the least of my worries, but I felt a slap of guilt about stealing and then losing it. That was another problem I would have to own up to. *If we get back to shore.* I gripped the oar tighter.

Clambering up to the bow, I leaned over and yelled to the waves, "Ambrose! Ambrose!" If he surfaced somewhere near, I could stick the oar out and drag him in. Panic rose in my throat, and I felt like I might throw up again. Where was he, in all those whitecaps? Salt water and tears stung my eyes. I clutched the oar and stared at the angry sea. "Ambrose!" I called again, my voice overshadowed by a clap of thunder. *I am not giving up.*

The sky lit up with lightning, shining a spotlight on Ambrose popping up from the deep. "Nell!" He was only a few feet to the right of the boat, but he was facing away from me.

"Behind you! I'm here!" I frantically rowed closer. Ambrose treaded with one arm, the other clutching something underwater. The glint of his signet ring showed me which way to go as the sky further darkened. "Look behind you!"

Finally, he turned and saw me. Who cares that I was crying like a baby and soaking wet. I wept a little harder because he was okay—or would be, so long as I could get to him.

I stuck the oar out. "Swim to me. Hurry!" The current and the wind had shifted and were moving the skiff quickly in the other direction, away from him.

Ambrose dipped under the waves. Now that I was so close, I could see him underneath the surface, moving through the churning water with speed and precision. Was Ambrose part fish or something? He could navigate the roughest surf I'd ever seen, and he could hold his breath underwater for a ridiculously long time. It wasn't normal. I shuddered. *Something weird is going on, and it's not just the weather.*

He surfaced right next to the side of the skiff, which teetered back and forth so much that he was only visible in between rocks of the boat. But I still saw that he barely gasped when he popped above the waves. "Take this!" he shouted. He held out an object to me—another oar? I dropped the one I was holding into the bottom of the boat and grabbed for it. It almost fell out of my hand because it had such a weird, slippery texture. Like the posts on that dock: wood that was slimy from years underwater and slick with algae.

Ambrose was beneath the waves again. I held my breath as I waited for him to surface. My lungs were bursting when he did. He grabbed hold of the skiff, clutching something with his right hand. The boat barely moved as he hopped in next to me. Or maybe I simply didn't notice it because of the waves.

"Where did you get this?" I held up the slimy oar. Another crack of thunder sounded, and a gust of wind washed a huge wave over us. I braced myself against the sides of the boat, shivering. My relief at Ambrose being safe was speedily being replaced by exhaustion. I wanted to be back at the cottage, in my little slant-ceilinged bedroom. I wanted to be curled up in a chair in the garden, reading. It seemed to be wishing for too much in the moment, but I wanted to be back in my New

York City apartment, watching TV on the perfect-size-for-three couch. Holding a bucket of microwave popcorn, with my parents on either side.

Ambrose's eyes were wet and shining. Maybe it was from the salt water and swimming, but it also looked like perhaps he had been crying. Otherwise, he was remarkably unruffled. His clothes were plastered to him, but he didn't shiver. The gusts of wind threatened to knock me over unless I crouched near the center of the skiff, but he sat up tall.

"I found it."

"Found what?" I asked. "The oar?" It would help us try to get home.

He shook his head. "Aye, but there's more. That oar is from the pinnace. Shipwrecked, half-buried in the sand."

Pinnace. Hadn't he said that his father had left on one of those? I felt a sinking sensation in my stomach, not related to the churning sea. *What if Ambrose's dad got shipwrecked?* Maybe that's why he never came back. I had to swallow three times over the catch forming in my throat before I could ask him. "What—what pinnace?"

"The one the colonists took."

I sucked in my breath so fast I gasped. "Wait—you found *it*? I mean, *them*? How do you know?"

"I could tell when I saw the boat. There were cannons on board, poking up out of the sand. I felt them with my hands.

Then I found this." He held out a tarnished object. "Take it; keep it safe," he said. "In your bag."

I grabbed it from him. It was rough and corroded, but I could tell what it once had been. "An old cup." I zipped it in my bag, which I slung across my body.

"A silver cup, the kind the colonists brought from England. One caused a big fight between the first group of Englishmen and the Aquascogoc people."

"Wow." It definitely looked old enough. "How are you so sure?"

"I also saw . . ." He trailed off, staring into the waves. "There *had* been a tempest that day. Most fierce." He stopped and cleared his throat. "Much like today. The storm blew up quickly, barely after they left the beach. Then they must have wrecked on a shoal. Alas, they ne'er got any farther." He grabbed the oar and clutched it to his chest. "All this time they have been so near," he said, his voice breaking a little.

I had the strangest feeling then, a cold shock. Like stepping into the freezer aisle at the grocery store on the hottest day of the year. *"There had been a storm. Much like this."* How in the world did Ambrose know that the colonists had left the island in a storm? What else did he see in that shipwreck to get the details?

Unless he knew all that before he found the wreck.

As I was about to ask, another huge wave hit the boat, stronger than any of the rest. Before I knew what was happening, the skiff flipped over. Ice-cold water filled my mouth, swirling over my head. The strap of my bag floated up and tugged on my neck. My hands moved through the water, one grasping an oar as it floated past my outstretched palm. With the other, I found the skiff's bench and hooked my elbow around it. I pulled myself into the pocket of air between the water and top of the boat, spitting out a mouthful and coughing. Thank goodness that at summer camp, they'd taught us how to flip a canoe.

"Nell! Hang on!" Ambrose swam up to me.

I clutched the bench and blinked the salt water out of my eyes. I could hardly breathe, much less speak. My bag settled back at my hip, but underwater.

"Pray pardon, do not move—I shall right us."

I was too weak to say anything, too weak to help. I don't know how he had the strength to overturn the boat, but as I clung to the seat, it flipped right side up again. I lay on the bottom, still hugging the oar Ambrose had rescued from the deep. Seconds later, Ambrose flung himself over the side and next to me. It must've been a huge effort because he looked as pale and weak as I felt. I was so cold, so tired. Rain pelted me. I wanted to let it fall onto my tongue, I was desperately thirsty. But exhaustion wouldn't let me open my mouth. *Water, water everywhere nor any drop to drink*. Everything else from the skiff, my water bottle and goggles and the other oar, was gone.

On the way to rest with the pinnace on the bottom of the sea. What was in my bag was surely ruined. *How are we ever going to get home?* I knew then what the answer was: We weren't.

We were lost now too.

My eyelids fluttered shut, even though I fought to stay awake. I felt myself slipping, slipping. The last thing I heard was Ambrose crying next to me. "I am so sorry, Nell. This is all my fault. Please forgive me. I never meant for this to happen. But—but be not afeard. You'll still be with me."

Barely do I possess the strength to write. More than a fort-night hath passed. With e'ry day, we grow weaker. We have little food remaining, only sparse grapes on the vines. The rest of our company hath given up all hope. They dismantled all the remaining homes and followed Manteo to his village on Croatoan. C-R-O, they carved into a tree, so the rest of our company would know whither they had gone.

Mother and I did intend to go.

But Mother, she is too weak and ill to journey. Whether lack of sustenance or an illness most wicked, I know not. A fever hath plagued her for days.

We shall wait hither. On Roanoke. By my troth, I know my father shall return.

E'ry morn, I walk yonder, to the edge of the sound. I wait for white sails on the horizon. Certes, my father shall find us.

This is my tale.

The story of how I journeyed across the sea, for a life in a new world.

Alas, to be lost!

Yet I still hope that by mercy we may be found.

Ambrose Viccars the Younger

CHAPTER THIRTEEN

$\mathcal{I}$ heard the barking first, so faintly that I thought I must be imagining it. The wind and rain had calmed a little, and the waves were still strong but not as scary. I struggled to sit up enough to see over the side of the skiff. Maybe we had drifted near the shore? But only open water surrounded us, at least as far as I could make out. Dusk had arrived, in addition to the darkness from the fading storm, and it was difficult to tell where the sea met the sky. *We must be out in the ocean now.*

"Ambrose." My voice came out all crackly and sent me into a coughing fit. My lungs ached. I tried again. "Ambrose, do you hear that?"

He was sitting next to me. Had he been holding my hand? Or did I dream that? My hands were so cold—all of me was. "Hear what?" He leaned into the wind. He looked almost fuzzy to me.

"Barking," I coughed. My face, covered in a layer of salt, felt stiff and brittle like limestone.

Ambrose stood up, not wobbly at all, and closed his eyes to better listen. That was when it appeared, off the starboard side.

I saw the light. Or rather, the *lights*.

The lights of a boat.

The barking got louder, too. My stomach was threatening to revolt and my head spun, but I'd never felt so happy in my entire life. Someone was coming to save us. Found. We were *found*.

A spotlight shined on Ambrose and me in the boat. I stuck up my hand to shade my face, then waved.

The spotlight stayed trained on us. "Ahoy, Nell! We found you!" The voice was of someone who knew it all. *Lila*. Never in my life did I think that I would be so excited to hear her. Joyful tears rolled down my frozen, salty cheeks. Next to me, Ambrose softly said, "See, Nell? Remember, what you think is lost may still be found."

Lila's mom boomed, "Sit tight, sweetheart! We'll be there in seconds!" The barking sounded close.

"Ambrose, we're saved!" I turned to hug him, but he was no longer there. I whipped around to see if he'd moved to steer us, or get a closer look at Lila's boat bumping across the chop. But the skiff was empty, except for my soggy bag, the pinnace oar, and me.

"Ambrose!" I shrieked. Had he fallen overboard? Did he jump in to swim back to the wreck? "Ambrose!" In the dusky light, I thought I saw him in the water, heading away from me.

The bow of the skiff bumped against the fishing boat, and the figures of Lila, her mom, and Sir Walter appeared in front of me like a mirage. I was so relieved to see that doggy grin. Then, amazingly, my mom popped up next to them. "Oh, my little sprout!" Her voice was raspy, like she'd been crying hard.

"Mom!" I shouted back. My mom, too scared to even get on a water taxi back home or wade in the calm water at the beach, had gone out to sea to rescue me—and in a storm! My heart swelled with pride for her.

"Nell, we'll help you off your boat," Kate called. Lila braced herself and held out her hand for me to grasp. Only her determined face peeked out of the bright orange rain gear she was wearing.

"Come on, Nell, I got you!"

I didn't budge. "Ambrose! Where are you?" I screamed past the empty skiff. If only I still had the life jacket to throw to him. . . .

Lila, her mother, and my mom exchanged worried looks. "Nell, take Lila's hand. We need you to get into the boat. It's going to be okay!" my mom pleaded. "We're taking you home."

Kate's strong arms held the skiff steady. I grabbed the oar and hobbled across so I was right next to them. "I know, but

Ambrose must've gone back in! We can't leave without finding him." I sobbed.

"You've been through a lot, Nell," Lila's mom soothed. "Just get on board with us, and we'll figure it out." Sir Walter barked as if to say, *Listen to her!*

I felt a rush of wooziness and knew they were right. We couldn't start looking for Ambrose while they were trying to coax me off the skiff. I let Lila guide me onto their boat. My legs were shaking so badly that I collapsed the second I set foot on deck. Sir Walter ran up to me and happily licked my stiff arms and legs. My mom lunged on top of me to give me a hug, one so tight that I thought she'd crack one of my ribs—but I hugged her back just as hard. Honestly, I never wanted her to let go. I clung to her shoulders and cried with relief. Lila hovered over us, watching. For once, she didn't seem to know quite what to do.

Her mom called, "Lila, grab a few blankets. Nell's freezing." Lila dashed off and came back with several huge, thick blankets. My mom bundled me up in them. They felt so good on my skin. Lila patted my shoulder awkwardly after my mom stopped hugging me for a second.

"Ambrose," I said weakly. "He's out there."

Lila and my mom exchanged those worried looks again. Kate finished tying my skiff to her big boat, I guess to drag it in with us.

"Nell," Mom said quietly. "What are you talking about?"

"Maybe he went back to the shipwreck. He knows how to dive. But it's so dark, I don't know how he could see." I was so cold and tired that I felt delirious, like when I'd get the flu as a kid. The colors of everything around me were all bleeding into one another like a watercolor painting, and sounds were getting fuzzy as though I was hearing everything through the front-door buzzer intercom.

"Shipwreck?" Lila perked up at that. "You found a ship-wreck?" She handed me a thermos. "Drink slowly or you'll be sick."

I took a sip; it was hot cocoa. It tasted like the most delicious thing in the world.

"Ambrose and I did, off the little island we washed up on out there. He swam out to the wreck. That oar is from it. So is the silver cup. In my bag." I coughed. "But Ambrose—we have to go back!"

"Wait, before I hear anything else . . ." Lila glanced, greed-ily, at the oar lying on the deck, like she was considering aban-doning the blanket-covered heap of me to inspect it. But then she yelled to her mom, who was back at the controls, "See if you can head back past the nearest sandbar! There might be a wreck there." Lila turned back to me. "Okay? Now you have to tell us what this Ambrose business is."

I squeezed my eyes shut, wishing we'd find him safe. "We were on the skiff together. I know you saw him. You shined your spotlight right on us. He was next to me when you waved and called my name. I turned to him and smiled. Sir Walter started barking again. Then somehow, he was gone."

Lila's eyes widened. "Nell. You were *alone* on that boat. I was watching the whole time after I turned on the spotlight. I didn't even *blink*. Nobody was ever with you." She patted my hand with concern. "I think you were hallucinating."

I sat up, thanks to strength from the cocoa. "No way." I tried to shake my head but that made me feel like I had roller coaster vertigo. "Ambrose was with me. He knew the oar was from a pinnace."

"Sprout, I saw you in the boat too," my mom said. "You were alone." She squeezed my shoulder to reassure me. "You've been through a lot. Perhaps you imagined someone was there with you." Mom bit her lip, nervous about the idea of her daughter hanging out in a boat with imaginary friends. "Try to rest. I'm going to see if Kate has any food for you." She gave me another hug, stood up, and left me, Lila, and Sir Walter on the deck. Sir Walter helpfully plopped down to cover my freezing feet.

"There is no Ambrose, Nell."

"But he's been all over Roanoke with me," I explained. "I first met him at the Festival Park. He found the flask—the one you stole, by the way—with me near the Watergate at the Elizabethan Gardens. He was the one who wanted to take the ring from the visitor center at Fort Raleigh. Because he was wearing an identical one! And I've seen him in the woods by my mom's vine, too. It's not like he's some boy I dreamt up while I was marooned in a skiff."

"Wait, you saw him in the woods by the vine?" Lila looked very excited all of a sudden.

"Yeah, once or twice."

"Think carefully: Did anyone else ever talk to him?" Her eyes glittered.

"Sure," I started. Then I thought about it. Ambrose never met my mom. At the gardens, he'd avoided the sticker lady. He conveniently disappeared whenever Lila and Sir Walter were nearby. The tightening in my chest lessened when I remembered that Lila's dad spoke to him, briefly. "Your dad talked to him—he said he'd seen him hanging around the fort. But he thought he was from the play. . . ." Which Ambrose, conveniently, had been very vague about—only saying that he "had been" a villager.

"I met his mom," I said. "I mean, I saw her. She was at the Festival Park. They both work there. They reenact the settlement." Yet I never saw him or her leaving work.

Lila shook her head. "So he's not our age? Because you have to be sixteen to work there. No exceptions." She scrunched up her eyebrows in thought. "Was his mom dressed like a colonist woman?"

I nodded. "She had on a heavy, old-fashioned dress."

Lila's eyes widened. "The people at the park reenact the 1585 colony, so it's historically accurate to only depict men. Although one supercool lady plays a blacksmith—but she still wears men's clothes."

Now I thought of how Ambrose never sweated. How he always wore the same tattered clothes. The lack of sound as he crashed through the forest and the lack of ripples as he moved through the sea. Ambrose didn't have a telephone, and he didn't go to school. He'd come from England with his family, only to have his father leave on a ship and never return.

"What is a pinnace?" I asked Lila.

"A small vessel. Large ships use them to ferry people around. I mean, large old sailing ships did."

"Ones like the colonists came here on?"

"Yup. In fact, the lost colonists still had a pinnace when John White returned to England." She frowned. "Wait a minute. Didn't you say—"

"Ambrose said his father left the island on one." Lila's mouth dropped open.

I thought of Ambrose in the water. He could hold his breath longer than any person I'd ever met, almost like he didn't really need to breathe—anymore. He seemed afraid of nothing except me getting hurt. When we were in serious danger during the storm and I thought I might die, he cried and comforted me. But what did he say? *"You'll still be with me."* I'd thought he meant trapped on the skiff. What if he'd meant something else?

Although he spoke briefly to Lila's dad, he let him be deceived into thinking he was an actor. Kind of like how I thought he worked as a reenactor.

Ambrose knew so much about the lost colony, almost as though he'd experienced it himself.

Then I knew the truth, with certainty as solid as the silver cup he'd recognized. *It's all so obvious now—how did I never see this before?*

"Nell, I think Ambrose was—" Lila started. I could finish her sentence.

"A ghost."

CHAPTER FOURTEEN

*L*ila ambushed me with questions the rest of the way to Roanoke, at least whenever her mom was at the controls and mine was out of earshot. "Let her rest!" Kate chided when she came out to check on us. My head spun from exhaustion but also from knowing the truth about Ambrose. And I *knew* it was true. I'd noticed his little quirks–like his funny slang, or his commitment to wearing reenactor clothes–and sensed that something was different about him. I thought it had been a city–country thing. An American–British thing. Or a North–South thing. Apparently it was actually a human–ghost thing.

When I'd told Lila that his name was Ambrose Viccars, her eyes widened like saucers.

"He *was* one of the colonists! I've seen that name at the visitor center, in the exhibit room with the wood paneling. Ambrose came here with his father, whose name was also Ambrose, and his mother, Elizabeth."

If my head didn't hurt so much, I'd have slapped my forehead. *Maybe if I'd read all the placards in the museum, I could've put two and two together.* But how was I supposed to know that?

"If I'd met him, *I* would've picked up on that, like, immediately," Lila added. That actually made me feel better: If I were going to die on the deck of their fishing boat, from seawater overdose or something, Lila probably wouldn't be acting like such a know-it-all. The universe was righting itself, and I was going to be just fine after I got home, took an extralong hot shower, and slept.

Still, I said, "Don't be a knave, Lila."

"I do know what that means," she replied.

The rain had mostly stopped when we finally docked. My mom got out to drive the Jeep close to the pier. I stood up, shaky on my sea legs, so Lila and Kate helped me step off the boat. Before they guided me into the idling car, Lila tugged on my arm. "I'll come by tomorrow. We need to talk about this"— she lowered her voice so our mothers couldn't hear—"ghostly new development."

I weakly nodded my okay. After Lila helped save me in that storm, I owed her some time and information. I also owed her for wrecking the metal detector—and I'd use the money I'd earned from my mom to pay for it. Although the balance between Lila and me seemed a little more equal now that I was the one who'd found both a shipwreck *and* a ghost.

Kate leaned into the driver's-side window, talking to my mom. "I'd keep a close eye on Nell tonight."

"Do you think she should go to a doctor? What about dry drowning or hypothermia? Or if all that salt water hurt her electrolytes . . ."

Kate wrote something down on a slip of paper. "The medical center's closed, but here's our family doctor's number. Call Dr. Parrish and let him know what happened—tell him the Midgetts referred you. Make sure Nell stays toasty and dry, keep an eye on her breathing, and give her lots of warm fluids. But I think she'll be just fine. She's one tough cookie."

As soon as we got back to the cottage, Mom had me take a hot shower. She actually wanted to stay in the bathroom with me, to make sure I didn't pass out or anything. But I wouldn't let her, so instead she checked in with the doctor. Afterward, Mom got Dad on the phone.

"Nell!" His voice sounded tinny and faraway. "Thank goodness you're okay. I—I don't know what I'd do if anything happened to you. . . ."

"I'm sorry, Dad." Even though it was so good to hear his voice, I could barely hold my head up, and I kept blinking away sleep. I hardly remember what he said because I was in such an exhausted daze. After a few minutes Mom took back the phone and I shuffled to my room, where I could still hear her muffled voice. For the first time since before we left for Roanoke—since my dad disappeared on us—she said, "I . . . love you, too," before hanging up the phone. I smiled as I ran a brush through my hopelessly tangled hair.

Mom didn't interrogate me, but just wrapped me up in all the blankets and told me to rest. I think she might've sat in my bedroom, watching me sleep, the whole night. The next morning, though, she may as well have thrown me on the griddle with the pancakes and bacon—because she really grilled me. "We both have a lot of explaining to do," she said as I limped into the kitchen. My *everything* was achy: head, knees, back, feet, eyes, neck. Even my hair hurt. I yawned and lowered myself into the chair next to her. Mom poured me a glass of juice.

I yawned again. "I might need coffee."

I was kidding, but Mom didn't find it funny. "No way. You're still dehydrated. Caffeine ban for you."

I sipped my juice. "I know I scared you. I didn't mean for that to happen."

Mom snorted, but not in a mean way. "'Scared' is a bit of an understatement. When I came home around lunchtime and you were gone, I was worried. Then your dad called in a panic, to tell me the message you'd left him about going on a boat. He'd tried your phone and it kept going to voice mail. Somehow, he knew something was very wrong. That's when I wasn't just terrified for you, but hurt, too. Imagine being a mom and knowing your child is not only in trouble, but was sneaking around on you."

I swallowed hard. "I wasn't trying to be sneaky. I figured that you'd worry if I told you where I was going, but I also knew I had to tell someone. That's why I sent the message to Dad."

"What you mean is, you 'figured' that I'd forbid you from going."

I studied the forkful of pancake I was holding. Eventually, I nodded. "Yeah. That was sneaky and wrong."

Mom's voice wavered. "If Lila hadn't known exactly what you were up to . . ." She trailed off.

"Wait." I set down my fork. "How *did* Lila know? I thought *you* asked them to go after me."

Mom shook her head. "Luke and I were at the vine when your father phoned, and on our way back to town Kate called to tell Luke that Lila was begging her to rescue you. Lila was convinced you were out to sea in that storm."

She really *had* saved me. But how had Lila known that I was out on the water? Was she following me that day? Whenever she came by, I had questions of my own for her.

My mom, waiting for me to explain myself, *ahem*ed from across the table.

"I guess you want to know why I was in the skiff?"

She nodded yes.

"I took the boat out to see if I could find clues about the

lost colony along the water's edge, where the land has eroded over the years. Ambr—" Oops, last thing I wanted to do was bring up that I'd spent the bulk of my time on the island hanging out with a risk-taking ghost boy. I was telling her the truth, but as much as she'd believe. "I've been trying to find evidence all summer. To figure out what happened to the colonists."

"With Lila?"

"More like in competition with her. She was trying to use her ghost-hunting stuff to locate the lost colony. That gave me the idea that Roanoke is a mystery Dad could write about. I thought if I could just find the clues for him . . ."

Mom sighed. "I see."

"But I never expected to get stuck out at sea in a storm." I paused. "I'm really, *really* sorry for scaring you, and for needing Lila and Kate to rescue me."

Mom tried to smile. "I accept your apology, but I think it goes without saying that I never, ever want you to do something like this again. And I'm going to have to think about appropriate consequences. Okay?"

I nodded. "Okay." In the silence that followed, I thought about what I'd realized while stranded in the skiff: that I wanted to paddle my own way out of problems now. "Well, I have some questions for you, too," I said. "If it's okay for me to ask them."

Mom looked me right in the eye and nodded. "That sounds like a good idea, sprout." For once, not a *we'll see* answer.

My voice wavering, I asked, "Why did Dad go to London so suddenly? What's going on with you guys? I want to know the truth."

Mom looked down at her coffee cup, rolling it in her hands. "Now *I* need to make an apology to you. I know it's been a rough summer. You've been concerned about your dad and everything that's been going on—and I haven't given you many answers. Hardly *any* answers. I'm very sorry for that."

A lump was forming in my throat. Ever since the day my dad disappeared, I'd longed to know what was going on with our family—even if it wasn't something I'd like to hear. Now that it seemed like Mom might tell me, though, I felt scared.

Mom continued, "Your dad and I . . . Things have been kind of hard for a while. We do love each other, and we love you. But it just hasn't been working between the two of us. We became very unhappy." She stopped to hold up the juice carton to offer me a refill. I shook my head no.

"Anyway, it got to a point that, well . . . I decided it might be good if your dad went away for a little while. On a trial basis," she added quickly. "So we both could see how things are when we're apart."

"*You* decided?" My head was spinning. This whole time, I thought my dad had walked out on us. But it was my mom's idea for him to go?

I'd spent so much time being upset with *him*, for leaving

not just me but *us*. I shuddered with guilt as I considered that maybe he'd disappeared only because Mom had told him to.

"It was sort of mutual. But ultimately, yes, it was my call." Mom cleared her throat. "He was so upset when I asked that he left immediately. We didn't plan it that way, to be so sudden and alarming. I should've told you that before. Pretending like Dad went away for work was a cop-out. It made things easier for me, and maybe for him, too, but not for you." Mom looked like she might cry. "I tried to explain a couple of times, but I felt so guilty. Because I was the one who uprooted us. I didn't want you to hate me for that." Mom brushed at her eyes. "Then after I found out he took a spontaneous trip to London, of all places, I was as angry as I was confused. I didn't want you to feel as lost as I felt. I'm afraid that we didn't handle this very well."

"Not at all!" I wanted to stomp out of the room, except there was that whole achiness thing. But I also wasn't finished asking questions. *This is scary, but I know now how brave I can be.* "So what's going on now? Are you guys getting divorced?" I heard her say the word "love" last night. Did divorced people say that to each other? Maybe only in times of crisis, like after their kid was trapped on a boat in stormy seas? I had no idea.

"The truth is—I don't know. But I promise I'll be honest with you from now on."

That didn't make me feel happy, or even relieved, but it was a start.

I spent the rest of the morning in the garden, reading my Shakespeare book. I opened it to a quote from *The Tempest* that chilled me: "Full fathom five thy father lies; of his bones are coral made; those are pearls that were his eyes: Nothing of him that doth fade, but doth suffer a sea-change into something rich and strange." It made me think of the watery resting place of Ambrose's dad. My heart was heavy with the truth about my parents, but I was so grateful I still had them both. I turned the page, and Lila bounded through the gate without even knocking.

"Have you seen him today?"

"Who?" I asked, still thinking of my dad.

"Ambrose! Your ghost!"

I sat up, shaking my head. "Nope. But I've been resting all day. Plus, he's never been to the cottage."

"Then we need to go find him. There's no time to waste."

"I would've thought you'd be more interested in going back to the pinnace wreck," I said.

"My mom and dad said we could check it out with the sonar, once the weather settles down. But maybe if we find your ghost friend, we can get information from him. That would be quicker than waiting for the archaeologists to brush the crud of four centuries off a shipwreck. Chop chop—get a move on! Aren't you leaving soon?"

We planned to go back to New York the next week, and I was basically on house arrest until then—Mom had decided to work from the cottage because she was too paranoid about leaving me home alone to get lost at sea or whatever. (Perhaps not paranoia, under the circumstances.)

"Yup. But I'm not allowed to go anywhere now. Grounded."

Lila shook her head. "Unacceptable. I'll talk to your mother. Give me a second or two." She dashed into the cottage, again without knocking. Minutes later, she and my mom came back.

"Nell, you can go with Lila—but I want you girls to stay together the whole time." Hands on hips indicated Mom meant business. "Take my phone with you." She handed it to me. "Call the cottage if *anything* happens." The only thing that had survived my waterlogged bag was the silver cup, which Lila had brought home to her dad. "Please be home for dinner. Lila, your family is eating here tonight."

"Great!" Lila grabbed my hand and tugged me up from my Adirondack chair. I still wasn't one hundred percent sure about this we're-acting-like-old-friends business, but she did kinda save my life yesterday. Also, it was nice to have a friend who was *living.* "Let's go!"

Lila had her bike, so I grabbed mine from the carport. Somebody had brought it back from the Elizabethan Gardens while I was sleeping.

"Where's Sir Walter?" I wasn't sure if I'd ever seen Lila without him.

"I left him at home. He slows me down on a bike."

Made sense. "Where are we going?"

"To find Ambrose! You first saw him by the Festival Park, right?"

I nodded. "He probably hangs out there because he can be incognito thanks to the reenactors' costumes."

Lila, forever an overachiever, pumped her legs furiously as she sailed down the quiet streets of Manteo. I trailed behind, biking extra slow partly because of my aches and general grogginess, and partly because I was frightened to find Ambrose. Knowing that the person I'd spent much of the summer with wasn't really a person was . . . bizarre. Did it undo the friendship I'd thought we had? What about how much I loved seeing his crazy mop of hair? Because if I was honest, being around Ambrose always gave me a few butterflies in my stomach, in that *maybe I'm developing a crush* kind of way.

Which begged the question: What kind of weirdo gets a crush on a *ghost*? I had no idea how I was going to explain all this to Jade.

But I was also scared that we wouldn't find Ambrose. I didn't want him to be lost, at least not to me. All that time, he'd been hiding the real story—not just about who he was but also about this place. The colonists. Where they'd lived. Why they'd disappeared. I'd spent the better part of a summer traipsing around *with* one of history's greatest mysteries. It was enough to make my head start spinning again.

Lila slowed down for me to catch up. "This probably goes without saying, but thanks for saving me," I said. "Even though I assume that means you were probably spying, right?"

She shrugged. "Well, of course I was spying on you, but I hadn't set out to. I was at the Waterside Theatre, taking some readings. I have to do that in the morning, before they start getting ready for the show. While I was poking around, I saw you in the distance—in that boat. You did *not* look like you knew what you were doing, and I could see the storm clouds rolling in." She grinned. "So I saved my friend, and I found a ghost colonist. Double win."

Friend. I wobbled a little on my bike. *Has Lila considered me one this whole time?* "Lila, I know I haven't been the friendliest to you." Worry flickered across her face. "Why didn't you give up on me?"

She shrugged. "First of all, I didn't want *you* to solve the mystery. I had to keep an eye on my competition. But also— after I bombed my *Lost Colony* audition, I didn't have anything going on. As much as I love spending my days with Sir Walter, I was just happy that I'd found a person to maybe hang out with. Especially one interested in history like I am."

I thought for a minute. "I guess I'm happy we found each other too."

We ditched our bikes on a rack. Lila sweet-talked the admission guy into letting us into the park for free, explaining that we had an important message to deliver to someone from her dad. I was starting to realize how much more effective my searching could have been if only I'd joined forces with Lila from the beginning. She knew how to get things done.

We ran to the settlement village. I tried to remember exactly where I'd seen Ambrose for the first time—*Near the blacksmith's!* "This way." I motioned to Lila. She followed me over to the thatched building.

We peeked inside and walked around it. I didn't see any signs of Ambrose. Lila pulled out her EMF detector, but it wasn't registering anything. The guy doing demos tried to get us to come over and use the lathe. Then he asked where our admission tickets were.

"Sorry, have to use the ladies'!" Before Lila bolted, she whispered to me, "*Follow my lead. Meet me at the entrance in a couple of minutes.*"

I pointed at Lila, dashing away. "She has mine." The guy shrugged and started chatting with an eager tourist.

Before I could follow her down the path, I heard someone whisper, "*Pray pardon, Nell.*" I turned to see Ambrose's mom. His *ghost* mom, I guess. She hovered near the edge of the village, holding a bonnet in her hands. She twisted it nervously.

Slowly, I stepped toward her, worried about what she might say. Could ghosts die? Did they get lost, too? Maybe she didn't know where Ambrose was.

Standing in the shade next to her, I tried to find any evidence that I wasn't speaking to a flesh-and-blood person—like the haze of an apparition. But she appeared as solid as I did, and just as Ambrose had. Maybe she was a little bit paler than he normally looked. I wished Lila were next to me, so we could see if her EMF detector picked up anything ghostly after all. I grabbed the cell phone Mom had given me. But it was acting as weird as mine used to in the Grandmother Vine woods, with no bars. *Maybe it's the ghost energy?*

"What is it?" I asked tentatively.

"Ambrose is e'er so sorrowful," she started.

"But he's okay?" Relief flooded me; he'd gotten back to his mom somehow. Ambrose was fine—even if he was still dead. What an odd, and sad, way to be reassured.

She nodded. Up close, Mrs. Viccars—Elizabeth—looked a lot younger than both of my parents. She shifted and smoothed the folds of her thick dress. "Prithee, Ambrose doth want to show ye. Yet he shall understand if thou didst hesitate to follow him e'er again."

"Where?"

"If thou wouldst meet him in the woods, yonder where thy mother goeth. Knowest thou the place?"

I nodded. She must mean where I'd bumped into Ambrose by the Grandmother Vine. "I think so."

She smiled. "Aye, he is there this morrow. Waiting."

"I'll go there," I said. "Thanks."

"Nay—grammercy." She reached out for me, instinctively. But then she pulled back her hand, and I realized that I had never touched Ambrose—our fingers hadn't brushed when we were exchanging the flask; I never clapped him on the shoulder when he did something cool or punched him lightly in the same spot if he did something stupid. And he'd always stopped himself before shaking hands or anything with me. Could that be part of being a ghost—not being able to have contact with living people anymore? *How lonely.* I hoped he could at least give his ghost mom a hug.

"Verily, thy companionship hath meant the world to him. I thank thee, Nell." She paused for a moment, before adding, "Eleanor would be so proud. Methinks Virginia, too." Then she waved and walked around the corner of the blacksmith building. I peeked behind after her, to see where she was heading. She was already gone.

I stepped out of the shade and back into the sunlight, thinking about what she'd said. Eleanor and Virginia *Dare*? So Ambrose must have told his mom about them being my ancestors.

I crunched along the wood-chip path, on my way to meet Lila. As I passed by the lathe guy, he gave me a funny look.

"You were having quite the conversation there, huh?" I was confused until I realized he had seen only me standing at the corner of the building—and not Ambrose's mom on the other side, to whom I'd been talking.

I patted my ear. "Wireless!"

"Aha! You can really never tell these days. Here I thought you were talking to a ghost." Little did he know.

"Where were you?" Lila stood outside the entrance, arms crossed and foot tapping impatiently on the pavement. "I've been waiting forever! We don't have all day."

"Relax! I know exactly where we need to go next."

Lila raised an eyebrow. "Oh?"

I nodded. "Ambrose's mother told me."

She sucked in her breath. "She's here? I want to see her! Oh, let me get out my EMF detector." As she fumbled with her backpack, I put out my hand to stop her.

"Hold on, she's already gone." Lila dropped her hands and pouted. "She appeared only to tell me where to find him."

"This is so unfair—I've been trying to encounter a ghost for years and *years*." Lila stamped her foot.

"Maybe you can meet Ambrose," I said. "Follow me."

Lila told me on the way to the vine that she'd always gotten her highest EMF readings along its road. "There are lots of haunted places on the island," she said. "But I never seriously thought that particular one had anything to do with the lost colonists. To think of all the time I've spent there and I had no idea . . . I mean, I bike past on my way to go swimming!"

But that's true, right? Sometimes it's the places we think we know the best that hold the most secrets: our streets, our backyards, and even our homes.

We left our bikes in a heap alongside the edge of the road. Lila started tramping into the woods right behind me, but I stopped her.

"Maybe you should wait here," I said, motioning to the vine.

"Are you kidding? And miss out on this?" She tightened her fingers around the EMF detector. "No way."

"Lila, Ambrose has always conveniently disappeared whenever you've come around. He thinks we're sworn frenemies. He might hide if I don't talk to him first. I don't really know the rules about when I can see him and when I can't. Obviously, he let your dad see him once or twice. But we don't know why."

Lila chewed on her bottom lip, thinking it over. "You're probably right. But please, *please* come find me after you explain. I've been waiting my whole life for this."

I promised I would try, and I meant it. She sat down in front of the vine, cross-legged, and holding her EMF detector on her lap. The meter was already waving around, like there was a lot of energy in the woodsy air—further convincing me that was why my phone had always acted so strangely in the area, like the compass spinning.

I hurried into the trees. Once I could no longer see Lila when I looked toward the vine and the road, just a curtain of loblolly pines and live oaks, I started calling his name.

"Ambrose? Are you here?" Silence; my voice had quieted even the birds. Sunlight dappled the forest floor around me, and a cool breeze tickled my arms. "Ambrose, please—I want to see you." Then I added, "I'm not mad."

I felt the eyes of the forest on me again, and I knew he was near. I turned to see Ambrose emerging from deep in the woods. Not much worse for wear from our misadventures, but that was understandable—nothing at sea could've hurt him. Ambrose carried something behind his back.

"Good morrow, Nell." He smiled at me, a little shyly.

"Hi, Ambrose." It made me sad to say hello, like this might be the last time. I tried to memorize how he looked gliding across the pine needles. His hair was crazy messy as always, his white shirt oddly crisp for something he'd been wearing for more than four hundred years. Dirty bare feet and pale skin. Those sad but sparkling eyes.

"I'm so happy that you are well," he said. "And I fear that I did make a grave mistake."

"How so?"

Now his twenty-first-century American speech was peppered with more Elizabethan words. "Aye, many things." He sighed. "Convincing you to go out in that mutinous storm. Lying to you about who I am, verily, and why I wanted to wander the island with you."

"Why *did* you want to spend time with me? You knew what happened to the lost colony. Because you're . . . a ghost."

"'Tis true. But I knew only what happened to my mother and me. Prithee take a walk with me, and I'll explain in good time?"

I fell into step with him as he led me deeper into the woods. "When I was alive—when all the colonists were—there was trouble on this island. The men in the 1585 colony were arrogant. Their violence ruined any chance of harmony with many of the tribes in the area. Verily, our company lacked the things to survive on this land, much less during a year of drought. After John White left, things became desperate, and with haste.

"Some of the men decided to sail away to finish our journey, settling at the mouth of the Chesapeake, as we had planned. My father was one of those who left on the pinnace. But my mother and I, like all the other women and children, stayed. Father promised that no matter what, he would come back for us. He swore that the words he used to say farewell would not be the last I'd hear from him."

I thought about the shipwreck we'd found, and a lump formed in my throat.

"But they didn't come back. A bad storm had arisen shortly after they set sail, and we feared the worst. Our group decided that if we were to survive, we must abandon the settlement. The Croatoan showed great compassion—they would let us live with them, in Manteo's village. So the remaining colonists dismantled our settlement, and we all prepared to leave. *CRO* was carved into the trees, so those who had left—like John White—would know where to find us. Yet by then most had given up hope for the group who had gone on the pinnace.

"Not I. By my troth, my father was always true to his word. My mother fell ill the day before our colony moved to Croatoan. She was in no shape to make the journey. I decided we should stay and wait for my father, where he left us. We watched as the others left the island in hopes of life on another. Then we waited."

"But nobody came back," I whispered.

"With every day we grew weaker. My mother's condition improved, but only slightly. We had the round grapes of these vines to sustain us, and what crabs I could catch in the marsh. I would walk yonder, to the edge of the sound, e'ry morn and wait to see white sails on the horizon. Alas, I knew that nothing in life would stop my father. Any day, certes, he would be back to take us to our new home. But what I ne'er knew was that a wreck had already taken him from this world. In time, not even the grapes were sustenance enough, and hunger and fever took my mother. Then me as well. Even after death, we have stayed here, keeping our vigil. Our souls have ne'er been at peace, not knowing what befell my father."

Ambrose stopped in front of a few tall trees. I cleared my throat, which ached with sadness. "I'm so sorry, Ambrose." Tears trickled down my cheeks.

"Grammercy, Nell." He revealed what he'd been hiding behind his back—a familiar round shape. *The flask!* "But because of what you and I found, we are no longer lost." Maybe it was my imagination, but his fingertips and the rest of his hands looked like the color was slowly draining out of them from holding it.

"Where did you get that—"

"Aye, I am the filch who stole it. I took it only to show my mother. But I owe that lass an apology, for letting the arrows of your accusation pierce her." He handed the flask to me. "'Twas my father's. I recognized it the moment you pulled it from the shore. I thought mayhap it meant that he *had* made his way back to Roanoke at some point in time. But the markings told me of what befell the ship in the storm. He scratched out those words as they took on water, and he threw this into sea, in hopes that it would reach my mother and me. Thusly, I knew I must leave the island to find his resting place and reunite. But for that, I needed your help."

"I'm happy I could help," I said slowly. "Even if, well, it

almost killed me." Ambrose shook his head with shame. I could tell he felt bad for putting me at risk. Although that would never be okay, I understood his desperation because I'd felt something similar. "Are you going to be okay now that you know the truth?"

Ambrose smiled. "It hath brought the peace for which my mother and I have been waiting for centuries. We are forever grateful. Now I want to help you discover the truth you have been seeking."

I gave him a questioning look. "What do you mean?"

"Aye, look up." He pointed to one of the oldest, tallest trees. It was as broad and tall as that ancient live oak at the Elizabethan Gardens. As I gazed up its trunk, I saw it. Carved faintly into the bark, very high above my head, were three letters. *C-R-O.*

I gasped. "This! This was where you all lived?"

Ambrose nodded. "Our village was in these woods, and over yonder is where my mother and I have remained for these years, tethered to this land. The grapes of that vine did help sustain us, so all this time I've looked after it—through storms and droughts and pestilence."

My mother would really freak out if she knew what had helped her special scuppernong live so long. Well, if she believed it.

"Verily, I saw you here for the first time, Nell. You were walking in these woods. Mother and I had stayed hidden from people until then—except that one man at Fort Raleigh. I watched him from time to time—I liked seeing what he did to preserve my history. A few times, I let him catch sight of me."

"But then why did I meet you at the Festival Park?"

"I do spend many a day there—the *Elizabeth II* is like the ship that ferried us from England, where I spent some of the last days with my father. But also, you'd have been afeard if I came out of these woods when I first saw you here. What's more," Ambrose added, "I could explain with ease my mother's and my clothing at the park."

"That's pretty smart." He was right—if an oddly dressed boy had jumped out from behind a tree that first day, that would have seriously weirded me out.

I remembered Lila, waiting for us up by the vine. "I'm not the only person you've come across. So why did you start talking to me?"

"You seemed familiar to me that day in the woods. 'Tis because you are a Dare. My mother said if I could trust anyone, certes would be you."

"Wow" was all I could say.

Ambrose gestured to the flask. "The longer I hold it, the more I fade." I gave him a questioning look. "Interacting with the living world—touching things, like this flask, or opening doors and rowing oars—it makes me less solid. Rest and scuppernongs help me regain myself."

"Is that why you made me do all the work?" I looked closer, and now Ambrose's arms up past his elbows were pale as snow and fuzzy-looking.

He nodded, kind of bashfully. "I beg your pardon for that, too."

"Apology accepted." Most of my questions were answered, so it was time to ask for a favor. "Do you think you could meet someone else? Because Lila—my friend—would love to meet you too."

"Friend?" It was Ambrose's turn to raise an eyebrow. "Nay, not a frenemy?"

"She pretty much saved my life yesterday. She's officially a friend now."

He nodded. "In truth, I had seen that lass before—she has come closer to discovering me, and this place, than anyone else on the island in four hundred years. But that beast was always with her." He shuddered.

Beast? "Her dog?" Ambrose nodded. "Wait, are you afraid of dogs?" I thought about how the only times I'd ever seen sleepy, friendly Sir Walter growl and bare his teeth were when Ambrose had been with me or nearby.

He nodded. "Most lily-livered. They can sense us better than any person can."

The irony of Lila's constant companion being the reason why she could never find a ghost was too funny. "Wait until I tell her that. But Sir Walter Raleigh's not around today. I promise." When he gave me an odd look, I added, "That's what she named her dog." Ambrose rolled his eyes. I guess some facial expressions are timeless.

We hurried through the forest, back to the vine. Once Lila was in view, I called her name. She shaded her eyes, looking in our direction. Her mouth dropped open, and then she jumped up, waving the EMF detector.

She was speechless when Ambrose and I reached her. "Lila, I'd like you to meet Ambrose. Ambrose, this is Lila."

"How now, good Lila," he said, giving her a shy smile.

Lila's mouth hung open, still.

"You can say hello back," I suggested.

"Hello!" she squeaked.

"Wait until you see what we have to show you." I grabbed her hand and turned to Ambrose. "Let's take her to see your home." The three of us headed back into the woods, the sunlight casting two long shadows behind as we raced toward the lost colony, found.

CHAPTER FIFTEEN

*A*fter we showed Lila the carved tree, she hurried back to the road (and away from all that ghostly energy) to call her dad at Fort Raleigh and tell him to come over *right away*. But I think she also knew that I needed a minute alone with Ambrose. To say good-bye.

"So what happens next? Where will you go?" Ambrose and I were sitting in the shade of the vine. He looked less fully human than ever before. Helping save me in the water had taken a lot out of him. Apparently, he'd also been the one to bring my bike back to the cottage. I loved thinking of a ghost riding my bike along Mother Vineyard Road, in the dead of night.

"Mother and I shall venture out to the wreck, once we have enough strength." Ambrose plucked one of the scuppernong grapes and popped it into his mouth. He looked maybe one smidge more solid as he chewed. Those grapes were the only thing he'd eaten in hundreds of years. How would people feel if they knew that the scuppernong jelly they ate was essentially made out of ghost food? He ate another, slowly, savoring it. "My father's spirit is there—I felt it in the air—just as my mother and I are here, in this ghostly form. Once we three are reunited, we won't need to be tethered to Roanoke anymore. In a way, my family will be going home. At long last." Ambrose smiled.

I swallowed hard. I wanted Ambrose to be happy, and to be "home," but I also didn't want to lose him. "Will I see you again?"

"Nay, I reckon not," he said, turning to face me. I stared into his bright eyes, and I felt tears well up in my own.

"Nell, sweet Nell, don't cry," he said. "Verily, you've helped me more than you can possibly know. 'Tis because of you that what was lost is found. For the first time in centuries, I am content."

I could see that he was right. His eyes weren't so sad, and there was a peacefulness in his face that I'd never seen before. "I'm happy about that. I'll just miss you as a friend." I wiped at the trail of a tear on my cheek and sniffed. I hated good-byes so much. I wondered, *Is it worse knowing that you will never see someone again? Or not knowing if you can?*

Ambrose took one last grape. "And I will miss thee terribly too." He sighed. "Mayhap 'tis time for us to head our separate ways." Slowly, he stood. He wiped his hazy right hand on his pants, and then he held it out to help me up.

I reached for him, trembling a little. He grasped my hand. Ambrose was stronger than I'd expected—especially for a ghost—but his palm was cold as ice, colder than any person should ever feel. I guess that's another reason why he always avoided contact with me. It was a dead giveaway. Ha.

Once I was standing up, he took a deep breath and then pulled me into a tight hug. I wrapped my arms around his freezing body and squeezed, shivering. "Thank you," I whispered in his ear. "Thank you for being my friend."

"'Twas my pleasure," he whispered back. He kissed my cheek, and my face flushed under his icy lips. Then he let me go.

"Anon, Nell. Tell the world what happened here." Hugging me had taken even more of him away. I could almost see the live oaks through his white shirt, the patterns of afternoon sunlight on grass through his feet. I realized this was my last chance for a picture—but I didn't need to take it. I'd remember that messy hair, those bright eyes, and that sad smile forever.

"I promise I will, Ambrose. Certes." Then he was off, gliding away through the forest. I shook with sobs, overcome by the sadness of his story and the grief of losing a friend. But I felt relief, too, knowing that he'd finally gotten the answers he'd longed for. And so had I.

Lila walked over and put her arm around my shoulders, pulling me into a half hug. "Hey, it's okay. You've still got me, and Sir Walter."

I took a deep breath. The thing about being alive is that you have to keep moving forward, right? Even when you're unsure about what's ahead. "About that—Ambrose told me something pretty interesting. You might want to rethink taking Sir Walter along on your ghost hunts." While we waited for our parents to arrive, I filled her in.

After four hundred years of quiet mystery, a lot happened very fast on Roanoke once we found the lost colony. The construction company happily went to plan B for their golf course. Even they didn't want to disrupt history—and Elizabethan Links' new spot on the mainland had a sweet view from across the water of where some actual Elizabethans had once lived. A new excavation project, led by Lila's dad, started the day after we showed him the site. Amazingly, within the first few hours, the crew had uncovered artifacts buried deep below the piney forest floor—including a chest that never made it to Croatoan or on board the ill-fated pinnace. As soon as I heard that they'd found it, I knew *exactly* whose it must be—Ambrose's family's, since they were the last to stay on the island. Sure enough, it held a well-preserved Bible that had "Ambrose Viccars the Elder" inscribed on the inside cover, in the same script with Gothic letters that I hadn't been able to read when we'd found the flask. But the most amazing thing was tucked under the Bible: twelve loose pages, on which my Ambrose had recorded his story—just in case it was ever found. The scientists said it was a miracle they were so well preserved. But I knew better. When Ambrose had said to *tell the world his story*, I didn't know he would be helping me.

That was when Lila and I decided to tell her dad the truth about Ambrose. He had a hard time believing us until I got to the part about Ambrose being at Fort Raleigh that day. Luke's face turned white as, well, a ghost. "That villager boy! I—I *knew* there was something different about him, but I thought he was just doing some kind of method acting." He stared out the window of his office. "I once caught him spying on me while I worked. When I tried to talk to him, he scurried away . . . wow." He shook his head. "Lila, if only I'd given your theories a little more consideration." For a second, she looked shocked, almost like she might burst into happy tears—and then she started to pester her dad about incorporating ghost-hunting methods into his archaeological work.

"Nell—knowing what these pages mean to you now, would you like to read them?" Luke opened a box on his desk, and took out a small stack of fragile-looking paper. I walked over to him, and he placed the pages in my hands. "Take your time," he added. "Lila, come here and tell me more about where you've gotten interesting readings with your EMF detector."

It was hard to read about the hopeful start of Ambrose's colony, knowing all that happened after—and because my eyes blurred as I slowly turned the pages. I squeezed them shut for a minute. *Hold it together, Nell.* I was afraid my tears would mar the writing. But as I kept reading, I realized that the fact that I was holding Ambrose's words in my hands was a joyful thing, too—his story needed to be known. As soon as the experts finished transcribing, people could read every word of it.

Finding the village site and the colonist shipwreck had turned Roanoke into major news. LOST COLONY FOUND! blared the headlines. GIRL DARE-D TO FIND THE TRUTH! People seemed especially excited about two things: that my dad wrote historical mysteries, and that I shared a lineage with the first English child born in America. It didn't seem fair that the articles focused on me, a New Yorker who hardly deserved full credit. So in every interview I did in the frenzy afterward, I pointed out that I couldn't have found any truths if a very determined local girl—my friend Lila—hadn't saved my life.

Apparently, super-old tree carvings—like the letters *C-R-O* that the colonists had left behind—are a thing people like Lila's dad and my mom study; they're called arborglyphs. *Smithsonian* magazine heard the news and asked my mom to write a special article about the bioarchaeology work she was doing at the site. Then my mom's museum decided that it wanted to put together an exhibit on both the lost colony artifacts and arborglyphs. She managed to convince them to do a joint exhibition with the Fort Raleigh visitor center, which meant that she'd be visiting the island and Lila's dad would be visiting New York City to put it all together. That meant lots of opportunities for me to see Lila again—about which I actually was thrilled. Who would have thought I would feel that way after our rocky start? Plus, there were still mysteries to solve—like what had happened to the colonists who'd traveled to Croatoan.

After extra days in Roanoke to deal with the media craziness and unexpected research work, Mom and I found ourselves back at the rental-car place, ready to fly home. The coffee vending machine spat a foamy, chemical-scented hot chocolate into a paper cup for me. I dumped a generous amount of coffee creamer into it to make up for the lack of real milk, then walked over to my mom, who was handing over the Jeep keys to the agent behind the desk.

"I hope you enjoyed your time in these parts." The agent smiled at me.

"We certainly did," I said.

"And you'll visit again sometime," she added.

"The next trip's already planned," Mom said, ruffling my hair. It was true—she would be back in a little over a month. This time, I was begging to come with her.

We both slept on the plane. As my mom put it, we were "bone tired." I didn't wake up until our wheels touched down at LaGuardia. For once, we didn't have to wait in the hour-long taxi line because as soon as we walked into the baggage claim area, I saw Jade, grinning and holding up a sign with DARE written on it in glitter paint.

"Jade!" I shrieked, running over to her.

"I figured we should take the car to get you—save you from the paparazzi, now that you guys are big news," she said. "We need a sleepover ASAP so I can get all the details. Anyway—sorry I missed a couple of your texts. It was fun hanging out with Sofia and stuff, and the red pandas at zoo camp were super cute, but I still missed my best friend. I'm so happy you're back!"

We hugged, and as soon as we broke apart she started in with the questions. "How did you find a lost colony? Are you going to be on *Good Morning America*? So are you friends with that Lila girl now? What's the deal with *Ambrose*? How come the news didn't mention him at all? And when the heck am I finally going to see a picture of him?"

"Jade! Give them a minute to grab their things," her mom scolded. But as Jade's parents helped us load our bags into their trunk, I started filling her in on everything that had happened. Not the full story about Ambrose, yet—that was definitely a conversation we needed to have without my mom scrunched in the backseat with us.

"For the record, you totally had the cooler summer," Jade said. I had to agree.

Their car whisked us through Queens and over the

Triborough Bridge toward home. Dusk was falling over Manhattan, and the peach-colored sky reminded me of our last sunset on Roanoke Island. As Mom and I were heading home from the Grandmother Vine woods, we'd driven past the sound. Over the ocean, the sky had taken on a beautiful sherbet-orange color.

"Look at that painterly sky, sprout," Mom had said. "You never see a sunset like that facing east."

I like to think that it was a sign from Ambrose and his mom—that somewhere out in that sea, they had reunited with his dad and were all finding their way home.

I could hardly contain my excitement when the car reached my neighborhood. *There's my pizza place!* My stomach growled for a greasy slice. *And my bookstore!* Finally, we turned onto my block. Our walk-up building looked the same as when we left it, except Mrs. Kim had fixed up her window boxes with some pretty violets. I jumped out of the car the second it stopped. Jade helped me drag my suitcase up the stoop.

"Sleepover tomorrow?" I asked. "I'll tell you the whole truth and nothing but."

She gave me a thumbs-up from the backseat. "You better!" As soon as their car pulled away, I left my bags in the entryway and called to Mom, "I'll go upstairs and open the door!" I bounded up all five flights, key in hand. But when I went to turn it in our lock, the door swung open. My dad stood inside, kind of awkwardly, in front of a banner that said WELCOME HOME!

"Dad!" I threw myself into his arms, almost knocking him over with a hug.

"Whoa, Nelly! I've missed you so much." He hugged me back just as hard. "I'm so proud of you. 'And though she be but little, she is fierce.'" He added, "That's from *A Midsummer Night's Dream.*" I heard footsteps on the landing, and then I felt a third body glom onto our hug.

"Welcome back, Celia."

Mom coughed kind of nervously, but smiled and replied, "Same to you." Not exactly a homecoming that suggested my family was back to normal—but at least we were all together. Including my mom's plants, which had survived a summer without us.

It was hard to let my dad out of my sight; I followed him from room to room in our apartment for the first hour or so we were home. When he sat down in his favorite easy chair, I plopped down by his feet instead of on the couch next to him (kind of like Sir Walter did to me, I guess). He was eager to hear everything firsthand—and he had a fresh writing notebook ready to fill with our story. But eventually I figured that maybe he and my mom could use a minute alone. I went to my room to "unpack," but really stared at them through the keyhole of my bedroom door and listened.

At first they sat awkwardly in the living room, glancing at each other. Finally my mom said, "So what was the deal with London?" Then Dad got up and pulled something out of his battered laptop bag. It looked like a restaurant menu. He handed it to her, and she looked up at him with surprise. "You went back to Arden?" I remembered my mom telling me about a romantic dinner at that restaurant, next to the Globe Theatre, when they were on their honeymoon.

"I thought I went to London to escape everything, but the day I found myself standing at its door I realized that, really, I had wanted to go back where we started."

Mom looked like she was going to cry again. I've seen enough movies to know that this was like a "grand gesture" on my dad's part, and I wanted her to jump up and kiss him (even though, ew) and then everything would be okay. But she stayed on the couch, sniffling. Finally, she said, "I miss that time too. If we could find our way back . . ." She reached out and put the palm of her hand on top of his.

After they were done talking, I unpacked for real. Putting away my toiletries in the bathroom, I smiled as I placed my toothbrush back in the holder. The tree held three brushes again. Whatever happened next—for right now, nothing was missing. Later that night, the three of us were curled up on our perfectly sized-for-three couch, stuffed with scallion pancakes and watching TV. My phone buzzed. I picked it up to see a message from Lila: Look! Found these by the Water-gate. The attached picture showed two new artifacts. The first was the flask—which I now understood had Ambrose's father's initials on it. The second was a small, bright signet ring, displayed in the palm of Lila's hand. I knew exactly to whom it had belonged.

My heart swelled. I glanced over at my parents, who leaned against each other on the couch. Outside our windows, the city played its nightly symphony of sirens and horns and dogs barking and laughter. I was *home*. I remembered what Ambrose had said to me in the woods, when I was frustrated about my dad and Lila and everything else going on in my life: "Never give up. What you think is lost may still be found." And in that moment I thought, *Truer words have never been spoken.*

AUTHOR'S NOTE

I can still picture the page of my elementary-school history textbook—especially the tiny black-and-white illustration showing confused Englishmen standing in front of a tree carved with *CRO*. The story of the lost colony of Roanoke was told in only a few short paragraphs—the arrival of the 117 men, women, and children; the struggles they had on the island to support themselves and coexist with the people whose home they occupied; the departure of their leader, John White; and their mysterious disappearance before his return. The most unbelievable part was that four hundred years later we still didn't know more about the fate of the first English settlement in America. The unsolved mystery of the lost colony never stopped fascinating me—and that is why this book is in your hands.

A note on Ambrose: The Viccars family really did travel to Roanoke as part of the 1587 colony. However, the real Ambrose was probably a small child during the time on Roanoke. For storytelling purposes, I made my Ambrose character closer in age to Nell.

THE HISTORY OF ROANOKE

Like most mysteries, the story of the lost colony of Roanoke is complex. It's important to note that while the colonists were the first English people to attempt to live permanently in North America, Roanoke Island was already home to many Native people. Carolina Algonquian tribes, including the Roanoke and Croatoan, had lived in the Outer Banks area for centuries. The arrival of European explorers and settlers dramatically, and tragically, changed their way of life. The story of Roanoke cannot be told without acknowledging that the determination, hopefulness, and wonder of the Europeans who crossed the sea would have cruel consequences for the Native people living there.

The Roanoke colony of 1587—the lost colony—was not the first to set foot on Roanoke Island. The English visited the area in 1584 while searching for a potential colony site between Spanish Florida and Newfoundland, and in 1585 a fortified camp was made on the island as a base for exploration of the coast and mainland. That group consisted of men only, mostly soldiers, miners, gentlemen, tradesmen, and sailors, and was led by Sir Richard Grenville. Shortly after arriving, the Englishmen lost a silver cup. They blamed the people of the Aquascogoc village for taking it—and responded by setting fire to their homes. After two months, Grenville decided to sail back to England for more supplies and left a small contingent of men on the island, with Ralph Lane as their governor. After Grenville's departure, the colony became a disaster. The men did not have enough food. Tensions with the local tribes, a result of the Englishmen's arrogant behavior and constant demands for food, erupted. Wingina, the leader of the Roanoke, convinced several tribes to plan an attack on the English settlement. But Lane's men struck first, and murdered Wingina. Their violence brought chaos to the region. When the explorer Sir Francis Drake passed by, the men begged him to take them back to England. Within weeks of their departure, Grenville arrived at the island. Finding the settlement deserted, he left another small group of men, with enough supplies to hold the fort for two years.

It was in that troubled environment that the 1587 colony tried to create a home. But, in fact, they never intended to settle permanently on Roanoke. Sir Walter Raleigh had sent them to start a new English colony, incorporated as the "Cittie of Ralegh," in the Chesapeake Bay—where they hopefully would have more success than the previous attempt. On their way, the colonists stopped at Roanoke Island to check on the men Grenville had left behind to maintain the fort, but upon arrival they made the grisly discovery that all had perished. The colonists' fate was sealed when the master and pilot of their fleet, a "scoundrel" and former pirate named Simon Fernandez, would not let them back on the ships to travel to the Chesapeake. They were abandoned at Roanoke.

That is where the tantalizing story of their disappearance begins. We know that the colonists struggled on the island—they didn't have enough supplies; they didn't have enough time to plant crops, as they arrived in late summer; and their relationships with the Native people were shadowed by the brutal behavior of the previous colony as well their own mistakes. Scientists studying tree rings today have learned that in 1587 the area suffered a serious, devastating drought. Even those who had lived there for many years would have struggled to survive as a result of it.

The floundering colonists had a lifeline in their friendship with Manteo, whose family ruled the Croatoan tribe. Manteo had returned to England with two explorers in 1584, as an honored guest. He had sailed back to Roanoke with the 1587 colony and helped them as a guide and translator. They never could have survived without Manteo's guidance and generosity. But even with it, their situation was dire.

In August 1587, the colonists convinced their governor, John White, to return to England for help. White was hesitant to go—he worried that it would look like he had abandoned his colony. He would be leaving behind his own family. His daughter, Eleanor, had given birth to the first English child born in

North America: Virginia Dare. But the best hope for the group was for White to seek help. He intended to come back right away, but three whole years passed before he was able to return. He finally made it back to Roanoke on August 18, 1590—his granddaughter Virginia Dare's third birthday. As you know, White found the colony abandoned. All the buildings had been taken down, and there were no signs of distress. Only the letters *CRO* carved into a tree and the word "Croatoan" into a post offered clues as to the colonists' whereabouts.

There are many theories about what the colonists' fate may have been. John White understood the *CRO* carving to mean that they had moved to Croatoan Island (called Hatteras today) to live in Manteo's village. He was unable to search for them there during his 1590 return because a brewing storm and problems with his ships forced him back out to sea. But it's impossible to know if he would have found the colonists on Croatoan at all. They could have suffered a devastating illness, or a hurricane could've ruined their settlement. They may have fought with a local tribe or been attacked by the Spanish. Or they may have traveled "fifty miles into the main," trying to finally get to the Chesapeake Bay. Perhaps the most likely scenario is some combination of those theories. Over the years, more clues have been found—from the "Dare stone" on which Eleanor Dare allegedly carved the story of the colony's fate, to tales of seventeenth-century European explorers encountering Native people using English building techniques inland—but we still don't have an answer. Research into what happened to the colonists is ongoing. During the summer of 2015, researchers announced important evidence that at least some colonists had traveled sixty miles from the island, to a site on the western shore of the Albemarle Sound. Concealed markings on a sixteenth-century map led researchers to a secluded North Carolina spot where they uncovered Border ware pottery—compelling evidence that some of the lost colonists had found their way there. Perhaps by the time you are reading this book, scientists will have discovered new clues!

Sir Francis Drake's coat of arms bore the Latin phrase *Sic Parvis Magna*—"greatness from small beginnings." It's an appropriate quote for the story of Roanoke. It's amazing to think about the legacy of this group of families that sailed from Plymouth, England, in 1587. They left everything they knew and loved for a chance at a better life in a world completely new to them. What bravery that required! Although we haven't yet found their fate on Roanoke, we have never lost their spirit.

ROANOKE TODAY

Roanoke Island is part of the North Carolina Outer Banks, a popular vacation destination as rich in scenery as it is in history. Across the sound, on Bodie Island, you'll find Kitty Hawk—site of the Wright brothers' first powered flight in 1903. Historic lighthouses and national seashores span the barrier islands from Bodie to Ocracoke, where the infamous pirate Blackbeard once made his home. The area is known as the Graveyard of the Atlantic, due to the many shipwrecks over the years.

Roanoke lies nestled between the barrier islands and the mainland. Its history goes beyond the English colonies—it was a Union stronghold during the Civil War and the site of a Freedmen's Colony, where thousands of former slaves found a safe home. It's also home to the longest-running outdoor symphonic drama in the world, *The Lost Colony*. The play is performed in the summer months at the Waterside Theatre at Fort Raleigh National Historic Site.

A few of the places in this book—like Renée's bookstore—are only part of the Roanoke in my imagination. (Although downtown Manteo is home to a lovely bookstore.) However, the four hundred-year-old scuppernong called the Mother Vine is very real. The vine is on private property, but you if you visit Roanoke, you can purchase jelly, juice, and even lip balm made from its grapes. The Festival Park and the sailing ship *Elizabeth II*, the Elizabethan Gardens, and Fort Raleigh are all real places where you can learn more about the many people who have made Roanoke Island their home.

BIBLIOGRAPHY

*Cerullo, Mary M. *Shipwrecks: Exploring Sunken Cities Beneath the Sea.* New York: Dutton Children's Books, 2009.

*Fritz, Jean. *The Lost Colony of Roanoke.* New York: G. P. Putnams's Sons, 2004.

*Hakim, Joy. *A History of US: The First Americans: Prehistory–1600.* 3rd ed. New York: Oxford University Press, 2003.

houston, lebame, and Barbara Hird, eds. *Roanoke Revisited: The Story of the Lost Colony.* Manteo, North Carolina: Penny Books, 1997.

Kupperman, Karen Ordahl. *Roanoke: The Abandoned Colony.* Lanham, Maryland: Rowman & Littlefield Publishers, Inc., 2007.

LaVere, David. "The 1937 Chowan River 'Dare Stone': A Re-Evaluation." *North Carolina Historical Review* 86, no. 3 (July 2009): 250.

Miller, Lee. *Roanoke: Solving the Mystery of the Lost Colony*. New York: Arcade Publishing, Inc., 2000.

National Park Service. "Fort Raleigh National Historic Site: Long-Range Interpretive Plan." May 2010. nps.gov/hfc/pdf/ip/2010-05-14-fora-finaldocument.pdf.

National Park Service. "Secrets in the Sand: Archeology at Fort Raleigh, 1990–2010: Archeology Resource Study." Manteo, North Carolina: National Park Service, 2011.

Quinn, David Beers. *The Lost Colonists and Their Probable Fate*. Raleigh, North Carolina: North Carolina Department of Cultural Resources, 1984.

Quinn, David Beers and Alison M. Quinn. *The First Colonists: Documents on the Planting of the First English Settlements in North America 1584–1590*. Raleigh, North Carolina: North Carolina Department of Cultural Resources, 2007.

The Outer Banks of North Carolina 2014 Official Travel Guide. Manteo, North Carolina: The Outer Banks Visitors Bureau, 2014.

Time Team America: Fort Raleigh, NC. United States: PBS Home Video, 2009.

Turnage, Sheila. *Compass American Guides: North Carolina,* 5th ed. New York: Random House, 2009.

*Yolen, Jane and Heidi Elisabet Yolen Stemple. *Roanoke, the Lost Colony: An Unsolved Mystery from History.* New York: Simon & Schuster Books for Young Readers, 2003.

*Resources for young readers

Selected Online Resources

Algonquian Indians of North Carolina, Inc.

ncalgonquians.com

"Croatoan Indians." NCpedia.

ncpedia.org/croatoan-indians

"Dare Stones." NCpedia.

ncpedia.org/dare-stones

Elizabethan Gardens (official website).

elizabethangardens.org

First Colony Foundation.

firstcolonyfoundation.org

Fort Raleigh National Historic Site.
nps.gov/fora/index.htm

Fort Raleigh: Time Team America, PBS.
pbs.org/time-team/explore-the-sites/fort-raleigh/

Harper, Douglas. Online Etymology Dictionary.
etymonline.com

"History of Muscadines and Scuppernongs."
scuppernongs.com/id2.html

Keiger, Dale. "Rethinking Roanoke."
Johns Hopkins Magazine, November 2011.
pages.jh.edu/~jhumag/1101web/roanoke.html

"Outer Banks Folklore." Outer Banks Information.
outerbeaches.com/OuterBanks/AllAboutOBX/Folklore/

"Virtual Jamestown: First-Hand Accounts."
virtualjamestown.org/fhaccounts_date.html

Roanoke Island Festival Park: Official Website.
roanokeisland.com/default.aspx

"Robert Cawdrey's A Table Alphabetical (1604)."
library.utoronto.ca/utel/ret/cawdrey/cawdrey0.html

Shakespeare's Words.
shakespeareswords.com

The Outer Banks of North Carolina.
outerbanks.org

"The Search for the Lost Colony." North Carolina Digital History.
learnnc.org/lp/editions/nchist-twoworlds/1835

"The Settlement at Roanoke: A Timeline." Durham University Library.
community.dur.ac.uk/4schools.resources/Roanoke/Timeline.htm

Additional resources and links to articles are available at
rebeccabehrens.com.

FOR EDUCATORS

To find out more about this book and the lost colony of Roanoke, visit the Resources page at rebeccabehrens.com. Available for download are:

***Summer of Lost and Found* Educator's Guide**
A Common Core Curriculum-aligned educator's guide for grades 4–7 as well as tips for struggling readers and enrichment activities for advanced readers.
Includes:
1) pre-reading questions
2) comprehension questions
3) classroom activities
4) bibliography for further research

American History/Social Studies Lesson Plan
The real history of the English colonists' interaction with Native peoples included in *Summer of Lost and Found* is an excellent point of entry into deeper historical study. This

lesson plan will guide students to research the people of Roanoke Island in the late 1500s and early 1600s.

Book-Club Discussion Guide
A guide with thought-provoking questions about *Summer of Lost and Found* for readers of all ages to discuss.

ACKNOWLEDGMENTS

This book found its way to you because of some extraordinary people, to whom I am very grateful:

Alyson Heller, my editor, who gave this book a home, and whose enthusiasm and insight enriched the story. The team at Aladdin is an author's dream. Many thanks to Laura Lyn DiSiena for creating such a beautiful design, to Robyn Ng for illustrating the gorgeous cover art and map, and to Mandy Veloso and Janet Rosenberg for making the words shine.

Suzie Townsend, who provides tireless support, guidance, and encouragement to her authors. She's a superwoman, and I am lucky to have an agent with her skill and kindness in my corner. Thanks to the whole team at New Leaf Literary for being such a wonderful and supportive agency.

My friends, especially Kim Liggett, Michelle Schusterman, and Tara Dairman, who offered wisdom, gentle criticism, and cheerleading in equal measure. Jordan Hamessley, thank you for loving this story—and for taking on the BISAC codes. A special acknowledgment to Laura Stiers, grammar-and-style savant. Every writer should be so lucky as to have Laura's eyes on her work.

Elizabeth Behrens, my sister, who read each draft with enthusiasm, and was always there with a life vest when things were looking rough.

Lebame Houston, historian of the Roanoke Island Historical Association, who graciously reviewed the manuscript for historical accuracy and taught me much about the island's people and history. Professor William E. Coleman pointed me in the direction of many resources on Elizabethan speech. Their expertise was invaluable in the creation of this book—and any mistakes within are my own.

My teachers, librarians, and booksellers, who opened the world to me through literature. It is thanks to them that I write, and this story in particular started way back in Mrs. Gerlach's fifth-grade class at Thoreau Elementary.

My parents, whose belief in me (and this book) never wavers. Thank you to my Behrens family—Bette, Margaret, Beth, Eyal, and Ben—and my Merriman family—Mark, Brigid, Elise, Grace, and Ben. Most of all, thanks to Blake. The best thing I've ever found is you.

TURN THE PAGE FOR A SNEAK PEEK AT

The Last Grand Adventure.

*I*t was the happiest place on Earth, or at least it was supposed to be. But I was hot, sticky from spilled lemonade, and unable to dislodge the nervous pit in my stomach. The crowds undulated around me, full of laughter and smiles and felt-and-plastic mouse ears. My father actually whistled as we strolled the park, Julie's arm hooked jauntily through his. Sally's sweaty palm pressed against mine as she squeezed with eagerness.

"I want to go to Tomorrowland! It's brand-new!" My stepsister's voice was high enough to be considered a squeal. The squeak of it fit with the mouse ears she was wearing. I already had a pair, so I'd passed. And I didn't like how Sally wanted to share everything with me—books and records and telephone calls and hairstyles. I felt like if I didn't turn the flimsy little latch on my bedroom door at night, I'd wake to find her curled up next to me with her head on half of my pillow, an arm hugging my old teddy bear.

"The grand opening was last week. It's not like we'll be the first to visit," I pointed out. I tugged on my paisley dress, which Julie had bought me. Somehow my stepmother had no problem selecting the right sizes for Sally, but this dress felt too short on me—and unfortunately, it wasn't supposed to be a miniskirt length. (All my parents said I was too young for those—maybe when I turned thirteen.) The bell-bottomed pants she'd brought home the week before were inches too long. Both were covered in bright, fashionable swirls that I wasn't so sure about wearing, even if Julie insisted they were just like something Twiggy wore in *Vogue*.

Julie patted Sally's shoulder. "Close enough," she chirped. My father was still whistling, and still oblivious.

I stared at the sign ahead of us. TOMORROWLAND: WHERE THE DREAMS OF THE FUTURE ARE REALITY TODAY. I felt a sharpness in my stomach again. Didn't any of these people get it? Sure, here the future looked exciting—with a PeopleMover train and clean white buildings and no litter on the street. Everybody singing along to show tunes and eating carnival food. But what about the world outside of amusement parks? What about all the war and rioting and terrible things to worry about?

There is a reason why there are no newsstands in Disneyland: to keep it the happiest place on Earth.

I'd been to the park once before, but it hadn't been with Sally or Julie. My mother, father, and I had celebrated my seventh birthday there. I drank so much lemonade I was almost sick on the carousel. We studied the park map and danced in New Orleans Square and laughed for the whole day, at least as I remember it. I watched them stitch our names into three matching pairs of black felt ears—Ken, Sheila, and Beatrice—like we were permanent. Back then, I thought that my family would always be together and that the world was a place you could understand, that there were some things you could count on no matter what, like your parents being in the same home to tuck you in at night.

Now I was in Anaheim with my father and a freshly minted stepmother and stepsister. Disneyland was a pit stop on the way to the home of a grandmother I had mostly met through birthday cards and calls on Christmas. When I thought about how things had changed since the last time I had been to the park, I had to wonder what else would be different the next time I came.

I started to get the panicked feeling again: as though the world were spinning like the Flying Dutchman at the playground, or as though the air had suddenly gotten thin. It had troubled me all spring, whenever a scary news report came on air, whenever my mother left town—and especially when my father remarried and Julie and Sally moved into our house.

Now the spinning feeling was back, while amusement-park cheer surrounded me at Disneyland. And it wasn't because I was on a ride. I rubbed my free palm along the hem of my too-short dress. I wished I had my journal with me, but it was in my suitcase in the trunk.

I didn't want to go into Tomorrowland and be fooled by its promise. I wanted to dig my heels into the paved walkway and stand still, to stay in the now. Or better yet, I wanted go back. *Wait a minute—here, I can.* I was in one of the few places in the world where you could actually stop time, by turning a corner and entering the past—or at least a pretty good imitation of it.

I let go of Sally's sticky hand and the crowds closed in, dropping like a curtain between my family and me. Craning my neck and standing on my tiptoes, I couldn't see a flash of Sally's matching paisley anywhere. They were gone, off into the future. I darted to the left, hurrying away from the gleaming white structures and toward knotty old wooden ones.

Howdy, Frontierland.

It was almost an hour later when my father, red-faced and huffing, found me cross-legged on a grassy spot of Tom Sawyer Island. The breeze ruffled my hair, and I felt as calm as I had in a while. Because of the too-shortness of my dress, grass clung to the backs of my legs when I shifted them to a more ladylike position as he hustled down the path in my direction.

Julie trailed behind him with Sally, who looked like she'd been crying.

"Beatrice," he sighed. "I've been looking everywhere for you. Do you know how long we had to wait in line for one of those boats over there?"

My father wiped the perspiration off his brow, then rubbed absentmindedly at his beard. That was a change too—he had been clean-shaven my whole childhood, up until he met Julie. It's like as soon as he and my mother divorced, he had to shed everything about our old life—except me—and then add facial hair.

"I'm sorry. . . . I got lost." Which was both true and untrue.

"Well, come on. We have only a few hours left, and Julie thought we should eat at Blue Bayou. After the Pirates of the Caribbean—Sally's begging for that."

She ran up to me then, a huge smile stretching her tearstained cheeks. "We found you!" It made me feel surprisingly touched: Sally seemed genuinely distraught by my running off. "*Now* can we go get in the line?" Or maybe she was just mad about missing time on the rides.

I wanted to stay on that fake adventure island, which, ironically, felt like a very safe and calm place to me. But I let my dad grab my hand and pull me up. I think we were both surprised that I had wandered off alone in the first place. It's just—in that sea of happy people in that fantasy world, I felt like the only one who could still spot the trash cans and utility poles. And nothing made me feel more alone, and unsure.

I think it was after Sally and I got into another fight—this time over some of my old paper dolls that she found in my closet and colored on—that my father got the idea of my going down to "visit with" my grandmother, Muriel, in Sun City. Julie was standing slightly behind him as he presented the idea to me while I watched TV, like she wasn't sure if she should be part of the conversation.

"Just for a few weeks—to help her settle in. I think she'd really appreciate it, and it would give you a chance to get to know her."

"But isn't my mom coming back soon?" I kept my eyes glued to the screen, but I could still sense the Look they exchanged.

"Sheila—your mom—phoned the other day and said she needs to go out to New Jersey first," Julie said. "Something about an assignment to cover a riot."

My mother is a writer. When I was small, she started writing little things for the newspaper—like household tips and recipes for new casseroles and the latest in home fashions. Then her friend from college, who had a job at *Look* magazine, gave her a few bigger stories—no more serving suggestions involving salads in hollowed-out watermelons. Around the time my parents split up, she started reporting on the really big things, like the Watts riots and troops going to Vietnam. In January, she'd traveled up to San Francisco to report on the "Human Be-In," when a bunch of hippies gathered in Golden Gate Park to . . . I wasn't really sure what they were doing. But now that it was summer, even more young people were flocking there to spread love and music and who knows what else, so my mother went back to witness the "Summer of Love," as people were calling it. She had been supposed to come home that week.

Even though I was hardly the only one of my friends whose parents had divorced, in most cases both their parents were still around. Their mothers packed lunches and set out trays of deviled eggs as a snack when you went over to study after school. Their dads picked them up on the weekends and whisked them away to go to the movies or to the beach. My mom flitted around the country with a notebook. When she was home in California, she spent as little time as possible in the tiny bungalow she rented in the nearby hills. I got it that she didn't want to hang around the suburbs, but I wondered—didn't she miss me?

Anyway, I thought about my options. I could stay at my house, which was no longer mine alone but also Julie's and Sally's. I could watch my stepmother and father coo at each other and my stepsister systematically take over the whole space. She was like the invading armies they talked about on the news. Nothing was off-limits—not even my pajamas. One night I wandered into the bathroom and found her brushing her teeth in my favorite pair. I was surprised she wasn't using my toothbrush, too.

Or my other option: go stay in an old-folk's community with a grandmother I barely knew. I didn't know what Sun City had to offer, other than no stepsisters constantly in your personal space. The only risk was boredom.

My mother always said she wanted to go wherever the stories took her, although lately she just went wherever *Look* magazine sent her. "Life is so short, Bea," she'd said. "And yet there is so much to experience in it." Visiting my grandmother's house wouldn't be an adventure. But at least it was *something*.

From behind my dad, I could see that Lassie was racing to Timmy's rescue. "All right. But just until my mother comes back."

Julie's smile stretched so wide, I thought it might split her pretty face. "That is so kind of you, Beatrice." She retreated into the kitchen, humming.

My father patted my shoulder. "I think you'll both enjoy getting to know each other."

The only person who seemed sad I was leaving was Sally, who grabbed on to my leg and swore she wouldn't let me go.

Later on I sat on my bed with a pencil and my two journals. One is my worry journal. Right before Mom left, I had trouble sleeping for weeks. Fears filled my head instead of dreams. My mother gave me a blank notebook and told me that whenever

I have a worry, I should write it down. "Sometimes it helps just to put your feelings to paper," she said. "Troubles might seem smaller. Or, if they don't, at least you've acknowledged them." She filled notebooks with writing, which I used to peek at sometimes. She wrote on and on about drudgery, some of it related to household chores (I had no idea what cruel and unusual punishment vacuuming was), and some of it related to my dad. Whenever I came across those entries, I snapped her notebook shut.

Eventually my mom's tight smiles and my dad's sighs turned to shouting. I started writing down everything that scared me, from the news reports about Russian missiles to the spelling bee at school to my parents' arguments. I think it helped, but I've also filled several notebooks. Looking at the pile of them in my closet always makes me a little sad—seeing just how many worries I've had to put to paper. And I'm sure there were some I forgot to write down.

The other is my adventure journal, and it is blank. My mother gave it to me after the separation, before she left on her first trip for a reporting assignment. "This is for you to write down all the wonderful adventures you have—big and small. You should scribble down the ones you hope you'll have someday, too. Because you're an adventurer—it's in your name. *Beatrice.* It comes from the Latin word for traveler, voyager."

The night I made the choice to go to my grandmother's,

I wrote in my worry journal: *I'm afraid to leave my house. What if I come back and Sally has overtaken it even more? What if she scratches up my Beatles album? What if Sally, my dad, and Julie become more of a family when I'm not around*—because *I'm not around? What if my mother comes back and then leaves again and I miss seeing her? What if my grandmother is strict and we do not get along at all? What if her new house starts to smell like old people?*

Then, in my adventure journal, I wrote: *Every adventure has to start somewhere. I suppose that could include a grandmother's retirement community.*

Did you LOVE reading this book?

Visit the Whyville...

IN THE MIDDLE BOOK HIVE

Where you can:

- Discover great books!
- Meet new friends!
- Read exclusive sneak peeks and more!

Log on to visit now!
bookhive.whyville.net